**Sapper** is the pen name  '88
at the Naval Prison in l ras
Governor. He served in vn
as 'sappers') from 1907 )ss
during World War I.

He started writing in France, adopting a pen name because serving officers were not allowed to write under their own names. When his first stories, about life in the trenches, were published in 1919, they were an enormous success. But it was his first thriller, *Bulldog Drummond* (1920), that launched him as one of the most popular novelists of his generation. It had several amazingly successful sequels, including *The Black Gang*, *The Third Round* and *The Final Count*. Another great success was *Jim Maitland* (1923), featuring a footloose English sahib in foreign lands.

Sapper published nearly thirty books in total, and a vast public mourned his death when he died in 1937, at the early age of forty-eight. So popular was his 'Bulldog Drummond' series that his friend, the late Gerard Fairlie, wrote several Bulldog Drummond stories after his death under the same pen name.

ASK FOR RONALD STANDISH
THE BLACK GANG
BULLDOG DRUMMOND
BULLDOG DRUMMOND AT BAY
CHALLENGE
THE DINNER CLUB
THE FINAL COUNT
THE FINGER OF FATE
THE ISLAND OF TERROR
JIM BRENT
JIM MAITLAND
JOHN WALTERS
KNOCK-OUT
MUFTI
THE RETURN OF BULLDOG DRUMMOND
SERGEANT MICHAEL CASSIDY RE
TEMPLE TOWER
THE THIRD ROUND

# SAPPER

*Bulldog Drummond*

## THE FEMALE
## OF THE SPECIES

HOUSE OF
STRATUS

This edition published in 2001 by House of Stratus, an imprint of
Stratus Books Ltd., 21 Beeching Park, Kelly Bray,
Cornwall, PL17 8QS, UK.

www.houseofstratus.com

Typeset, printed and bound by House of Stratus.

A catalogue record for this book is available from the British Library
and the Library of Congress.

ISBN 1-84232-547-7

# CONTENTS

# CHAPTER 1

*In which I make Drummond's acquaintance*

Even now, after three months calm thought, I sometimes feel that I must have dreamed the whole thing. I say to myself that this is England: that I am sitting at lunch in my club hoping that that gluttonous lawyer Seybourne will not take all the best part of the Stilton: that unless I get a move on I shall be very late at Lord's. I say all that just as I always used to say it – particularly about Seybourne. And then it suddenly comes over me – the events of those amazing days.

I don't suppose anybody will believe me: I wouldn't believe the story myself if somebody else told it to me. As I say, I sometimes think it must be a dream. And then I turn back my left sleeve nearly to the elbow and look at a three-inch scar, still red and angry, though it's healing nicely now. And I know it was no dream.

Was it a joke? If so, it was the grimmest and most desperate jest that has ever been cracked, and one wherein the humour was difficult to find. Moreover, it was a joke that would have brought the propounder of it to the gallows – had we but been able to catch her. For there was a woman at the bottom of it, and women can suffer the death penalty in England for murder.

No: it was no dream: no jest. It was grim, stern reality played for a stake sufficient to crack the nerve of the principal player on our side had he been possessed of nerves to crack. A game played against time: a game where one mistake might have proved fatal.

Personally, I am a peace-loving individual of mild appearance: I like my rubber of bridge at the club and my round of golf: I am not averse to letting people know that I was wounded in the leg in France. Moreover, I fail to see why I should gratuitously add the information that I was in the horse-lines at the time, and Heaven alone knows where the bullet came from. I mention these points merely to show that I am just a very ordinary sort of person, and not at all of the type which seems to attract adventure. In fact, until that amazing Whitsun, the only thing in any way out of the ordinary which had ever happened to me was when I, on one occasion, tried to stop a runaway horse. And the annoying thing then was that the driver assured me he had the horse under control. Three weeks had elapsed, and I was still in hospital, so I didn't argue the point.

The truth is that I am not one of those enviable men who are at their best when in a tight corner, or when confronted with the need for immediate action. If, as I read somewhere once, men consist of two classes – those who can stop a dog fight and those who can't – honesty compels me to admit that I belong to the latter. In fact, put in a nutshell, I am a rabbit.

And yet I wouldn't have missed that adventure for anything. I can't flatter myself that I did very much: indeed, there were times when I fear I was merely in the way. For all that, never once did a single member of the extraordinary bunch of men who were playing on our side say any word of reproach or irritation. They never let me feel that I was a passenger, even when the strain was greatest.

However, enough of this preamble. I will start at the beginning. For many years it has been my custom to spend a few days round Whitsuntide with some old friends of mine called Tracey. They have a charming house not far from Pangbourne – Elizabethan, and standing in delightful grounds. There is generally a small party – perhaps a dozen in all – and I may say that the keyword to the atmosphere of the house is peace. It may be that I am a little old-fashioned, but the pleasure to be derived from what is sometimes described as an evening's jolly seems to me to be over-rated.

As usual, I went to them this year, arriving on the Thursday before Whitsuntide. The motor met me at the station, and, having shaken Jenkins, the chauffeur, by the hand, I got in. Somewhat to my surprise, he did not at once drive off: he appeared to be waiting for someone else.

"Captain Drummond, sir," he said to me, "who is stopping at the house, came down to get a paper."

"Captain Drummond, Jenkins," I mused. "Do I know him?"

"I think not, sir," he answered, and it seemed to me that a very faint smile twitched round his lips. In fact, there was a sort of air of expectancy about Jenkins – excitement almost – that was most unusual. Jenkins I have always regarded as a model servant.

"Five to one, my trusty lad. That's better than breaking your false teeth on a plum stone."

I turned at this somewhat astounding utterance and regarded the speaker. He was still immersed in the paper, and for the moment I couldn't see his face.

"Put anything on Moongazer?"

" 'Alf a dollar each way, sir," said Jenkins, so far forgetting himself as to suck his teeth in his excitement.

"You'll get your money back. Second at fours. That's not so bad for the old firm."

"Pity about cook, sir," said Jenkins earnestly. "She don't 'old with backing both ways. Moongazer – win only – she was."

He consulted a small notebook, apparently to verify the statement.

"That sheds a bit of gloom over the afternoon, Jenkins."

Captain Drummond lowered the paper, and seemed to become aware of my existence for the first time.

"Hullo! hullo! hullo!" he exclaimed. "The new arrival. Home, Jenkins – and for God's sake don't break it to the cook till after dinner."

He got into the car, and it struck me that I had seldom seen a larger individual.

"Do you think it is quite wise to encourage the servants to bet?" I enquired a little pointedly as we started.

"Encourage, old lad?" he boomed. "They don't want any encouragement. You'd have to keep 'em off it with a field-gun."

He waved a friendly hand at an extremely pretty girl on the pavement, and I took off my hat.

"Who was that?" he said, turning to me.

"I don't know," I answered. "I thought you waved at her."

"But you took off your hat."

"Because you waved at her."

He pondered deeply.

"I follow your reasoning," he conceded at length. "The false premise, if I may say so, is your conclusion that a friendly gesture of the right hand betokens previous acquaintance. I regret to say I do not know the lady: I probably never shall. Still, we have doubtless planted hope in her virginal bosom."

He relapsed into silence, while I glanced at him out of the corner of my eye. A strange individual, I reflected: one, somehow, I could hardly place at the Traceys'. Now that he was sitting beside me he seemed larger than ever – evidently a very powerful man. Moreover, his face was rather of the type that one associates with pugilism. He certainly had no claims to good looks, and yet there was something very attractive about his expression.

"*The Cat and Custard Pot*," he remarked suddenly, and Jenkins touched his hat.

"It's nearly an hour," he said, turning to me, "since I lowered any ale. And I don't really know Bill Tracey well enough to reason with him about his. The damned stuff isn't fit to drink."

The car pulled up outside a pub, and my companion descended. I refused his invitation to join him – ale is not a favourite beverage of mine – and remained sitting in the car. The afternoon was warm, the air heavy with the scent of flowers from a neighbouring garden. And in the distance one got a glimpse of the peaceful Thames. Peaceful – the *mot juste*: everything was peaceful in that charming corner of England. And with a feeling of drowsy contentment, I lay back and half-closed my eyes.

I don't know what drew my attention to them first – the two men who were sitting at one of the little tables under a tree. Perhaps it was that they didn't seem to quite fit in with their surroundings. Foreigners, I decided, and yet it was more from the cut of their clothes than from their actual faces that I came to the conclusion. They weren't talking, but every now and then they stole a glance at the door by which Drummond had gone in. And then one of them turned suddenly and stared long and earnestly at me.

"Who are those two men, Jenkins?" I said, leaning forward.

"Never seen 'em before today, sir," he answered. "But they was 'ere when the Captain stopped for his pint on the way down. Lumme – look there."

I looked, and I must admit that for a moment or two I began to have doubts as to Drummond's sanity. He had evidently come out by some other door, and he was now standing behind the trunk of the tree under which the men were sitting. They were obviously quite unaware of his presence, and if such a thing hadn't been inconceivable, I should have said he was deliberately eavesdropping. Anyway, the fact remains that for nearly half a minute he stood there absolutely motionless, whilst I watched the scene in frank amazement. Then one of the two men happened to glance at me, and I suppose my face must have given something away. He nudged his companion, and the two of them rose to their feet just as Drummond stepped out from behind the tree.

"Good afternoon, my pretties," he burbled genially. "Are we staying long in Pangbourne's happy clime – or are we not?"

"Who the devil are you, sir?" said one of the men, speaking perfect English, except for a slightly guttural accent.

Drummond took out his case and selected a cigarette with care.

"Surely," he remarked pleasantly, "your incompetence cannot be as astounding as all that. Tush! tush! – " he lifted a hand like a leg of mutton as the man who had spoken started forward angrily. "I will push your face in later, if necessary, but just at the moment I would like a little chat. And since the appearance of you both is sufficient to shake any man to the foundations, let us not waste time over unnecessary questions."

"Look here," snarled the other angrily, "do you want a rough house, young man?"

"Rough house?" said Drummond mildly. "What is a rough house? Surely you cannot imagine for one minute that I would so far demean myself as to lift my hand in anger against my neighbour."

And then the most extraordinary thing happened. I was watching the strange scene very closely, wondering really whether I ought not to interfere – yet even so I didn't see how it was done. It was so incredibly quick, and as far as I could tell, Drummond never moved.

The two men seemed to close in on him suddenly with the idea obviously of hustling him out of the garden. And they didn't hustle him out of the garden. Far from it. There came a noise as of two hard bodies impinging together, and the gentleman who had not yet spoken recoiled a pace, holding his nose and cursing.

I sympathised with him: it is a singularly painful thing to hit one's nose hard on somebody else's head. In fact, the only completely unmoved person was Drummond himself.

"You shouldn't kiss in public places, laddies," he remarked sadly. "It might make the barmaid jealous. And I do declare his little nosey-posey is beginning to bleed. If you ask the chauffeur nicely he might lend you a spanner to put down your back."

The two men stood there glaring at him, and they were not a prepossessing pair. And then the one who had done the talking drew his friend of the damaged nose on one side, and spoke to him in a low tone. He seemed to be urging some course on the other which the latter was unwilling to accept.

"My God, sir," muttered Jenkins to me, "the bloke with the bleeding nose has got a knife."

"Look out, Captain Drummond," I called out. "That man has a knife."

"I know, old lad," he answered. "He's been playing at pirates. Not going, surely? Why, we've never had our little chat."

But without a backward glance, the two men passed through the gate and started walking rapidly down the road in the direction of the station. And after a time Drummond sauntered over to the car and got in.

"After which breezy little interlude," he murmured, "the powerful car again swung forward, devouring mile after mile."

"Would you very much mind explaining?" I remarked dazedly.

"Explaining?" he said. "What is there to explain?"

"Do you usually go about the country molesting perfect strangers? Who are those men?"

"I dunno," he answered. "But they knew me all right."

He was staring at the road ahead and frowning.

"It's impossible," he muttered at length. "And yet –"

He relapsed into silence, while I still gazed at him in amazement.

"But," I cried, "it's astounding. If I hadn't seen it with my own eyes, I couldn't have believed it possible."

He grinned suddenly.

"I suppose it was a bit disconcerting," he answered. "But we're moving in deep waters, laddie – or, rather, I am. And I tell you frankly I don't quite know where I am. Why should those two blokes have followed me down here?"

"Then you have seen them before?"

He shook his head.

"No. At least, I saw them when I stopped for some ale on the way down to the station. And they aren't very clever at it."

"Clever at what?"

"The little game of observing without being observed. Apart from their appearance, which made them stick out a mile when seen in an English country inn, the man whose nose suffered slightly positively hissed into the other's ear when he first saw me. In fact, I very nearly dealt with them then and there, only I was afraid I'd be late for your train."

"But why should they follow you?" I persisted. "What's the idea?"

"I wish to God I knew," he answered gravely. "I don't think I'm losing my nerve, or anything of that sort – but I'm absolutely in the dark. Almost as much as you are, in fact. I loathe this waiting game."

"Of course," I remarked resignedly, "I suppose I am not insane. I suppose there is some sense in all this, though at the moment I'm damned if I can see it."

"Presumably you read Kipling?" he said suddenly.

I stared at him in silence – speech was beyond me.

"A month ago," he continued calmly, "I received this."

From his breast pocket he took a slip of paper, and handed it to me. On it some lines were written in an obviously feminine hand.

"When the Himalayan peasant meets the he-bear in his
       pride,
He shouts to scare the monster, who will often turn aside.

8

But the she-bear, thus accosted, rends the peasant tooth
    and nail.
And the point, I warn you, Drummond, is discovered in
    the tail."

I handed the paper back to him.

"What do you make of it?" he asked.

"It looks like a stupid joke," I said. "Do you know the writing?"

He shook his head.

"No; I don't. So you think it's a joke, do you?"

"My dear sir," I cried, "what else can it be? I confess that at the moment I forget the poem, but the first three lines are obviously Kipling. Equally obviously the fourth is not."

"Precisely," he agreed with a faint smile. "I got as far as that myself. And so it was the fourth line that attracted my attention. It seemed to me that the message, if any, would be found in it. It was."

"What is the fourth line?" I asked curiously.

"'For the female of the species is more deadly than the male,'" he answered.

"But, surely," I cried in amazement, "you can't take a thing like that seriously. It's probably a foolish hoax sent you by some girl you cut at a night club."

I laughed a little irritably: for a man to take such a message in earnest struck me as being childish to a degree. A stupid jest played by some silly girl, with a penchant for being mysterious. Undoubtedly, I reflected, the man was a fool. And, anyway, what had it got to do with the two men at the *Cat and Custard Pot*?

"'The female of the species is more deadly than the male,'" he repeated, as if he hadn't heard my remark. "No hoax about it, old lad; no jest, believe you me. Just a plain and simple warning. And now the game has begun."

For a moment or two I wondered if he was pulling my leg; but he was so deadly serious that I realised that he, at any rate, believed it was genuine. And my feeling of irritation grew. What an ass the man must be!

"What game?" I asked sarcastically. "Playing peep-bo behind the trees?"

He let out a sudden roar of laughter.

"You probably think I'm bughouse, don't you?" he cried. "Doesn't matter. The only real tragedy of the day is that the cook didn't back Moongazer each way."

Once again he relapsed into silence, as the car rolled through the gates of the Traceys' house.

"Good intelligence work," he said thoughtfully. "We only decided to come down here yesterday. But I wish to the Lord you'd learn to control your face. If you hadn't given a life-like representation of a gargoyle in pain I might have heard something of interest from those two blighters."

"Confound you!" I spluttered angrily.

"You couldn't help it." He waved a vast hand, and beat me on the back. "I ought to have warned you. Must have looked a bit odd. But it's a pity – "

The car pulled up at the door, and he got out.

"Little Willie wants a drink," he remarked to Tracey, who came out to greet us. "His nervous system has had a shock. By the way, where's Phyllis?"

"Playing tennis," said our host, and Drummond strolled off in the direction of the lawn.

"Look here, Bill," I cried, when he was out of earshot, "is that man all there?"

"Hugh Drummond all there?" he laughed. "Very few men in England more so. Why?"

"Well, if he hits me on the back again I shan't be. He's rammed my braces through my spine. But, honestly, I thought the man was mad. He's been talking the most appalling hot air on the way up, and he assaulted two complete strangers at the *Cat and Custard Pot.*"

Bill Tracey stared at me in surprise.

"Assaulted two strangers at the *Cat and Custard Pot!*" he repeated. "What on earth did he do that for?"

"Ask me another," I said irritably. "Two foreign-looking men."

"That's funny," he remarked thoughtfully. "Rodgers – the gardener – was telling me only a few minutes ago that he had seen two foreign-looking men hanging round the house this morning, and had told them to clear off. I wonder if they were the same."

"Probably," I said. "But the fact that they were hanging round here hardly seems an adequate reason for Captain Drummond's behaviour. In fact, my dear Bill – What's the matter?"

He was staring over my shoulder in the direction of the lawn, and I swung round. Drummond was running towards us over the grass, and there was a peculiar strained look on his face. He passed us without a word, and went up the stairs two at a time. We heard a door flung open, and then we saw him leaning out of his bedroom window.

"I don't like it, Algy," he said. "Not one little bit."

A somewhat vacuous-looking individual with an eyeglass had joined us, whom the remark was obviously addressed to.

"Ain't she there, old bean?" he remarked.

"Not a trace," answered the other, disappearing from view.

"Can't understand old Hugh," remarked the newcomer plaintively. "I've never seen him in this condition before. If I didn't think it was impossible I should say he'd got the wind up."

"What's stung you all?" said Bill Tracey. "Isn't Mrs Drummond playing tennis?"

"She was – after lunch," answered Algy. "Then she got a note. Your butler wallah brought it out to her on the court. It seemed to upset her a bit, for she stopped at once and came into the house."

"Where," remarked Drummond, who had joined us, "she changed her clothes. It was a note, was it, Algy: not a letter? I mean, did you happen to notice if there was a stamp on the envelope?"

"As a matter of fact, old lad, I particularly noticed there was not. I was sitting next her when she took it."

The butler passed us at that moment, carrying the tea-things.

"Parker," said Drummond quietly, "you gave a note to Mrs Drummond this afternoon, I understand."

"I did, sir," answered the butler.

"Did you take it yourself at the front door?"

"I did, sir."

"Who delivered it?"

"A man, sir, who I did not know. A stranger to the neighbourhood, I gathered."

"Why?" snapped Drummond.

"Because, sir, he asked me the nearest way to the station."

"Thank you, Parker," said Drummond quietly. "Algy, it's quicker than I expected. Hullo! Jenkins, do you want me?"

The chauffeur touched his cap.

"Well, sir, you know you asked me to adjust your carburettor for you. I was just wondering if you could tell me when the car will be back."

"Be back?" said Drummond. "What do you mean?"

"Why, sir, the Bentley ain't in the garage. I thought as 'ow Mrs Drummond had probably taken it out."

And if anything had been needed to confirm my opinion that this vast individual was a little peculiar, I got it then. He lifted his two enormous fists above his head and shook them at the sky. I could see the great muscles rippling under his sleeves, and instinctively I recoiled a step.

The man looked positively dangerous.

"Thrice and unutterably damned fool that I am," he muttered. "But how could I tell it would come so soon?"

"My dear fellow," said Bill Tracey, gazing at him apprehensively, "surely there is nothing to get excited about. Mrs Drummond is a very good driver."

"Driver be jiggered," cried Drummond. "If it was only a question of driving, I wouldn't mind. I'm afraid they've got her. For the Lord's sake, give me a pint of ale. Yours is pretty bad – but it's better than nothing."

And then he suddenly turned on me of all people.

"If only you could have kept your face in its place, little man, I might have heard something. Still, it can't be helped. God made you like it."

"Really," I protested angrily, but this extraordinary individual had gone indoors again. "The man is positively insulting."

"Nothing to what he can be if he dislikes you," said the being called Algy placidly. "He'll be all right after he's had his beer."

# CHAPTER 2

*In which I find a deserted motorcar*

Now, in view of the fact that this is my first essay in literature, I realise that many of my relatives may feel it to be their bounden duty to buy the result. Several, I know, will borrow a copy from one another, or else will endeavour to touch me for one of the six free copies which, I am given to understand, the author receives on publication. But most of them, in one way or another, will read it. And I am particularly anxious, bearing in mind the really astounding situations in which I found myself later, that no misconception should exist in their minds as to my mood at the beginning.

Particularly Uncle Percy – the Dean of Wolverhampton. He is, I am glad to say, a man of advanced years and considerable wealth. He is also unmarried, a fact which has never occasioned me great surprise. But few women exist who would be capable of dealing with his intellect or digestion, and so far he does not seem to have met one of them.

For his benefit, then, and that of others who know me personally, I may state that when I saw Captain Drummond engaged in the operation, as he called it, of "golluping his beer with zest", I was extremely angry. He, on the contrary, seemed to have recovered his spirits. No longer did he shake his fists in the air; on the contrary, a most depressing noise issued from his mouth as he put down the empty tankard on the table. He appeared to be singing, and, incredible though it may seem, to derive some pleasure from the operation. The words of his dirge seemed to imply that the more we were together the merrier we would be – a statement to which I took the gravest exception.

I was to learn afterwards the amazing way in which this amazing individual could throw off a serious mood and become positively hilarious. For instance – on this occasion – having delivered himself of this deplorable sentiment, he advanced towards me. Fearing another blow on the back, I retreated rapidly, but he no longer meditated assault. He desired apparently to examine my cuff-links, a thing which did not strike me as being in the best of taste.

"You approve, I trust?" I said sarcastically.

He shook his head sadly.

"I feared as much," he remarked. "Or have you left 'em at home?" he added hopefully.

I turned to Bill Tracey.

"Have you turned this place into a private lunatic asylum?" I demanded.

And all Bill did was to shout with laughter.

"Cheer up, Joe," he said. "You'll learn our little ways soon."

"Doubtless," I remarked stiffly. "In the meantime I think I'll go and have some tea."

I crossed the lawn to find several people I knew assembled in the summer-house. And, having paid my respects to my hostess, and been introduced to two or three strangers, I sat down with a feeling of relief beside Tomkinson, a dear old friend of mine.

"Really," I said to him under cover of the general conversation, "there seem to be some very extraordinary people in this party. Who and what is that enormous man who calls himself Drummond?"

He laughed, and lit a cigarette.

"He does strike one as a bit odd at first, doesn't he? But as a matter of fact, your adjective was right. He is an extraordinary man. He did some feats of strength for us last night that wouldn't have disgraced a professional strong man."

"He nearly smashed my spine," I said grimly, "giving it a playful tap."

"He is not communicative about himself," went on Tomkinson. "And what little I know about him I have learned from that fellow with the eyeglass – Algy Longworth – who incidentally regards him as only one degree lower than the Almighty. He has got a very charming wife."

He glanced round the party.

"You won't see her here," I remarked. "She has apparently taken his Bentley and gone out in it alone. Having discovered this fact, he first of all announces 'They've got her!' in blood-curdling tones, and then proceeds to lower inordinate quantities of ale. And his behaviour coming up from the station – "

"What's that you said?"

A man whose face was vaguely familiar turned and stared at me.

"Why, surely you're Mr Darrell!" I cried. "You play for Middlesex?"

He nodded.

"I do – sometimes. But what's that you were saying about Drummond having said 'They've got her?'"

"Just that – and nothing more," I answered. "As I was telling Tomkinson, Mrs Drummond has apparently gone out in his Bentley alone, and when he heard of it he said, 'They've got her.' But who 'they' are I can't tell you."

"Good God!" His face had suddenly become grave. "There must be a mistake. And yet Hugh doesn't make mistakes."

He made the last remark under his breath.

"It all seems a little hard to follow," I murmured with mild sarcasm.

But he paid no attention: he had glanced up quickly, and was staring over my shoulder.

"What's this I hear about Phyllis, old boy?" he said.

"The Lord knows, Peter."

Drummond was standing there with a queer look on his face.

"She got a note delivered here by a stranger. It came while I was at the station. And Algy said it seemed to upset her. Anyway, she went indoors and changed, and then went out alone in the Bentley."

A silence had fallen on the party which was broken by our hostess.

"But why should that worry you, Captain Drummond? Your wife often drives, she tells me."

"She knows no one in this neighbourhood, Mrs Tracey, except your good selves," answered Drummond quietly. "So who could have sent a note here to be delivered by hand?"

"Well, evidently somebody did," I remarked. "And when Mrs Drummond returns you'll find out who it was."

I spoke somewhat coldly: the man was becoming a bore.

"If she ever does return," he answered.

I regret to state that I laughed.

"My dear sir," I cried, "don't be absurd. You surely can't believe, or expect us to believe, that some evilly-disposed persons are abducting your wife in broad daylight and in the middle of England?"

But he still stood there with that queer look on his face.

"Peter," he said, "I want to have a bit of a talk with you."

Darrell rose instantly, and the two of them strolled away together.

"Really," I remarked irritably, when they were out of earshot, "the thing is perfectly preposterous. Is he doing it as a joke, or what?"

Algy Longworth had joined them, and the three of them were standing in the middle of the lawn talking earnestly.

"I must say it does all seem very funny," agreed our hostess. "And yet Captain Drummond isn't the sort of man to make stupid jokes of that sort."

"You mean," I said incredulously, "that he really believes that someone may be abducting his wife? My dear Mary, don't be so ridiculous. Why should anyone abduct his wife?"

"He's led a very strange life since the War," she answered. "I confess I don't know much about it myself – neither he nor his friends are very communicative. But I know he got mixed up with a gang of criminals."

"I am not surprised," I murmured under my breath.

"I'm not very clear about what happened," went on Mary Tracey. "But finally Captain Drummond was responsible somehow or other for the death of the leader of the gang. And a woman, who had been this man's mistress, was left behind."

I stared at her: absurd, of course, but that bit of doggerel at the end of Kipling's verse came back to me. And then common sense reasserted itself. This was England: not a country where secret societies flourished and strange vendettas took place. The whole thing was a mere coincidence. What connection could there possibly be between the two men at the *Cat and Custard Pot* and the fact that Mrs Drummond had gone out alone in a motorcar?

"It seems," Mary Tracey was speaking again, "from what Bill tells me, that this woman vowed vengeance on Captain Drummond. I know it sounds very fantastic, and I expect we shall all laugh about it when Phyllis gets back. And yet – " she hesitated for a moment. "Oh! I don't want to be silly, but I do wish she'd come back soon."

"But, Mrs Tracey," said someone reassuringly, "there can be no danger. What could happen to her?"

"I quite agree," I remarked. "If on every occasion a woman went out alone in a motorcar her friends and relations panicked about her being abducted, life would become a hideous affair."

And then by tacit consent the subject dropped, and we dispersed about our lawful occasions. I didn't see Drummond, but Darrell and Longworth were practising putting on the other side of the lawn. I strolled over and joined them.

"Your large friend," I laughed, "seems to have put the wind up most of the ladies in the party fairly successfully."

But they neither of them seemed to regard it as a subject for mirth.

"Let us hope it will end at that," said Darrell gravely. "I confess that I have rarely been so uneasy in my life."

And that, mark you, from a man who played for Middlesex! Really, I reflected, the thing was ceasing to be funny. And I was just getting a suitable remark ready, when Longworth suddenly straightened up and stared across the lawn. Bill Tracey was coming towards us, and at his side was a police-sergeant. And Bill Tracey's face was serious.

"Where's Drummond?" he called out.

"He said he was going to stroll down to the river," said Darrell.

He cupped his mouth with his hands and let out a shout that startled the rooks for miles around. And very faintly from the distance came an answering cry.

"What's happened?" he said curtly.

"I don't know," answered Bill uneasily. "Quite possibly it's capable of some simple explanation. Apparently the Bentley has been found empty. However, we'd better wait till Drummond comes, and then the sergeant can tell his story."

I noticed Darrell glance significantly at Longworth; then he calmly resumed the study of a long putt. With a bang the ball went into the hole, and he straightened himself up.

"My game, Algy. So Hugh was right: I was afraid of it. Here he comes."

We watched him breasting the hill that led down to the river, running with the long, easy stride of the born athlete. And it's curious how little things strike one at times. I remember noticing as he came up that his breathing was as normal as my own, though he must have run the best part of a quarter of a mile.

"What's up?" he said curtly, his eyes fixed on the sergeant.

"Are you Captain Drummond?" remarked the officer, producing a notebook.

"I am."

"Of 5a, Upper Brook Street?"

He was reading these details from the book in his hand. Drummond nodded.

"Yes."

"You have a red Bentley car numbered ZZ 103?"

"I have," said Drummond.

With maddening deliberation the worthy sergeant replaced his notebook in his breast pocket. And another curious little thing struck me: though Drummond must have been on edge with suspense, no sign of impatience showed in his face.

"Have you been out in that car today, sir?"

"I have not," said Drummond. "But my wife has."

"Was she alone, sir?"

"To the best of my belief she was," answered Drummond. "She left here when I was down at the station in Mr Tracey's car meeting this gentleman."

The sergeant nodded his head portentously.

"Well, sir, I have to report to you that your car has been found empty standing by the side of the road not far from the village of Tidmarsh."

"How did you know I was here?" said Drummond quietly.

"The constable who found the car, sir, saw your name and address printed on a plate on the instrument board. So he went to the nearest telephone and rang up your house in London. And your servant told him you was stopping down here. So he rang up at the station in Pangbourne."

"But why take all the trouble?" said Drummond even more quietly. "Surely there's nothing extraordinary about an empty car beside the road?"

"No, sir," agreed the sergeant. "There ain't. That's true. But the constable further reported" – his voice was grave – "that he didn't like the look of the car. He said it struck him that there had been some sort of struggle."

"I see," said Drummond.

Quite calmly he turned to Darrell.

"Peter – your Sunbeam, and hump yourself. Algy – ring up Ted and Toby, and tell 'em they're wanted. Put up at the hotel. Sergeant – you come with me. Tracey, ring up the railway-station and find out if two foreign-looking men have been seen there this afternoon. If so, did they take tickets, and for what destination? Let's move."

And we moved. Gone in a flash was the large and apparently brainless ass; in his place was a man accustomed to lead, and accustomed to instant obedience. Heaven knows why I got into the Sunbeam: presumably because I was the only person who had received no definite instructions. And Drummond evinced no surprise when he found me sitting beside him in the back seat. The sergeant, a little dazed at such rapidity of action, was in front with Darrell, and except for him none of us even had a hat.

"Tell us the way, sergeant," said Drummond, as we swung through the gates. "And let her out, Peter."

And Peter let her out. The worthy policeman gasped feebly once or twice concerning speed limits, but no one took the faintest notice, so that after a time he resigned himself to the inevitable and concentrated on holding on his hat. And I, having no hat to hold on, concentrated on the man beside me.

He seemed almost unaware of my existence. He sat there, motionless save for the swaying of the car, staring in front of him. His face was set and grave, and every now and then he

21

shook his head as if he had arrived at an unpleasant conclusion in his train of thought.

My own thoughts were frankly incoherent. Somehow or other I still couldn't believe that the matter was serious – certainly not as serious as Drummond seemed to think. And yet my former scepticism was shaken, I confess. If what the sergeant said was right: if there were signs of a struggle in the car, it was undoubtedly sufficiently serious to make it very unpleasant. But I still refused to believe that the whole thing was not capable of some simple solution. A tramp, perhaps, seeing that an approaching car contained a woman alone had stopped it by the simple expedient of standing in the middle of the road. Then he had attacked Mrs Drummond with the idea of getting her money.

Unpleasant, as I say – very unpleasant. But quite ordinary. A very different matter to all this absurd twaddle about gangs of criminals and dead men's mistresses. Moreover, I reflected, with a certain amount of satisfaction, there was another thing that proved my theory. On Drummond's own showing he attached considerable importance to the two foreign-looking men at the *Cat and Custard Pot*. Now it was utterly impossible that they could have had anything to do with it since they were sitting there in the garden at the very time that Mrs Drummond must have left Tracey's house in the car. Which completely knocked Drummond's conclusion on the head. The whole thing was simply a coincidence, and I said as much to the man beside me. He listened in silence.

"Ever been ratting?" he asked when I'd finished.

Once more did I stare at this extraordinary individual in amazement. What on earth had that got to do with it?

"Well – have you?" he repeated when I didn't answer.

"In the days of my youth I believe I did," I answered. "Though the exact bearing of a boyish pastime on the point at issue is a little obscure."

"Then it oughtn't to be," he remarked curtly. "It's only obscure because your grey matter is torpid. When a party of you go ratting, you put a bloke at every hole you know of before you start to bolt your rats."

He relapsed again into silence, and so did I. The confounded fellow seemed to have an answer for everything. And then just ahead of us we saw the deserted car.

A constable was standing beside it, and a group of four or five children were looking on curiously. It stood some three or four feet from the left-hand side of the road, so that there was only just room for another car to pass. And the road itself at this point ran through a small wood – barely more than a copse.

"You've moved nothing, constable?" said the sergeant.

"Just as I found it, sergeant."

We crowded round the car and looked inside. It was an ordinary open touring model, and it was obvious at once that there were signs which indicated a struggle. The rug, for instance, instead of being folded, was half over the front seat and half in the back of the car. A lady's handkerchief, crumpled up, was lying just behind the steering-wheel, and one of the covers which was fastened to the upholstery by means of press studs, was partially wrenched off. It was the cover for one of the side doors, and underneath it was a pocket for maps and papers.

"This is your car, sir?" asked the sergeant formally.

"It is," said Drummond, and once more we fell silent.

There was something sinister about that deserted car. One felt an insane longing that the rug could speak: that a thrush singing in the drowsy heat on a tree close by could tell us what had happened. Its head, of course, was pointed away from Pangbourne, and suddenly Drummond gave an exclamation. He was looking at the road some fifteen yards in front of the bonnet.

At first I noticed nothing, though my sight is as good as most men's. And it wasn't until I got close to the place that I could see what had attracted his attention. Covered with dust was a pool of black lubricating oil – and covered so well that only the sharpest eye would have detected it.

"That accounts for one thing, anyway," said Drummond quietly.

"What is that, sir?" remarked the sergeant, with considerable respect in his voice. I was evidently not the only one who had been impressed with the keenness of Drummond's sight.

"I know my wife's driving better than anybody else," he answered, "and, under normal circumstances, if she pulled up, she would instinctively get into the side of the road. So the first question I asked myself was why she had stopped with the car where it is. She was either following another car which pulled up in front of her, or she came round the corner and found it stationary in the middle of the road, not leaving her room to pass. And the owners of the car that did not leave her room to pass wanted to conceal the fact that they had been here, if possible. So, finding they had leaked oil, they tried to cover it up. God! if only the Bentley could talk."

It was over in a moment – that sudden, natural spasm of feeling, and he was the same cool, imperturbable man again. And I felt my admiration for him growing. Criminal gangs or no criminal gangs, it's a damnable thing to stand on the spot where an hour or two earlier your wife has been the victim of some dastardly outrage, and feel utterly impotent to do anything.

"Do you think it's possible to track that car?" said Darrell.

We walked along the road for a considerable distance, but it was soon obvious that the idea was impossible. Far too much traffic had been along previously, and since there had been no rain the chance of following some distinctive tyre marking had gone.

"Hopeless," said Drummond heavily. "Absolutely hopeless. Hullo! one of those kids has found something."

They were running towards us in a body led by a little boy who was waving some object in his hand.

"Found this, governor, in the grass beside the road," he piped out.

"My God!" said Drummond, staring at it with dilated eyes.

For "this" was a large spanner, and one end was stained a dull red. Moreover, the red was still damp, and when he touched it, it came off on his finger.

Blood. And the question which rose in all of our minds, and the question which none of us dared to answer was – Whose? As I say, none of us dared to answer it out loud: I think we all of us had answered it to ourselves.

"You don't recognise the spanner, I suppose, sir?" said the sergeant. "Is it one from your car or not?"

"I do recognise it," answered Drummond. "It's the regular set spanner I keep in the pocket with the maps and papers and not in the tool-box, because it fits the nut of the petrol tank."

"The pocket that was wrenched open," I put in, and he nodded.

"Show us just where you found it, nipper," said the sergeant, and we all trooped back to the Bentley.

"Here, sir," said the urchin. "Behind that there stone."

He was pointing to a place just about level with the bonnet, and it required no keenness of vision such as had been necessary to spot the dust-covered pool of oil to see the next clue. From the stone where the spanner had been found to a point in the grass opposite where the other car must have stood, there stretched a continuous trail of ominous red spots. Some were big, and some were small, but the line was unbroken. Blood once again – and once again the same unspoken question.

"Well, sir," said the sergeant gravely, "it's obvious that there has been foul play. I think the best thing I can do is to get back to the station and phone Scotland Yard. We want a look-out kept all over the country for a motorcar containing a wounded lady."

Drummond gave a short laugh.

"Don't be too sure of that, sergeant," he remarked. "It was only my wife who knew where that spanner was kept. I should be more inclined, if I were you, to keep a look-out for a motor containing a wounded man. Though I tell you candidly if this thing is what I think it is – or, rather, what I know it is – you're wasting your time."

And not another word would he say.

# CHAPTER 3

*In which I get it in the neck*

It was hopeless, of course, as I think we all realised from the beginning. But it was impossible to sit still and do nothing. And for the rest of that afternoon, until long past the time for dinner, we scoured the country. Drummond drove the Bentley alone – he was in no mood for talking – and I went with Darrell.

It was in the course of that wearisome and fruitless search that I began to understand things a little more clearly. My companion amplified Mary Tracey's vague remarks, until I began to ask myself if I was dreaming. That this affair was the work of no ordinary person was obvious, but for a long time I believed that he must be exaggerating. Some of the things he told me sounded too incredible.

They concerned a man called Carl Peterson, who, it appeared, had been the head of the gang our hostess had alluded to. This man was none other than Wilmot, of airship fame. I, naturally, remembered the name perfectly – just as I remembered the destruction of his airship, mercifully after all the passengers had disembarked. Wilmot himself was killed – burned to death, as were the rest of the crew.

And here was Darrell, in the most calm and matter-of-fact way, stating something completely different.

27

"I was one of the passengers that night," he said. "I know. Wilmot – or rather, Peterson, as we prefer to call him – was not burned to death. He was killed by Drummond."

"Killed!" I gasped. "Good God! what for?"

Darrell smiled grimly.

"It was long overdue," he answered. "But that was the first opportunity there had been of actually doing it."

"And this woman knows that he killed him?" I said.

"No – and yes," he said. "She was not there at the time, but four days later she met Drummond by the wreckage of the airship. And she told him the exact hour when Peterson had died. I don't know how to account for it. Some form of telepathy, I suppose. She also told him that they would meet again. And this is the beginning of the meeting."

"So that verse was sent by her, was it?"

He nodded.

"But it seems rather an extraordinary thing to do," I persisted. "Why go out of your way to warn a person?"

"She is rather an extraordinary woman," he answered. "She is also a most terribly dangerous one. Like all women who have a kink, they are more extreme than men. And I don't mind telling you, Dixon, that I'm positively sick with anxiety over this show. An eye for an eye, and a tooth for a tooth – you know the old tag? I'm afraid it's going to be a life for a life."

"You mean they may kill Mrs Drummond?" I cried in horror.

"Just that and nothing more," he said gravely. "Drummond killed her lover: she will kill his wife. She would have no more scruples over so doing than you would have over treading on a wasp. The only thing is – does it suit her book? Is she going to try and get Drummond into her power by using his wife as a lever? And only time will tell us that."

"What sort of a woman is she?" I said curiously.

"To look at she is tall, dark, and very *soignée*. She's handsome rather than pretty, and I should think has some Southern blood in her."

He smiled slightly.

"But don't run away with the impression that she'd be likely to look like that if you met her. Far more probably would she be a wizened-up crone covered with spectacles, or a portly dame with creaking corsets. So much for her appearance. Her character is a thing to stand aghast at. She has the criminal instinct developed to its highest degree: she is absolutely without mercy: she is singularly able. How much, of course, was her and how much Carl Peterson in the old days is a thing I don't know. But even if it was him principally, to start with, she must have profited considerably by seeing him at work. And a final point which is just as important if not more so than those I've already given, she must be a very wealthy woman. Peterson's life was not a wasted one as far as other people's money was concerned."

"It sounds a tough proposition," I murmured.

"It is," he agreed gravely. "A damned tough proposition. In fact, Dixon, there is only one ray of sunshine that I can see in the whole business. To do them both justice, in the past they have never been crude in their methods. In their own peculiar way they had a sense of art. If that sense of art is stronger now with her than her primitive desire for revenge, there's hope."

"I don't quite follow," I said.

"She will play the fish – the fish being us. To kill Mrs Drummond offhand would be crude."

"I fail to see much comfort," I remarked, "in being played if the result is going to be the same. It's only prolonging the agony."

"Quite so," he said quietly, "but is the result going to be the same?"

A peculiar smile flickered for a moment round his lips.

"You probably think I'm talking rot," he went on. "At least, that I'm exaggerating grossly."

"Well," I admitted, "it's all a little hard to follow."

"Naturally. You've never struck any of these people before. We have. We met them quite by accident at first, and since then we've almost become old friends. We know their ways: they know ours. Sometimes we've fought with the police on our side: sometimes we've fought a lone hand. And up to date on balance we have won hands down. That is why I cannot help feeling – at any rate hoping – that this woman would not regard the slate as being clean if she merely killed Mrs Drummond. It has been our wits against theirs up till now. She wants a much fuller revenge than such a crude action as that would afford her."

"I am glad you feel optimistic over the prospect," I murmured. "*Chacun à son gout.*"

"Of course," he went on thoughtfully, "I may be wrong. If so – it's hopeless from the start. They've got Drummond's wife: if they want to they can kill her right away. But somehow or other – "

He broke off, staring at the road ahead. The light was of that half-and-half description when headlamps are useless and driving is most difficult.

"Anyway, I'm afraid this is a pretty hopeless quest," I said. "We don't even know what sort of a car we are looking for – "

He touched the accelerator with his foot.

"What's that dark thing there beside the road?" he said. "It's a car right enough, and you never can tell."

We drew up beside it, and the first thing I noticed was a pool of lubricating oil in the road, under the back axle. Only a coincidence, of course, I reflected, but I felt a sudden tingle of excitement. Could it possibly be the car we were looking for?

We got out and walked up to it; the car was empty – the blinds of the back windows drawn down. "We'd better be careful," I said a little nervously, "the owner may be in the field."

"On the other hand, he may not," said Darrell coolly, and opened the door.

It was an ordinary standard limousine, and at first sight there seemed nothing out of the normal to be seen. There was no sign of disorder, as there had been in the Bentley: the rug on the seat was carefully folded. And it was almost mechanically that I opened one of the back doors, to stand nearly frozen with horror at what I saw. The covering of the front bucket seat beside the driver's was saturated with blood from the top right down to the floorboards.

"Good God!" I muttered, "look here."

Darrell came and looked over my shoulder, and I heard him catch his breath sharply.

"This evidently," he remarked, "is the car we are after. There's a torch in the pocket of the Sunbeam: get it, like a good fellow."

By its light we examined the stain more closely. The average width was about six inches, though it narrowed off towards the bottom. But one very peculiar point about it was that near the top were a number of strange loops and smears, stretching away out of the main stream. They were the sort of smears that a child might make who had dipped its fingers in the blood, and had then started to draw patterns.

"The person who sat in this seat must have bled like a pig," said Darrell gravely. "From a wound in the head obviously."

Whose head? Who was it who had sat in the seat? Once again the same ghastly question, unasked and unanswered, save in our own minds. But I remember that to me all his hopes and ideas about crudeness and art suddenly became rather pitiful. To me there seemed no doubt who it was who had sat in that seat. And I felt thankful that Drummond wasn't there with us.

One could picture the poor girl sitting there, probably unconscious, with the blood welling out from some terrible wound in her head, while the devil beside her drove remorselessly on. A hideous thought, but what alternative was there?

"What do you make of it, Dixon?"

Darrell's voice cut into my thoughts.

"I'm afraid it's pretty obvious," I said. "And I'm afraid it rather disposes of your hopes as to crudity and art. This is the crudest and most brutal attack on a woman, that's all."

"You think so?" he said thoughtfully. "And yet it's all a little difficult to understand. Why did they stop here? What has become of them?"

"It's a road without much traffic," I answered. "Probably they changed into another car to put people still more off the scent. Don't forget that if they had garaged this car anywhere for the night they would have had some pretty awkward questions to answer."

"That's true," he agreed. "And yet it presupposes that the thing had been arranged beforehand."

"It probably was," I pointed out. "They were anyway going to change cars, and the fact that the poor girl was so terribly wounded did not make them alter their plans."

"But why mess up two cars?" he argued. "That's what I can't get at."

He once more switched the torch on to the stained cover.

"You know," he said, "those loops and smears puzzle me. What on earth can have caused them? What possible agency can have made that stream of blood divert itself like that? Hold the torch a moment, will you? I'm going to copy them into a notebook."

"My dear fellow," I remarked, "what on earth is the use? Do it if you like, but I should say that the best thing we can do is to make tracks for the nearest police-station and give them the number of this car. We want to find out the owner."

"It won't take a moment," he said, "and then we'll push off. There – is that about right?"

He handed me his rough sketch: a copy of it is before me as I write.

"Yes," I remarked, "that's pretty well how it looks. But I'm afraid it's not going to help us much."

"You never can tell," he answered. "Those marks didn't come there accidentally – that I swear. It's a message of sorts: I'm certain of it."

"It may be a message, but it's absolute gibberish," I retorted. "Now don't you think we'd better push on to a police-station. I've got the number of this car – ZW 3214."

He looked at me thoughtfully.

"Can you drive my Sunbeam?" he said.

"I blush to admit it," I answered, "but I'm one of those extraordinary people who have never driven a car in my life."

"That's a pity," he remarked. "Because I was going to propose that I stopped here, while you went. I think one of us ought to remain, in case anything happens."

"Good God!" I said, "hasn't enough happened already? However, I don't mind staying. Only get a move on: I'm beginning to feel like dinner."

"Stout fellow," he cried. "I'll be as quick as I possibly can."

He got into his car, and in half a minute was out of sight.

Now as I have already explained I am not one of those fortunate individuals to whom battle, murder, and sudden death come as the zest of life. And honesty compels me to admit that at no period of my career have I more bitterly regretted not having had lessons in driving. Moreover, I am essentially a town man: the country always seems to me to be so full of strange noises. Especially at night – and it was dark by now.

I lit a cigarette – quite unaware of the horror with which Drummond would have viewed such a proceeding. To see and not be seen, to hear and not be heard, was a dictum of his I was to learn later.

All sorts of weird whispering sounds came to my ears as I stood there beside the car. And once I gave a terrific start as a shrill scream came from the field close by.

"An animal," I reflected angrily. "A rabbit caught by a stoat. Don't be such a fool."

I began pacing up and down the middle of the road, conscious of an absurd desire for someone to speak to even if it was only an inebriated farm labourer. And then by way of forcing discipline on my mind, I made myself go over the whole amazing business from the beginning.

What was the letter that had made Mrs Drummond leave the house? Where did the two men at the *Cat and Custard Pot* come in? Why had this car stopped here and what had happened after? And finally those strange smears. Were they indeed some message, and if so who had written it? Was it that poor girl trying to write some final communication as she felt her life slipping away from her?

My thoughts turned to Drummond, and I felt most bitterly sorry for my earlier sarcasm. Still, there had been some excuse: I defy any ordinary person to have viewed his behaviour without feeling some doubts as to his sanity. The fact remained, however, that I owed him the most abject apology. Not that my apology would be much use to the poor devil in exchange for his wife.

I ground my cigarette out with my heel, and stared down the road. Surely it was about time for Darrell to get back. And as I stood there leaning against the bonnet, a bird got up with a sharp cry from a point in the hedge some hundred yards away. It was the cry of sudden alarm from which a poacher might have read much, but I read nothing.

And then a twig cracked: I heard it distinctly and stiffened. Another – and yet another, whilst I stood there motionless peering into the darkness. Did my eyes deceive me, or was there something dark moving cautiously along the grass beside the road, in the shadow of the hedge? I recalled times in France when strange things took shape in No Man's Land: when men became as bushes and bushes as men. And putting my hand to my forehead I found it was wet with sweat.

I listened again: all was silent. The stealthy mover, if there was a mover, was moving no more. My imagination probably, and with a shaking hand I extracted my cigarette-case. Damn it! what was there to be frightened at?

"Lawks sakes – look at this 'ere!"

The voice came from the hedge not ten yards away, and in my fright I dropped my case in the road. Then with an effort I pulled myself together: to be frightened at my time of life by a mere yokel was not good for one's pride.

"Look 'e 'ere, mister."

"Where are you?" I said. "I can't see you."

The fellow gave a cackling laugh which made me think he was not quite right in his head. And then came another remark which caused me to start forward in horror.

"A dead 'un."

"Where?" I cried, moving towards him slowly. My mouth felt suddenly dry: it required all my will power to force myself to go. I knew what I was going to see: I knew that there in the darkness just ahead of me I would find some half-witted yokel staring inquisitively at the body of the unfortunate girl. There would be a terrible wound in her head, and at each step I took my reluctance increased. I loathed the thought of having definite proof: up to date there had been a doubt, however shadowy.

"Where?" I said thickly, once again, and then I saw him just in front. His back was towards me, and he was bending over something that lay in the ditch close to the hedge. He was chuckling to himself in an idiotic way, and I heard a voice croak at him: "Shut up!" It was my own.

I reached his side, and bent over, too. And for a moment or two I stood there staring, hardly able to believe my eyes. True, a body was there, lying in that peculiar twisted position which tells its own tale. True, there was a terrible wound in the head, clearly visible even in the darkness. But it was not a woman; it was a man. And the feeling of relief was stupendous.

I turned to the yokel foolishly: turned and froze into immobility. The idiotic chuckling had ceased, and the face that was thrust near mine wore a sarcastic smile.

"Too easy," he remarked.

A pair of hands fastened on my throat, and I began to struggle desperately. Dimly I realised that it was a trap: that the man had been acting a part so as to draw me into an advantageous position in which to attack me. And then all other thoughts were blotted out by the appalling knowledge that as far as strength went I was a child in his hands. There was a roaring in my ears, a ghastly tightness in my throat. And I remember that my last coherent thought before I became unconscious was that if Drummond had been in my place the result would have been very different.

It was fitting, therefore, that the first man I should see when I opened my eyes was Drummond himself. For a moment or two I couldn't remember what had happened, and I stared foolishly around. I was lying on the grass beside the road, and my head and coat were sopping wet. Drummond with Darrell and another man were standing close to me in the light of the headlamps of a car.

"Hullo!" I said feebly.

They swung round.

"Hullo! little man," said Drummond. "You gave us a nasty shock. What fun and laughter have you been engaged in?"

"Where's the dead man?" I cried, sitting up.

They all stared at me.

"What's that?" said Drummond slowly. "A dead man, you say?"

I struggled to my feet, and stood swaying dizzily.

"Steady, old man," said Drummond. "Easy does it."

"There *was* a dead man," I repeated, and then I stared round. "Where's the other car?"

"Precisely," agreed Drummond. "Where is it? It wasn't here when we arrived."

"Not here," I repeated stupidly, "I don't understand. What's happened?"

"That's easily told," said Drummond. "By mere chance I ran into Peter at the police-station, and when I heard what you'd found I came along with him and this officer. We must have gone half a mile beyond here before he knew we'd gone too far. So we turned and came back. And the pool of oil told us where the car had been. Peter knew you couldn't drive, so we thought you must have been abducted in the car. And then quite by chance the officer found you in the ditch. You looked like a goner at first, but we sluiced you with cold water, and you'll be as fit as a trivet in a minute or two. When you do let's hear what happened to you."

"I'm all right now," I said. "A bit dizzy, that's all. Let me sit down in the car for a little."

It was quite true. My head was quite clear, and, except for a most infernally stiff neck, I felt none the worse for my experience. And I told them exactly what had taken place. They listened in silence, and it was only when I hesitated a little over saying who it was I had expected to find in the ditch that Drummond spoke.

"I understand," he said curtly. "Go on."

I finished my story, and then he spoke again.

"If any confirmation is needed," he remarked, "the ditch should supply it. Where was the body lying?"

I got out of the car and led them to the spot. As he had said, the ditch did supply it. A great pool of blood showed up red and sinister in the light of Darrell's torch, but of the body of the man whose blood it was there was no trace.

"So what happened," said Drummond thoughtfully, "is fairly easy to spot. But the reason for it is a little more obscure. The gentleman who caressed your windpipe had evidently been sent back to retrieve car and corpse. Finding you here he gave you the necessary medicine. Then he removed corpse in car. But if that was the great idea, why were car and corpse left here in the first place?"

"Would you recognise the man who attacked you, sir?" said the police-officer, speaking for the first time.

"I think I'd recognise him," I said, "but I couldn't give you a description of him that would be the slightest help."

"Well, there doesn't seem much use our standing here any more," remarked Drummond at length, and his voice was weary. "We know the number of the car, so the owner can be traced. But I shall be very much surprised if we find that helps us much."

He sighed, and lit a cigarette.

"Come on, Peter, we'd better be getting back. My stomach is flapping against my backbone, for want of food, and we can't do any more good here."

And I, for one, agreed with him fervently.

# CHAPTER 4

*In which we get the semblance of a clue*

Looking back on it now after the lapse of time, I find it hard to recall my exact state of mind that night. I remember that amongst certain members of the house-party I found myself in the position of a popular hero. To have been assaulted and left for dead conferred an air of distinction on me, which I found rather grateful and comforting. The tacit assumption seemed to be that only abnormal strength of constitution on my part had saved my life.

I also remember experiencing a distinct feeling of pique that amongst other members of the party my adventure seemed to cut no ice at all. They appeared to regard it as the most ordinary thing in the world. Two new arrivals had come – the two whom Longworth had been told to summon under the names of Ted and Toby. Their surnames were respectively Jerningham and Sinclair, and Tracey had managed to squeeze them into the house. And it was in describing the events of the afternoon and evening to these two that the point of view of this second section of the party became obvious. Not, I mean, that I wished it to be exaggerated in any way: at the same time I admit that I felt, when all was said and done, that whilst Drummond and Darrell had been in perfect safety at a police-station, I had had a murderous assault made on my life. And to have it described by Darrell as getting a clip over the ear-hole struck me as somewhat inadequate. The replies of the audience also left, I thought, a certain amount to be desired.

Jerningham said: "Pity you didn't ladle the bloke one back."

Sinclair said: "Splendid! So we know one of them by sight, anyway."

Then they all dismissed the matter as trifling, and resumed the interminable discussion. Not that I minded, you understand – but it struck me that it showed a slight lack of a proper sense of proportion.

However, I waived the matter: it was not my wife who had been forcibly dragged from her car in broad daylight. Had it been I should have been insane with worry. And that was the extraordinary thing about Drummond. Outwardly he seemed the most self-possessed of us all, and only the strained look in his eyes showed the mental condition he was in.

Bill Tracey was absolutely beside himself. That such a thing should have happened in his house made him almost incoherent. And it was characteristic of Drummond that in spite of his own agonising suspense, he should have gone out of his way to ease things for Bill.

"My dear fellow," he said more than once, "please don't blame yourself. The fact that it happened to take place here is nothing whatever to do with you. They waited till they were ready and then they struck. That they happened to become ready when we were staying with you, is just pure chance."

Which, though perfectly true, did but little to alleviate his feelings of responsibility. It was his house, and the bald fact remained that one of his guests, and a woman at that, had been decoyed away from it and been made the victim of foul play. And apart from his natural grief at such a thing happening, the prospect of the notoriety involved concerned him, of course, more than any of us save Drummond himself. It was Jerningham who summarised the situation after a while.

"Let's just see," he said, "that we've got this thing clear. Whilst playing tennis this afternoon Phyllis got a note delivered by hand of such importance that she stops playing and goes out alone in the Bentley. At that time Hugh was having a bit of back chat with the two foreign-looking blokes – "

"Who have not been traced at the railway-station," put in Tracey.

"Who have since disappeared," went on Jerningham. "But it is generally agreed that they had something to do with it, though what we don't know. Shortly after the Bentley is found deserted, showing every sign of having been the scene of a struggle."

"She dotted him one, Ted," said Drummond with certainty. "She dotted him good and hard with that spanner. In fact she killed him – glory be to Allah!"

They pondered this point in silence for a while.

"It stands to reason, old boy," went on Drummond, "that the man Dixon saw lying in the ditch is the same man whose trail we followed on the grass beside the Bentley."

"Very well then," said Jerningham, "make it so. She dotted him one. Finding herself suddenly attacked she out with the spanner and slogged him good and hard. So then the other bloke – there must have been at least one more – bunged Phyllis into the back of the other car, stuffed his pal into the seat beside him, and pushed off."

"It don't sound right to me, Ted," said Drummond slowly.

"What's wrong?" demanded Jerningham.

"All the last part. If you were driving a motorcar in broad daylight, and had to take with you a fellow who was bleeding like a pig from a wound in the head, would you put him on the seat beside you? Especially if you did not want to draw attention to yourself."

He took a long gulp of beer.

"Not so, old lad: you'd bung him on the floor at the back. And from Peter's description of the blood in the car that's what happened. If he'd been sitting in the seat beside the driver, the front of it would have been stained, too. It wasn't – only the back."

"I don't see that it matters much, anyway," I remarked. "Back or front the result is the same. Perhaps Mrs Drummond was beside the driver."

"Good Lord!" said Drummond, sitting up and staring at me. "I hadn't thought of that. Perhaps she was."

"What's stung you?" said Darrell, surprised, and we all looked at him curiously. He seemed strangely excited.

"Supposing Phyllis was sitting in that seat," he remarked. "Supposing the man was bleeding to death behind. Supposing she managed to get her hand over the back of the seat, with the idea of getting some message through by dipping her finger in the blood and writing on the cover."

His excitement infected us all, though, for the life of me, I couldn't see what he was getting at.

"Well – get on with it," said Darrell.

"Don't you see that the writing would be upside down?" cried Drummond. "Where's your notebook, Peter? Turn the page the other way round."

We crowded over his shoulder and stared at the rough sketch.

"It is," shouted Drummond. "Smeared letters, or I'll eat my hat. There's a K there: two Ks. And L: and E. What's that first word? Something KE... LUKE is it?"

"Like," I hazarded. "That first letter might be L."

"Then it's LIKE LAK," said Drummond, and we stared at one another a little blankly. If that was the solution it didn't seem to advance us much. Like Lak: it was meaningless. Probably not realising that it was useless the message had continued into the stream of blood where it had been obliterated. But that was no help.

"Anyway," said Drummond quietly, "it proves one thing. She wasn't unconscious."

He got up and went to the open window, where he stood with his back to us, staring out into the darkness. His shoulders were a little bowed: his hands were in his pockets. And, by Jove! I felt for the poor chap. Somewhere out under those same stars – perhaps twenty miles away, perhaps a hundred – his wife was in the hands of this infamous gang. Up-to-date action had kept him going, even if it had only consisted of futile motoring up and down roads. Now the time of forced inaction had come. There was nothing to distract his thoughts: nothing to take his mind off the ghastly possibilities of the situation.

There was no use sympathising with him: the matter had passed beyond words. Besides, it struck me that he was of the brand that is apt to shy away from sympathy like a frightened colt. And so we sat on in silence, hardly daring to meet one another's eyes, with the same fear clutching at all our hearts.

It didn't seem to matter very much whether or not Mrs Drummond had been conscious in the car. Was she conscious now? Was she even alive? It seemed too incredible to be sitting there in that peaceful room, contemplating such an appalling thought. And yet what was there to be done? That was the maddening part of it. Literally the only clue in our possession was the number of the car – ZW 3214. It was true that I might recognise the man who had nearly throttled me, but even on that point I felt doubtful. And that wasn't going to be much use, unless I saw him again.

The same applied to the two men at the *Cat and Custard Pot*. Both Drummond and I would recognise them again – but where were they? And even if they were found they would probably prove to be only very minor characters in the cast. The telephone on Tracey's desk rang suddenly, sounding unnaturally loud in the silence, and we looked at it almost apprehensively. Was it some further complication, or was it news?

"Hullo!" said Tracey, picking up the receiver. "Yes – speaking."

Drummond had swung round, his hands still in his pockets. And he stood there, his face expressionless, while the metallic voice from the machine, punctuated by occasional grunts from our host, droned on. At last Tracey replaced the receiver, and shook his head gloomily.

"Nothing, I'm afraid," he said. "It was the police. They've traced the car, and it belongs to a man called Allbright in Reading. He's a retired grocer, and absolutely above suspicion. He is away from home at the moment, and the car must have been coolly stolen from his garage this morning. He has a deaf housekeeper, who is also above suspicion, and who was in complete ignorance that the car had gone until visited by the police this evening."

Once more silence fell on the room, and Drummond, with the faintest perceptible shrug of his shoulders, again turned his back on us and stared into the darkness. Our only positive clue gone – or at any rate valueless: the outlook blacker, if possible, than before. The butler brought in a tray of drinks, and Tracey waved his hand at it mechanically.

"Help yourselves," he remarked, but nobody moved.

And then at last Drummond spoke. His back was still towards us: his voice was perfectly quiet.

"This situation is too impossible to continue," he said. "Something is bound to happen soon."

And as if in answer to his remark the telephone bell jangled a second time.

"I told you so," he said calmly. "This is news."

Tracey had again taken the receiver: and again we watched him with a kind of feverish anxiety. Was Drummond right? Or was it some further futile communication from the police?

"A lady wishes to speak to you, Drummond," said Tracey, and the tension suddenly became acute. "She won't give her name."

Drummond went to the instrument, and we waited breathlessly. And if there is a more maddening proceeding during a time of suspense than having to listen to one end of a telephone conversation, I have yet to experience it. We heard the metallic voice of the other speaker; we saw Drummond give an uncontrollable start, and then freeze into absolute immobility.

"So it is you," he said in a low voice. "Where is Phyllis?"

Again that metallic voice, and then quite clearly a laugh.

"Damn you," said Drummond, still in the same quiet tone. "What have you done with her?"

This time the voice went on for nearly a minute, and all we could do was to watch the changing expressions on his face, and try to imagine what was causing them. Anger, bewilderment, and finally blank surprise were all registered, and it was the latter which remained when the voice ceased.

"But look here!" he cried. "Are you there? Damn it – she's gone!"

He rang the bell furiously for exchange.

"Where did that last call come from?" he asked. "London. Can you possibly get me the number?"

We waited eagerly, only to see him lay down the receiver wearily.

"The public call-box at Piccadilly Circus," he said.

"It was Irma?" almost shouted Darrell.

"Yes – it was."

He stood there frowning, and we waited eagerly.

"It was that she-cat right enough. I'd know her voice anywhere. And she's got some dirty game up her sleeve."

45

"What did she say?" asked someone.

"She first of all said that she was charmed to renew her acquaintance with Phyllis, and that it seemed quite like old times. She went on to say that so far she had only been able to have a very brief chat with her, but that she hoped for many more in the near future. She was sure I would like to know that she was unhurt, but that how long that condition of affairs lasted depended on me entirely. That I should have a letter from her in the morning making things quite clear, and that all she could advise me to do for the present was to have a good night in. Then she rang off."

"Well – that's something," said Darrell. "We know she's unhurt."

"Yes – I don't think she would lie," agreed Drummond. "But what's she getting at? How can it depend on me?"

"That seems fairly obvious," said Jerningham gravely. "You're going to be put through it, old man, and if you don't play nicely Phyllis is going to suffer. There's no good not facing facts, and she's got you by the short hairs."

Drummond sat down heavily.

"I suppose you're right," he said slowly. "I'll do anything – anything. I wanted to ask her tonight if she would take me instead of Phyllis, but she's rung off."

Darrell laughed shortly.

"I don't think the answer would have been very satisfactory even if she hadn't," he said. "You're not a very comfortable person to have about the house, old boy."

"Hell!" said Drummond tersely.

Then he stood up, and the expression on his face made me feel profoundly thankful that I was never likely to come up against him.

"I'm going to take one of your boats, Tracey," he remarked. "Don't wait up for me: I shan't go to bed tonight."

The next moment he had vanished through the open window.

"Poor devil," said Bill. "I'm sorry for him. But I don't see that there's anything to be done."

"There isn't," said Darrell. "We can only wait for this letter tomorrow morning."

He helped himself to a whiskey and soda, and I followed his example. That was all we could do – wait for the letter. But it was impossible to prevent oneself speculating on the contents. What test was Drummond going to be put to? Was he going to be told to commit some crime? Some robbery possibly with his wife's safety depending on his success?

What a ghastly predicament to be in! To have to run the risk of a long term of imprisonment, or else to know that he was putting his wife in danger. And even if he ran the risk how could he be sure that the others would stick to their side of the bargain? Avowedly they were criminals of the worst type, so what reliance could possibly be put on their word?

The others had gone off to the billiard-room, leaving Tracey and me alone. And suddenly the utter incredibility of the whole situation came over me in a wave. Not twelve hours ago had I been sitting peacefully in my club, earnestly discussing with the secretary whether the new brandy was as good as the last lot. He had said yes: I had disagreed. And it had seemed a very important matter.

I laughed: and he looked up at me quickly.

"I don't see anything very humorous in the situation," he remarked.

I laughed again.

"No more do I, Bill, not really. But it had just occurred to me that if I was suddenly transported to the smoking-room of the club, and I told the occupants that since I last saw them a lady had been kidnapped from your house, I had found a dead man in a ditch, and finally had been nearly murdered for my pains – they might not believe me."

He grunted.

"You're right," he said. "They might not. At times I hardly believe it myself. Damn this accursed woman Irma – or whatever she calls herself!"

He mixed himself a drink savagely.

"We're going to have hordes of newspaper men round the place, poking their confounded noses into everything. And, being Whitsuntide, they'll probably run special steamers to view the scene of the crime. I tell you, Joe, I wouldn't have had it happen for worlds. Of course I'm very sorry for Drummond – but I wish it had taken place somewhere else."

"Naturally," I agreed. "At the same time, Bill, don't forget that everything that happened did take place somewhere else. The dead man I found was twelve miles from here – and he has since disappeared. The car has disappeared, too. In fact there's nothing to connect the matter with this house."

"What do you mean?" he said. "Nothing to connect it with this house! What about Mrs Drummond? Wasn't she staying here?"

"She was – undoubtedly. But hasn't it occurred to you – mind you, I only put it forward as a possibility – that Drummond may be compelled by the gang who have got her to keep the fact of her disappearance quiet?"

"But the police know it already," he cried.

"They know she went out in a car, and that the car was found empty. That does not necessarily mean that she has disappeared. We know she has, but that's a very different matter. And if, as I surmise, Drummond is going to be ordered to commit a crime as the price for his wife's life – or at any rate safety – the first essential is that he should keep the police out of it as much as possible."

"Commit a crime!" He stared at me for a moment or two and then put down his glass on the table. "You really think that that is going to be the next move?"

48

"I don't know any more than you do," I said. "The whole thing is so absolutely amazing that no ordinary rules seem to apply. If they had murdered the poor girl outright as an act of revenge it would at any rate have been understandable. But this new development can only mean that they are going to put pressure on him through his wife."

"Well, I must frankly admit," he said at length, "that the less that is known about this affair the better I shall be pleased. At the same time I'd hate to know that Drummond was running round the country robbing churches or something of that sort."

He paused, struck by a sudden thought.

"It might be a case, not of blackmail exactly, but of ransom. On the payment of a sum of money she will be returned."

"Is he a wealthy man?" I asked.

"Quite well off. Do you think that's the solution, Joe?"

"My dear old man," I cried, "ask me another. I don't think I've ever been so hopelessly at sea in my life. I shall put a cold compress round my neck, and go to bed. Presumably all our questions will be answered tomorrow morning."

And to bed I went – but not to sleep. Try as I would I could not stop thinking about the affair. That last idea of Bill Tracey's had a good deal to be said for it. And what would happen if Drummond wouldn't pay – or couldn't? People of the type we were up against were not likely to ask a small sum.

Would they go on keeping her a prisoner until he had scraped together the money? Or would they murder her? I shuddered at the thought: this was England, not a bandit-infested desert. They would never dare to run such an appalling risk. They might threaten, of course, but at that it would stop. And then as if to mock me I saw once again that evil face with its cynical smile: heard that voice: "Too easy," felt those vice-like hands on my throat. Would they stop at that?

At last I could bear it no longer. I got up, and lit a cigarette: then I went and sat down by the open window. A very faint breeze was stirring in the trees: from the other end of the lawn came the mournful cry of an owl. And somewhere out there in the darkness was that poor devil Drummond, on the rack with anxiety and worry.

Suddenly the moon came out from behind a cloud, throwing fantastic shadows across the lawn – the clear-cut black and white shadows of the night. And after a while I began to imagine things: to see movement where there was no movement – to hear noises when there was no noise. Every board that creaked in the house seemed like the footsteps of a man, and once I started violently as a bat flitted past close to. In fact I came quite definitely to the conclusion that during the hours of darkness Piccadilly was good enough for me. With which profound reflection I got back into bed, and promptly fell asleep. But what the footman thought, I don't know. Because when a motorcar with blood spouting from the radiator is on the point of knocking you down, and you see that it isn't really a radiator, but the face of a man with a cynical smile who continually says "Too easy," it is only natural that you should push that face. I did – and it was the footman's stomach. The only comfort was that he had already put down the tea.

# CHAPTER 5

*In which the letter arrives*

And now I come to the beginning proper of the amazing adventure which was to occupy us for the next few days. The happenings of the preceding day were only the necessary preliminaries, without which the adventure could not have started.

As I have said, the two alternatives which I had in my mind as I went downstairs the next morning could be summed up in the two words ransom or crime. And it was with a queer feeling of excitement that I saw Drummond standing in the hall holding a bulky letter in his hand. THE letter.

"How's the neck?" he remarked.

"So so," I said. "You've heard from that woman?"

He nodded his head thoughtfully.

"I have. And I'll be damned if I can make out if I'm mad or if she is. Go and hit a sausage, and then we'll have a council of war."

I went into the dining-room, to find that the rest of his pals had nearly finished. None of the women were down yet, so conversation was non-existent. And ten minutes later we all duly assembled in Tracey's study.

"I've read this letter twice," said Drummond, coming straight to the point, "and as I said to Dixon I don't know whether I'm mad or she is."

He looked a bit fine-drawn, I thought, but much less worried than he had done the previous night.

"I should think the best thing to do is for me to read it aloud to you," he went on. "The post-mark on the envelope is of no assistance. It was posted in London, and that doesn't help. Somewhat naturally also there is no address."

He spread out the sheets and began.

"Mon Ami,

"In case you have forgotten, I wish to recall to your memory the circumstances of our last meeting. A little more than six months ago you may remember we met beside the wreckage of the airship. And I told you then that I knew you had killed Carl. It matters not how I knew: some things are incapable of ordinary explanation. But if it is of any interest to you, I did, as a matter of fact, make further enquiries from people who had been on that last voyage. And from them I learned that I was right, and that you did kill him.

"Six months ago, Drummond, and during those six months you have never been out of my thoughts for long. There was no hurry, and during a winter spent in Egypt, I have been indulging in the luxury of anticipation. They say it is better than realisation: the next few days should decide that point as far as this particular case is concerned. There was another reason also which necessitated a little delay. Various arrangements had to be made in England – arrangements which took time. These have now been made, and I trust that in the near future you will find them satisfactory.

"However, I go too fast. The first thing I had to decide was what method I should adopt for punishing you adequately. My revenge, if I was to enjoy it to the full, had to be carefully thought out. I wanted nothing crude"; (I caught Darrell's eye at that moment) "I wanted something artistic. And above all I wanted something long drawn out.

"And so your brilliant intellect will at once perceive that no mere death coming suddenly out of the blue could fit into my ideas. You smile, perhaps: you recall that in the past you were frequently threatened with death and that you are very much alive today. Agreed, *mon ami*; but do not forget the little verse I sent you. Doubtless you have inspected the message contained in it, and it is up to me to prove that that message is no empty boast.

"For example, it would have been the easiest thing in the world to have killed your dear Phyllis yesterday afternoon. And her positively murderous assault on one of my most trusted assistants really made me very angry for a while. The poor man is quite dead.

"In parenthesis, *mon cher*, who on earth is the funny little man you left to guard the car when you found it? From the description I've heard he's a new one on me."

"Damn the woman!" I spluttered, and even Drummond grinned suddenly. Then he went on.

"To return, however. It would have been very easy to have killed her, but so far from doing so the dear girl is sitting with me as I write. Not only easy – but just. We should have been all square. But I want more satisfaction than that, Drummond: much more. And so I will come down to my little scheme.

"In the past your physical strength has always excited my warmest admiration. But I have never been quite so certain about your mental ability. Luck, I think, has entered a good deal into the matter, and though I should be the last person to belittle luck, yet it is apt to affect the issue somewhat unfairly.

"And so on this occasion I propose to test your brain. Not unduly, I trust, but enough to afford me a certain amount of amusement. Do not be alarmed – your physical strength will be tested also. If you emerge triumphant your dear Phyllis will be restored to your bosom. If on the other hand you fail, then I shall claim my pound of flesh. In other words, what might have so easily been done yesterday afternoon will merely have been postponed.

"The test is expressed simply by two words: Find Phyllis. You raise your eyebrows: that, you say, is somewhat naturally the test. But wait, *mon ami*, and I will explain a little further. You have doubtless heard of hidden treasure hunts: perhaps joined in one yourself. This is going to be run on the same rules. You will receive clues which you will interpret to the best of your ability. These clues will lead you to various places, where further clues will await you. They will also lead you to various places where you may or may not enjoy yourself. Things will happen which you may or may not like. In fact, my dear Drummond, to put the matter in a nutshell, you may or may not pull through. As I said, I have made my arrangements with some care.

"One further word. This little matter is between you and me. I have no objection to your roping in your friends – in fact, the more the merrier. But I don't want the police butting in. You could not avoid it yesterday afternoon, I know, so you are forgiven for that. But get them out of it now – quickly. Another thing, too. I don't want Uncle Percival, or whatever he calls himself, asking absurd questions from any of the Broadcasting Centres. If that should happen our little game would cease abruptly. So bear those two points in mind: no police, no broadcasting. And that, I think, is all. You will get your first clue today."

Drummond laid down the letter, and lit a cigarette.

"What do you think of it?" he said.

"The thing is a fantastic leg pull," cried Tracey.

But Drummond shook his head doubtfully.

"I wonder," he said. "What do you think, Peter?"

"That she means every word of it, old boy," answered Darrell, positively. "That's no leg pull: it's damned grim earnest."

"Hear, hear," said Jerningham. "We're for the trail again."

"You mean to tell me," spluttered Tracey, "that this woman has hidden your wife, and now expects you to go chasing round the country till you find her! Dash it – it's absurd."

"Absurd or not absurd," said Drummond gravely, "that is exactly what this woman has done. And from what I know of her it's going to be some chase."

He got up, and suddenly, to my amazement, an almost ecstatic grin spread over his face.

"Gosh! boys," he said, "if it wasn't that it was Phyllis, what a glorious time we should have. Why did we never think of it before with Carl? We might have had two or three games in our spare time."

Then he became serious again.

"Look here, Tracey," he said: "and you, too, Dixon, may I rely on you not to say a word of this even to the ladies? The fewer people who know about it the better. If this came to the ears of a newspaper man, we'd have the whole of Fleet Street on our heels. So – not a word to a soul."

"A police-sergeant to see you, sir."

The butler was holding the door open.

"Mind," said Drummond urgently – "not a word."

The officer who had gone with us to the deserted Bentley the previous afternoon entered the room.

"Good morning, sergeant," said Drummond quietly. "Found Mr Allbright's car yet?"

The policeman shook his head.

"I'm afraid not, sir," he said. "May I ask if you have any news of your wife?"

Drummond frowned suddenly: then he gave a short laugh.

"Yes – I have. Look here, sergeant – you're a man of discretion."

I looked at him covertly: what tale was he going to tell?

"Well, sir," said the officer, with a slightly gratified smile, "they don't make you a sergeant for nothing."

"Precisely," said Drummond. "Well – the fact of the matter is this. My wife has run away – bolted. With another man."

He lit a cigarette with a sort of savage resignation. "I didn't say so yesterday, but I feared even then that that note that was brought her was from the swine who – "

He broke off abruptly – words had failed him – and strode to the window.

"Poor old Hugh," said Sinclair sadly. "It's a devilish business. That dirty little sweep of all people, too."

Drummond invoked the Deity twice, while the sergeant stared at him blankly.

"But look here, sir," he said, "what about all that blood?"

"That, sergeant," remarked Drummond, "is the staggering part of the whole business. When my wife rang me up last night to tell me that she had – she had left me, she said – 'I suppose you've found the Bentley by now.' I said to her – 'But what about the blood on the grass?' She said 'What on earth are you talking about? If it's a riddle I haven't got time to buy it now.' Then she rang off. She knew nothing about it, sergeant – absolutely nothing."

The officer's face was blanker than before.

"Since then," went on Drummond, "we've been trying to reconstruct what happened. And the only possible conclusion we can come to is this. The car belonging to Mr Allbright was stolen by two or three men. Driving along the road, they came on the deserted Bentley. Well, if they'd steal one car, they'd steal another. So they decided to steal that, too. And then they fell out – why, Heaven alone knows. Probably one of them was already at the wheel of the Bentley – and there was a struggle in which somebody got hit over the head with the spanner. Much harder than was intended. They all became frightened, and bundled the wounded man into the closed car. Of course," he continued modestly, "it's only crude amateur deduction: there are doubtless many objections to our theory – "

"Many," agreed Darrell, staring out of the window.

"Which your trained brain will spot," went on Drummond. "But the great point as far as we are concerned is this. As far as I am concerned, I should say. The whole thing is merely an amazing coincidence. The blood we saw on the road, the blood in Mr Allbright's car, has nothing to do with my wife's disappearance. And since I still have hopes that she will realise the error of her way, and come back to me, the last thing I want is to run any risk of hardening her heart by worrying her with police enquiries."

"You know my views, Hugh," said Jerningham.

"And I damned well don't want to hear them again," snapped Drummond.

"A lounge lizard like that!" cried Jerningham scornfully. "How you can dream of forgiving her I don't know."

"Lounge lizard, gentlemen?" said the bewildered policeman.

"That's right, sergeant," Jerningham pointed an outraged finger at space. "A lounge lizard. A ballroom snake. What matter that his Black Bottom is the best in London?"

"My Gawd! sir," gasped the other. "His 'ow much?"

"What matter, I say?" swept on Jerningham. "Is that a thing which should commend itself to reasonable decent men?"

"I should 'ardly say so myself, sir," agreed the sergeant fervently.

Jerningham paused to recover his breath.

"What is the gent's name, sir?" said the sergeant, producing his pencil and notebook.

"Albert. Albert Prodnut," said Jerningham, and Drummond sat down abruptly.

"And his address?"

"I wish we knew," answered Jerningham. "If we did, doubtless by this time Captain Drummond would have removed his liver with a rusty penknife. I speak metaphorically."

"So you don't know where he is, sir?"

"Somewhere on the Continent," said Drummond in a hollow voice.

"And your wife, too?"

Drummond groaned and hid his face in his hands, while Jerningham rose and took the sergeant by the arm.

"No more now, sergeant," he whispered confidentially. "He is strung up to breaking point. In a week or two, perhaps. Or a month. And in the meantime you will treat what we have told you as absolutely confidential, won't you?"

He propelled him gently towards the door.

"It's all very strange, sir," he said in a worried voice.

"If you knew Albert Prodnut you'd think it was a damned sight stranger," said Jerningham feelingly. "One of those strange cases of mental aberration, sergeant – almost I might say of psycho-sclerosis – which baffle the cleverest doctor. Leave him to us now."

The door closed behind the harassed officer, and Jerningham held up his two thumbs.

"Prodnut," said Drummond weakly. "Why Prodnut?"

"Why not? It's very difficult to think of a name when you're suddenly asked for one. There is a ring of sincerity about Albert Prodnut that carries entire conviction."

"Look here, you fellows," said Tracey seriously, "this is getting beyond a joke. You can't expect any man out of a lunatic asylum to believe that absurd rigmarole."

"We had to say something," remarked Drummond. "Personally I think we told the tale rather well."

"Yes – but what about me?" said Tracey. "It's a tissue of lies from beginning to end."

"We can't tell the truth," answered Drummond gravely. "Look here, Tracey, I'm very sorry about this, and I quite appreciate the difficulties of your position. In the bottom of your mind you probably think that that woman's letter is a bluff. I know it isn't. We've got to keep the police out of this if we possibly can. And I really couldn't think of anything better on the spur of the moment."

"You still mean," said Tracy amazed, "to take that woman at her word! To go hunting about all over England on clues she sends you, and which will probably lead you nowhere nearer your wife than you are at present!"

"What else can I do?" cried Drummond. "She's in the position of being able to dictate terms."

Once again the door opened and Parker came in: this time with a telegram on a salver.

"For you, sir," he said, handing it to Drummond.

He tore open the yellow envelope, and as he read the message a look of complete bewilderment spread over his face. "Well, I'm damned!" he muttered. "No answer, thank you, Parker. Listen here, you fellows," he went on as the butler left the room, "what in the name of fortune do you make of this?

"My first a horse may draw or even two the rest is found at York and aids the view and when you've solved that bit by dint of trying an inn you'll find where fishermen are lying."

"It's the first clue," said Jerningham excitedly. "She said you'd get it this morning."

"But it's hopeless," cried Drummond in despair. "The simplest crossword reduces me to a jibbering wreck. If I've got to try and solve these damned things, I'm done before I start."

"There are half-a-dozen perfectly good people to help you, old boy," said Darrell. "Sling the paper over. Let's put it down as it's meant to be – in the form of a verse."

He scribbled the words on a piece of paper, while we leaned over his shoulder. And even Tracey seemed impressed by this sudden new development.

"Now then," said Darrell, "does that make it any better?"

> "My first a horse may draw, or even two;
> The rest is found at York, and aids the view.
> And when you've solved that bit by dint of trying,
> An inn you'll find where fishermen are lying."

"If line three is right," I said, "the first two are a complete clue in themselves."

"That's so," agreed Tracey. "But what sort of a clue? Is it the name of a man or a town or what?"

"Let's assume it's a town to start with," said Jerningham. "There's an inn mentioned in the last line."

"What's found at York?" demanded Drummond gloomily.

"Ham, dear old boy," burbled Algy Longworth.

"And Archbishops," said Sinclair hopefully.

"I don't know that it can be truthfully maintained," said Tracey mildly, "that either ham or Archbishops aid the view."

"Hold hard a bit," remarked Darrell. "Let's start at the beginning. 'My first a horse may draw, or even two.' Presumably that means two horses. So it's a horse-drawn vehicle suitable for one or two horses."

"By Jove! Peter, you're a blinking marvel," cried Drummond. "Cart, cab, wagon."

"You don't have a two-horse cab," objected Jerningham.

"Wagon sounds possible," said Darrell. "There must be places beginning with Wagon. Got a map, Tracey?"

"Here's the *Times Gazetteer*," he answered. "By Jove! Wagonmound."

"Got it!" shouted Drummond. "There's bound to be a mound at York."

But Tracey was shaking his head.

"Sorry. I spoke too soon. The darned place is in New Mexico. And that's the only place beginning with Wagon that's mentioned."

"Hell!" said Drummond, and relapsed into silence.

"What about Dray," I remarked. "You speak of a one-horse dray and a two-horse dray."

"Stout fellow," cried Drummond. "Look up Dray, Tracey."

"There are about forty Draytons," he said. "Lots of Draycotts: Drayminster, Drayney."

"Drayminster!" I yelled. "Minster, York Minster."

"I believe you've got it," said Darrell. "It fits at any rate as far as the first two lines are concerned."

"By Jove! you fellows," cried Jerningham. "Listen here. This is the AA handbook. Drayminster. Population 2,231, Sussex. 55 miles to London. Now brace yourselves for it. Hotel – the *Angler's Rest*. We *have* got it."

For a while we all stared at one another too excited to speak. Was there a mistake? Fishermen lying; *Anglers' Rest*. No one could say that York Minster was not an aid to the view: a dray could certainly be drawn by one or two horses. It fitted, every clue fitted.

"Get packed, boys," cried Drummond. "We lunch at the *Angler's Rest*. Gosh! I feel better. We've started. Beer, Tracey, old lad – pints of beer. And you and Dixon shall wish us good hunting."

The beer arrived, and then Drummond raised his hand as for some solemn rite. Slowly he waved it to and fro, and once more did the words of his favourite refrain burst forth with vigour:

"The more we are together – together – together: the more we are together the merrier we shall be."

"A new music-hall song?" I enquired politely.

And all they did was to roar with laughter.

"When we start hunting, boys," he said, "that shall be the war-cry. Don't forget – once for the rally, twice for danger."

I suppose it was foolish of me, but I really couldn't help it. There was something contagious about the spirits of this extraordinary gang which must have infected me.

"I must learn the tune," I said. "For if you'll allow me I should very much like to join you in whatever is coming."

They all stared at me, and then, a little doubtfully, at one another.

"Of course," I said stiffly, "if you'd prefer I didn't."

"It isn't that," interrupted Drummond. "Look here, Dixon, if you're going to come in on this thing, you'd better be under no delusions. You got a taste last night of the sort of people we're going to be up against. And believe you me that's nothing to what we shall strike. I want you to understand quite clearly that if you do join us you'll be taking your life in your hands at most hours of the day and night. I mean it – quite literally. It's not going to be a question of merely solving little puzzles."

"I'll chance it," I answered. "As a matter of fact I dislike most strongly the implication behind the phrase funny little man."

Once more the whole lot burst out laughing.

"Right," said Drummond. "That settles it. But don't say you weren't warned if you get your ear bitten badly."

# CHAPTER 6

*In which I get the second clue*

The village of Drayminster is one of the beauty spots of England. Somewhat out of the beaten track, it is as yet unspoiled by motor coaches and hordes of trippers. The river Dray meanders on its peaceful way parallel to the main street, and in the very centre of the village stands the *Angler's Rest*. A strip of grass separates it from the water's edge, and moored to two stakes a punt stretches out into the stream from the end of which the energetic may fish for the wily roach and perch. A backwater – but what a pleasant backwater.

"Your lady friend," I said to Drummond, "has undoubtedly an artistic eye."

We were sitting on the lawn after lunch, and he grunted thoughtfully. The others had departed on a tour of exploration, and save for the motionless figure of the landlord's son at the end of the punt, we were alone.

"If only I could be absolutely certain that we were right," he remarked. "That we aren't wasting our time sitting here."

"Unless the whole thing is a stupid hoax," I said reassuringly, "I'm certain our solution was correct."

It was the inaction that chafed him, I could see. I think he had expected to find another clue waiting for us on our arrival. But there had been nothing, and gradually his mood of elation had left him. He had kept his eyes fixed so searchingly on an elderly parson and his daughter during lunch, that the poor man had become quite hot and bothered. In fact, it wasn't until our host had assured him that the reverend gentleman had come to the hotel regularly for the last twenty years, that he desisted.

"It's not a hoax," he said doggedly. "So why the devil, if we're right, haven't we heard something more?"

"Quite possibly that's all part of the game," I answered. "They may know that that is a method of rattling you."

"By Jove!" he cried, "I hadn't thought of that."

He looked quite relieved at the suggestion.

"There's one thing we might do," I went on. "It may not be any good, but it can't do any harm. Let's find out if there are any houses in the neighbourhood that have recently changed hands. If they are hiding your wife, a house is the most likely place to do it in."

"Dixon," he said, "you're the bright boy all right. My brain at the moment is refusing to function altogether. Hi! John – or whatever your name is – cease tormenting fish, and come here a moment."

Obediently the boy put down his rod and approached.

"Now, you know all the big houses in the neighbourhood, don't you?"

The boy nodded his head.

"That's right, mister. There be the Old Manor – that be Squire Foley's. And there be Park House. That do belong to Sir James – but he be away now."

"Has there been any house sold round about here recently," I put in.

The boy scratched his head.

"There be Widow Maybury's," he said. "She did sell her little cottage, and be gone to live with her darter near Lewes."

"Who bought it?" I cried.

"They do say he be a writer from Lunnon, or sommat fulish like that. He just comes occasional like."

"Is he here now?" asked Drummond.

"Ay," said the boy. "He come last night. There was a young leddy with him."

I caught Drummond's eye, and it was blazing with excitement.

"They come in a motorcar," went on the boy.

"Where is the cottage?" said Drummond.

"End o' village," he replied. "'Lily Cottage', it do be called."

Drummond had already risen to his feet, and the boy looked at him doubtfully.

"He be a terrible funny-tempered gentleman," he said. "He set about Luke Gurney with a stick, he did – two or three weeks ago. Had to pay Luke five pounds, he did, or old Gaffer Gurney would have had him up afore the beak."

"My lad," said Drummond, "there is half a crown. You may now resume your occupation of catching fish."

He turned to me. "Are you coming?" he said.

"Well," I said a little doubtfully, "we'd better be careful, hadn't we? This fellow may be a perfectly harmless individual."

"In which case we will withdraw gracefully," he cried. "Damn it, man, I believe we're on the scent. Why – Good God! Phyllis may be actually there now."

"All right – I'll come," I said. "Only – cautious does it."

But for the moment Drummond was beyond caution. The thought that possibly his wife was within half a mile of him had sent him completely crazy, and it was only with the greatest difficulty that I restrained him from bursting straight into the house when we got there.

"You can't, my dear fellow," I cried. "We must have some sort of excuse."

It was a small cottage standing back a little from the road. A tiny patch of garden in front was bright with flowers, and two pigeons regarded us thoughtfully from a dovecot.

"We'll ask if it's for sale," he said, and then suddenly he gripped my arm like a vice.

65

"Look up at the top left-hand window," he muttered.

I did so, and got a momentary glimpse of the saturnine, furious face of a man glaring at us. Then like a flash it was gone.

"Dixon," he said hoarsely, "we've done it. She's in there. And I'm going through that house with a fine comb."

A little dubiously I followed him up the path. Nothing that I could have done would have stopped him, but even before he knocked on the door I had a shrewd suspicion that he was making a blazing error. It seemed impossible that, after all the chat and bother there had been, the solution should prove so simple.

And a blazing error it proved. The door was flung open and the man we had seen peering at us through the window appeared. And to put it mildly he was not amused.

"What the – " he began.

"Laddie," interrupted Drummond firmly, "something tells me that you and I will never be friends. Nevertheless I am going to honour your charming cottage with a call."

He extended a vast hand and the other man disappeared into the hat-rack – an unstable structure. Drummond disappeared upstairs. And the scene that followed beggared description. The hat-rack, in falling, had pinned the owner underneath. Moreover, as far as I could see, one of the metal pegs was running straight into the small of his back. Then came a shrill feminine scream from above, and Drummond appeared at the top of the stairs, looking pensive. He was still looking pensive when he joined me.

"I fear," he murmured, "that someone has blundered."

A rending crash from behind announced that the hat-rack was still in the picture, and we faded rapidly down the street.

"A complete stranger," he remarked. "With very little on. Most embarrassing."

I began to shake helplessly.

"But I maintain," he went on, "that no man has a right to possess a face like that. It's enough to make anyone suspicious."

A howl of rage from behind us announced that the battle of the hat-rack was over.

"Pretend," said Drummond, "that I'm not all there."

"Hi, you, sir," came a shout, and we paused.

"You are addressing me, sir?" remarked Drummond majestically, as the other approached.

"You scoundrel," he spluttered. "How dare you force your way into my house?"

"My Prime Minister will raise the point at the next meeting of Parliament," said Drummond. "Do you ever hit yourself hard on the head with a heavy spanner? Hard and often. You must try it. It's so wonderful when you stop. The audience is terminated."

He turned on his heel, and strode off down the street, whilst I touched my head significantly.

"Good God!" said the other. "Is he mad?"

"Touched," I murmured. "Result of shell shock. He'll probably be quite all right in an hour or two, when he'll have completely forgotten the whole incident."

"But the cursed fellow ought to be locked up," he cried angrily.

"His relatives don't want it to come to that if it can be avoided," I said. "I much regret the incident, sir – but…"

"Bring me a mushroom omelette without…"

Drummond had suddenly returned, and was staring fixedly at his late victim.

"Without?" stammered the other nervously. "Without what?"

"Without mushrooms, you fool. Damn it – the man's not right in his head. What else could it be without? Come, fellow, I would fain sleep."

He seized me by the arm, and stalked off in the direction of the *Angler's Rest*, leaving the other standing speechless in the road.

"Did we put it across him?" he said when we were out of hearing.

"More or less," I answered. "He said you ought to be locked up."

"I really don't blame him," he conceded. "She was a pretty girl, too," he continued irrelevantly as we arrived at the hotel. "Very pretty."

Darrell and Jerningham were both on the lawn, but the others had evidently not yet returned.

"Any luck?" they asked as we pulled up a couple of chairs.

"Damn all," said Drummond moodily. "I pushed a bloke's face into a hat-rack, and contemplated a charming lady with very little on, but we never got the trace of a clue. What's worrying me, chaps, is whether we ought to sit still and wait, or run round in small circles and look."

"After your recent entertainment," I remarked mildly, "I should suggest the former. At any rate for a time."

"Perhaps you're right," he agreed resignedly. "All I hope is that it won't be for long."

"But you don't imagine, do you, old boy," remarked Jerningham, "that Phyllis is likely to be round about here? Because, I don't."

"What's that?" said Drummond blankly.

"This is but the beginning of the chase. And I don't think Mademoiselle Irma would have run the risk of bringing her to the place where all of us would certainly be, granted we solved the first clue. All we're going to get here is the second clue."

"And probably have a darned sticky time getting it," said Darrell.

He stretched out his legs and closed his eyes, and after a while I followed his example. The afternoon was drowsy, and if we were going to have a sticky time, sleep seemed as good a preparation for it as anything. And it seemed only a moment afterwards that a hand was laid on my shoulder, and I sat up with a start.

The shadows had lengthened, and at first I saw no one. The landlord's son had ceased to fish: the chairs that the others had occupied were empty.

"You will, I am sure, excuse me," came a pleasant voice from over my shoulder, "but your snores are a little disconcerting to the sensitive ear."

"I beg your pardon," I said stiffly as I rose. "Falling asleep when sitting up is always dangerous."

He regarded me affably – a pleasant-faced little white-haired man.

"Don't mention it," he said. "I do to others as I would they should do to me. And I feared you might collect a crowd, who would misconstrue the reason of the uproar, in view of the proximity of the *Angler's Rest*."

He sat down in the seat recently occupied by Drummond.

"You are staying long?" he enquired pleasantly.

"That largely depends," I answered.

"A charming village," he remarked. "A bit of old-world England, the like of which I regret to say is becoming all too rare. They tell me it was fifth – or was it sixth – in the competition for the most beautiful village."

He frowned.

"How annoying. Was it fifth or sixth?"

"Does it," I murmured, "make very much difference?"

For a moment or two he stared at me fixedly.

"It might," he said gravely, "make a lot."

Then he looked away, and I felt a sudden pricking feeling of excitement. Was he implying something? Was there a hidden meaning in his apparently harmless remark? Was he one of those people who really are worried by failing to remember some small, insignificant detail such as that – or was it the beginning of a new clue?

"Only, I should imagine, to the lucky inhabitants," I said lightly. "For my own part I am content with it whatever place it occupied in the list of honour."

He nodded.

"Perhaps so. It is certainly very lovely. And the inn is most comfortable. I always feel that in such a setting as this the old-time English beverage of ale tastes doubly good – a point of view which was shared, I think, by a very large individual who was sitting in this chair half an hour or so ago."

"I know the man you mean," I answered. "He is a very prolific beer-drinker."

"He crooned some incantation which seemed to assist his digestion," he went on with an amused smile. "You are all one party, I suppose?"

"As a matter of fact we are," I said politely, restraining a desire to ask what business it was of his. If there was anything to be got – I'd get it.

"We are here," I added on the spur of the moment, "on a quest."

"Indeed," he murmured. "How interesting! And how mysterious! Would it be indiscreet to enquire the nature of the quest?"

"That I fear is a secret," I remarked. "But it concerns principally the large individual of whom you spoke."

"My curiosity is aroused," he said. "It sounds as if a lady should be at the bottom of it."

"A lady is at the bottom of it," I answered.

He shook his head with a whimsical smile.

"What it is to be young! I, alas! can only say with the poet 'Sole – sitting by the shores of old romance.'"

Once again did he give me a peculiar direct stare before looking away.

"At the moment," I remarked, "the quotation eludes me."

"It may perhaps return in time," he smiled. "And prove of assistance."

"In what possible way can it prove of assistance?" I said quickly.

"It is always an assistance to the mind when a forgotten tag is recalled," he remarked easily.

I said nothing: was I imagining things, or was I not? He seemed such a harmless old buffer, and yet...

"As one grows older," he went on after a while, "one turns more and more to the solace of books. And yet what in reality are words worth? *'Si jeunesse savait: si vieillesse pouvait.'* The doctrine of life in a nutshell, my friend."

Still I said nothing: why I know not, but the conviction was growing on me that there was a message underlying his remarks.

"Words may be worth a lot," I said at length, "if one fully understands their meaning."

For the third time he gave me a quick, penetrating stare.

"To do that it is necessary to use one's brain," he murmured. "You will join me in a little gin and vermouth?"

"Delighted," I said perfunctorily. Then – "May I ask you a perfectly straight question, sir?"

He returned to his seat from ringing the bell.

"But certainly," he said. "Whether I give you a perfectly straight answer, however, is a different matter."

"Naturally," I agreed. "Do you know why we are here, or do you not?"

"You have already told me that you are in quest of a lady."

He raised his glass to his lips.

"*Votre santé, m'sieur* – and also to the success of your search. If any stray words of mine have assisted you, I shall be doubly rewarded for having aroused you from your slumbers."

He replaced his glass on the table.

"Exquisite, is it not – the gold and black of the colour scheme? But alas! the air grows a little chilly *pour la vieillesse.* You will pardon me, I trust – if I leave you. And once again – good hunting."

He went indoors and I sat on, thinking. More and more strongly was the conviction growing on me that the second clue lay in our conversation: less and less, could I see a ray of light. Was it contained in that quotation – 'Sole – sitting by the shores of old romance'? He had said it might prove of assistance – and then had passed off his remark.

Who had written it, anyway? It came back to me as a dimly remembered tag, but as to the author my mind was a blank. Had the well-known old French proverb any bearing on the case?

His voice from a window above me cut into my reverie.

"I feel sure that you are tormenting yourself over the author of my little quotation," he chuckled. "It has suddenly occurred to me that his name was actually mentioned in our conversation."

The window closed, leaving me staring blankly at it. Mentioned in our conversation! No author's name had been mentioned: to that I could swear. And yet would he have said so if it was not the case? It seemed stupid and unnecessary.

Once more I ran over it, trying to recall it word by word. It was maddening to think that I was now possibly in actual possession of the information we wanted, and yet that I couldn't get it.

I ordered another gin and vermouth: perhaps, after all, I had been mistaken. An old gentleman in all probability with an impish delight in the mysterious who was deliberately playing a little joke on me. And then the window above me opened again.

"Goodbye, my friend. I am sorry to say that I have to leave this charming spot. And I trust for all your sakes that your brain will prove equal to my little problem."

I got up quickly: surely that remark clinched the matter. He was one of the others, and I'd make him tell me more. A Ford was standing by the door, and a minute or two later I saw him getting into it.

"Look here, sir," I said, "I must insist on your being more explicit. You *do* know why we are here; you *have* been giving me the second clue."

He raised his eyebrows.

"You have told me why you are here," he answered. "And as for the second clue, the phrase sounds most exciting. And as for me I have a train to catch. To the station, driver."

The car started, leaving me standing there blankly. And then he put his head out of the window.

"Good hunting."

I suppose Drummond would have pulled him out of the car by the scruff of the neck: I wasn't Drummond. I watched the car disappear up the road, then I went back to my neglected gin and vermouth, swearing under my breath.

"Who," I said to the landlord, who came out at that moment, "is the old gentleman who has just driven off?"

"He entered himself in the book, sir, as Mr Johnson of London. More than that I can't tell you."

Evidently disposed for a chat he rambled on, whilst I pretended to listen. And suddenly – I don't know what the worthy man was talking about at the moment – I fired a question at him.

"Have you got any books of poetry in the hotel?"

It must have been a bit disconcerting, for he stared at me as if I had taken leave of my senses.

"I believe the missus has," he said in an offended voice. "I don't hold with the stuff myself. I'll ask her."

He went indoors to return in a few moments with the information that she had Longfellow, Shelley, Wordsworth, Keats. I cut short the catalogue with a yell, and this time the poor man looked really alarmed.

"Wordsworth," I said. "Please ask her to lend me Wordsworth."

He again went indoors, and I sat there marvelling at my denseness. "And yet what in reality are words worth?"

At the time the phrasing had struck me as peculiar, a little pedantic. And there it had been sticking out right under my nose. Now there was nothing for it but to go clean through until I found the quotation, and then if my reasoning was right we should find the clue in the context.

Mine host handed me the book with an air of hurt dignity, and retired once more indoors, whilst I started on my lengthy task. In couples the others came back looking moody and disconsolate, and disinclined for conversation. They took no notice of me, and I, for fear I might raise false hopes, said nothing. Plenty of time to talk if I proved right.

Dinner came, and over the steak and kidney pie, I found it.

"Lady of the Mere,
Sole – sitting by the shores of old romance."

I stared at the page blankly. Lady of the Mere. What earthly good was that? Had all my time been wasted? Was the old man a harmless jester after all?

"Everything to your satisfaction, gentlemen?"

The landlord came up to our table, and I drew a bow at a venture.

"Tell me, landlord," I said, "is there in this neighbourhood any place called the Mere?"

He stared at me for a moment or two without speaking.

"There is," he answered at length, and his jovial expression had vanished. "May I ask why you want to know, sir?"

"Curiosity," I said, hardly able to keep the excitement out of my voice. "Is it a pond – or what?"

"It's a house," he said. "An old house. About three miles from here."

"Who is the owner?" I cried.

"Owner!" he gave a short laugh. "There ain't been no owner, sir, for nigh on ten years. And there ain't never likely to be."

"What's the matter with the place?"

"I bain't a superstitious man, gentlemen," he said gravely, "but it would take more'n a bag of gold to get me across the threshold of the Mere – even by day. And by night, I wouldn't go – not for all the money in the Bank of England."

"Haunted, is it?" I prompted.

"Maybe – maybe not," he answered. "There be grim things, sir, black things go on in that house. Ten years ago the owner, old Farmer Jesson, were murdered there. A fierce man he was: used to keep the most awful savage dogs. And they do say that he found his young wife with a lad – a powerful-tempered boy. And they had a terrible quarrel. The lad, so the story goes – 'e struck the old man and killed him after an awful struggle. And as he died he cursed the lad and his young wife. He cursed the house: he cursed everything he could think of. Certain it is that the lad and the lass disappeared: folks do say they died where they stood, and then were mysteriously removed. As I say, I bain't superstitious, and I don't rightly hold with that story. But what I do know is that since then there be strange lights and noises that come from the old place – for I've seen 'em and heard 'em myself. And I do know that there come a young gentleman from London who heard the tales and didn't believe them. He went there one night, and they found him next day on the ground outside, lying on his back and staring at the sky – as mad as a hatter. No, no, gentlemen – take my advice and give the Mere a wide berth, or you'll regret it."

He bustled off to attend to a new arrival.

"How fearfully jolly," I remarked.

The others were staring at me curiously.

"Why this incursion into local superstition?" asked Darrell.

"No particular reason," I answered on the spur of the moment. "As I said, just idle curiosity."

# CHAPTER 7

*In which we come to the Mere*

I really don't know why I didn't tell them at once. Somehow or other the whole thing seemed so terribly thin – as I ran over it in my mind. And told second-hand it would have sounded even thinner. A tag from Wordsworth: the coincidence of a name. And that was positively all.

I felt that something more definite was wanted, and there seemed only one way of getting it. I would go there myself and reconnoitre. I admit that I didn't like the idea particularly: that bit about the man who was found on the ground outside, as mad as a hatter, was so wonderfully reassuring. At the same time I'd had three cocktails, and I was now having my second glass of port. And the suspicion that this cheery band regarded me as a rabbit rankled. Their opinion would change pretty rapidly if I came back with the next clue in my pocket.

After all it was I who had solved the first one and spotted Drayminster, and though I might not be their equal in mere physical strength it was brain that was needed on a show like this. And in that department I ventured to think the boot was on the other leg.

I ordered another glass of port. Just local superstition, of course: good enough for inebriated yokels wandering home at night. They would hear noises and see lights anywhere. But for an educated man to be put off by such an absurd story was nothing short of ridiculous. I'd borrow a bicycle after dinner, and have a look round the place. Only three miles mine host had said: I'd be back comfortably by eleven o'clock. And if I'd found nothing, I would not mention my conversation of before dinner.

The others had drifted away from the table, and were sitting in the lounge outside as I went through. They seemed bored and depressed, and with difficulty I repressed a smile as I thought of the change that would occur when I came back with the goods. I should have to solve it for them too in all probability: in fact it had been a very fortunate moment for them when I had decided to help them.

The first thing to do was to get hold of a bicycle, and in that I was successful at once. The landlord's son would be only too pleased to lend me his, and after a few minutes it was brought round to the front door.

"Be you going far, mister," he said, "because there bain't too much oil in the lamp."

"I'm going to the Mere," I answered as casually as possible. "Which is the way?"

The boy's jaw dropped, and he stared at me speechlessly.

"To the Mere," he stammered at length. "But you can't go to the Mere at night. It bain't safe."

I smiled a little pityingly.

"Rot, my good boy," I said. "Anyway, I'll chance it. Now, which is the way?"

"Straight along the road," he answered, pointing up the street. "And when you get about two mile out of Drayminster, you'll find a turning going down to the right. Take that, and in about another half-mile or so you'll see the house in front of you."

He hesitated for a moment: then he burst out with a further warning.

"It ain't safe, sir: it be a terrible place at night."

"Light the lamp, my lad," I said. "Your bicycle will be quite safe, anyway."

He fumbled with a match, and I glanced in through the open door. The others were still in the lounge, and just for a moment or two I hesitated. Should I tell them, after all? When all was said and done it was their show more than mine, and the thought of Drummond beside me had much to commend it. And then I dismissed it: was I, a grown man, going to admit that I was frightened of a stupid story?

"The lamp be lit, sir," said the boy. "But you be terribly foolish to go."

He turned away and slouched in at the back door, while I got ready to mount. Foolish or not, I was going, and the sooner I started the sooner I'd be back.

It was a beautiful night, warm and without a breath of wind, and I was soon clear of the village. The moon had not yet risen, but there was no mistake about the road which ran for the first mile beside the river. Then it swung away to the left over some high ground. I found the turning the boy had spoken of without difficulty – one that evidently would lead back towards the river. The surface was poor – it was scarcely more than a lane, and little used at that – and very soon some high trees made the darkness so intense that the going was hard. In fact, after a short time I dismounted and pushed on, on foot.

Now I make no bones about it, but the fact remains that with every step I took I found myself wishing more heartily that I had listened to the boy's advice. Whether it was due to the effects of the port wearing off, or whether the reality was worse than what I had anticipated, is immaterial. But after I'd walked about fifty yards it was only by the greatest effort of will that I prevented myself turning and fleeing incontinently.

There was a sort of dank feeling about that lane which got on my nerves, and the feeble little circle of light from the lamp dancing about in front of me as the bicycle jolted, only seemed to make the surrounding darkness more impenetrable. And at last, acting on a sudden impulse, I blew it out, and left the bicycle standing against the hedge. If the landlord's three miles was right I must be very near my destination.

Came a sudden jink in the lane, and there within fifty yards of me stood the house. I stopped instinctively: what a fearsome-looking place it was. Trees were all round it except on one side where a large pool of water lay stagnant and unruffled – doubtless the pool that had given the place its name. The house itself was a big one, and gave an impression of indescribable gloom. It seemed to squat there in its setting of trees like a dead thing. No gleam of light came from any window: no sound broke the absolute silence.

I sat down on the bank beside the lane: some plan of action had to be decided on. Up till now I hadn't really thought what I was going to do when I got there: now it had to be faced. Obviously there was no use in sitting down and looking at the place: the clue, if my supposition was right, was not likely to be obtained that way. It would be inside the house, and if I wanted to get it that is where I should have to go. And the more I thought of it the less did I relish it.

I tried to find excuses for myself. How, for instance, could I get in? The answer to that was obvious – I certainly couldn't tell unless I tried. Was it wise for a man to attempt such a thing single-handed? The answer to that consisted of one word – coward. Had I come all this way – made all this song and dance in my own mind – merely to run away when I arrived? I forced myself to view the matter from a commonsense point of view.

"Here," I said out loud, "is an old untenanted house – set, it is true, in gloomy surroundings, which look all the more gloomy because it happens to be dark. But it is merely a house consisting of bricks and mortar. You are a man of the world. Are you going to admit to yourself that you are afraid of exploring those bricks and mortar? Are you going to allow yourself to be influenced by an ancient story of something that happened ten years ago? At any rate go a bit closer and have a look."

At that I compromised to start with. I would go a bit closer and have a look. Very likely I should find everything shut and barred: if so I should have no alternative but to go home. Skirting along the undergrowth I approached the house. Stone steps covered with weeds led up to the front door, which was overhung with trailing creepers and ivy. For a moment I hesitated: then I went up the steps and cautiously tried the handle of the door. To my great relief it was locked, and the feeling that honour was satisfied was very strong. I could now go back to the *Angler's Rest* in order to get something to open the door with. And even as I so decided I seemed to hear Drummond's voice saying – "What about the ground-floor windows? Didn't you try them?"

Right! I would. And then there would be no possibility of any backchat. Keeping close in to the wall I skirted round the house. And I hadn't gone twenty yards before I was brought up standing. There in front of me was a wide-open window. All I had to do was to put my leg over the sill and I should be inside the house.

I peered in doubtfully: dimly I saw a table, some chairs, and, on the other side of the room, an open door. The musty smell of long disuse was overpowering, and I knew that if I hesitated for long I should hesitate for good. I flung a leg over, and stepped on to the floor.

The dust was thick everywhere. It rose in choking clouds, and deadened the sound of my feet as I crept towards the open door. It was almost like walking on a carpet, and it struck me that whatever might have happened in the past no one could have been in the house for months, if not years. So what was the good of going on? I paused in the doorway to consider that new point. If no one had been in the clue could not be in the house: it must, if I was on the right track, be in the garden outside.

In front of me was the hall. I could just see the staircase to my right, and opposite me was a piece of furniture that looked like a hat-rack. I peered across at it: was it my imagination, or was there something white that was hanging on one of the pegs – something that might be a piece of paper? Was it possible that here was the actual clue I was searching for?

I tiptoed across the hall: and almost trembling with excitement I struck a match. One word was written on it – "Excelsior".

The match burned out, and I did not light another. No need to rack one's brain to interpret that message. True, it proved I was on the right track, which was gratifying to my pride as a solver of conundrums, but it also indicated with painful clearness the next move. There was only one way to Excelsior in that house, and that was to go upstairs. And the thought of going upstairs left me chilled to the marrow.

I stood staring at the dim outline of the staircase fading into utter blackness at the top. Where I was a faint light did come from the open door by which I had entered. Above the darkness was absolute. Should I, or should I not? And though I say it myself, I consider that a certain amount of credit was due to me for deciding in the affirmative. I'd go and have a look at the top of the stairs.

Still on tip-toe I crossed the hall to the foot of them. A mouldering carpet existed in patches, and I began to ascend cautiously for fear of tripping up. But no care on my part could prevent the stairs creaking abominably, and in the silence of the house each step I took sounded like a pistol-shot.

At last I reached the top. Now that I was there the darkness was not quite so intense: a little of the light from the open door below managed to filter up. To my right and left ran a passage, and putting my hand in my pocket I counted the coins. Odd to the left: even to the right. There were seven, and I started feeling my way towards the left. And I can't have taken more than half a dozen steps when a strange creaking noise came from the hall, and at the same moment I realised it was getting darker. I stopped abruptly, and peered below. And what I saw froze me stiff with fright. The door by which I had entered was closing, and even as I looked at it, it shut with a bang. Then once more absolute silence.

For a moment or two I gave way to blind panic. I rushed as I thought in the direction of the stairs, and hit a wall. I turned round and rushed another way, and hit another wall. Then I forced myself to stand still: I'd lost my bearings completely – I hadn't an idea where the stairs were. Like a fool that I was I had walked straight into the trap, and the trap had shut behind me.

My first instinctive thought was to light a match – anything seemed better than this impenetrable blackness. And then prudence won. If there were people round me, all I should do would be to give myself away. I was safer in the dark. At any rate we were on equal terms.

I crouched against the wall, with my heart going in sickening thumps and listened. Not a sound. The silence was as complete as the darkness. And I began to wonder if there was anyone in the house – any human that is. Was it a material agency that had shut that door – or was it something supernatural? Would some ghastly thing suddenly hurl itself on me: something against which even Drummond with all his strength would be powerless? Every ghost story I'd ever heard of came back to me, along with the comforting reflection that I had always ridiculed the idea that there were such things. But it is one thing to be sceptical in the smoking-room of your club, and quite another when you are crouching in inky darkness in a deserted house from which your line of escape has been cut off.

Suddenly I started violently: an odd slithering noise had begun. It was rather as if a sack full of corn was being bumped on the floor, and it seemed to come from my left. I peered in what I thought was the right direction, while the sweat ran off me in streams. Was it my imagination, or was there a faint luminosity in the darkness about three feet from the ground? I stared at it and it moved. With each bump it moved, and it was coming closer. Step by step I backed away from it: step by step it kept pace with me. And for the first time in my life I knew the meaning of the word terror. Frightened I had been many times: this was stark, raving horror. I was stiff and paralysed with fear. Was this the thing that had sent the other man mad?

Then, as if a veil had suddenly been torn away, came the change. One instant there had been merely a faint lessening of the darkness: the next I found myself staring into a shining yellow face of such inconceivable malignity that I almost screamed. It was not two feet away, and about on a level with my chest. I hit at it blindly, and found my wrist caught in a grip of steel. Then I felt a hand creeping up my coat, until it reached my throat, and I began to struggle wildly.

I kicked into the darkness, and my foot hit something solid. There was a grunt of pain, and the grip on my throat tightened savagely. The face drew nearer, and there came a roaring in my ears. And I had just given myself up as finished, when a thing happened so staggering that I could scarcely believe my eyes.

Out of the darkness from behind the shining face there came a pair of hands. I could see them clearly – just the hands and nothing more, as if they were disembodied. There was a curious red scar on the middle finger of the right hand, and the left thumb-nail was distorted. With the utmost deliberation they fastened on the throat of my assailant, and began to drag him backwards. For a while he resisted: then quite suddenly the grip on my throat relaxed. Half insensible I sank down on the floor, and lay there watching. For the moment my only coherent thought was relief that I could breathe again, that the yellow face was going. Writhing furiously, its mouth twisted into a snarl of rage, it seemed to be borne backwards by those two detached hands. And even as I tried foolishly to understand what it all meant, there came from down below a well-known voice – "The more we are together." The relief was too much: I did another thing for the first time in my life. I fainted.

I came to, to find the whole bunch regarding me by the light of half a dozen candles.

"Look here, little man," said Drummond, "what merry jaunt have you been up to this time?"

"How did you know I was here?" I asked feebly.

"The landlord's son told us you'd borrowed his bicycle," he answered. "And since they all seemed very alarmed at the pub we thought we'd come along and see. We found your machine outside, and then we found you here unconscious. What's the worry? Have you seen a ghost?"

"Seen and felt it," I said grimly. "A ghastly shining yellow face, with fingers like steel bars that got me by the throat. And he'd have killed me but for a pair of hands that came out of the darkness and got him by the throat as well."

They looked at me suspiciously, until Jerningham suddenly peered at my neck.

"Good God!" he said, "look at the marks on his throat."

They crowded round, and I laughed irritably.

"You don't imagine I dreamed it, do you? The thing that attacked me had a grip like a man-trap."

"Tell us again exactly what happened," said Drummond quietly.

I told them, starting with my conversation with the old gentleman that afternoon. And when I'd finished he whistled softly.

"Well done, Dixon: well done! It was a damned sporting thing to come here alone. But, laddie, don't do it again – I beg of you. For unless I'm greatly mistaken, but for our happening to arrive when we did your only interest by this time would have been the site for your grave."

He lit a cigarette thoughtfully.

"Phosphorous evidently on the man's face who attacked you. An old trick. Probably our headlights alarmed them, and the owner of the hands dragged him off. So that there are at least two unpleasing persons in this house, beside us."

He rubbed his hands gently together.

"Splendid! At last we come to grips. Blow out those candles, boy: there's no good advertising our position too clearly. And then I think a little exploration of the old family mansion."

Once more we were in darkness save for the beam of Drummond's torch. He had it focussed on the floor, and after a while he stooped down and examined the marks in the dust.

"What an extraordinary track," he remarked. "There doesn't seem to be any sign of footmarks. It's one broad smear."

We crowded round, and it certainly was a most peculiar trail. In width about eighteen inches to two feet, it stretched down the middle of the passage, as far as we could see. And suddenly Drummond turned to me with a queer look in his eyes.

"You say this face seemed to be about on a level with your chest," he said.

"Just about," I answered. "Why?"

"Because it strikes me that you've had even a narrower escape than we thought," he remarked. "The thing that attacked you hadn't got any legs. It was a monstrosity: some ghastly abnormality. The owner of the pair of hands dragged it after him, and that's the trail it left."

"It is a jolly house," murmured Darrell. "What does A do now?"

"What the devil do you think?" grunted Drummond. "A follows the trail, and for the love of Mike don't get behind the light."

Now I don't suppose I should ever have thought of that. I could see Drummond in front, his right arm fully extended, holding the torch, while he kept over to the left of the passage. Behind him, in single file, we all of us followed, and, once when

I drifted over to the right, Sinclair, who was just behind me, pulled me back.

"If anyone shoots," he muttered, "they shoot at the torch. Keep in line."

And the words had hardly left his mouth when there came an angry phut from in front of us, and a splintering of wood from behind. Simultaneously Drummond switched off the light. Silence, save for our heavy breathing – and then once again did I hear that ominous slithering noise.

"Look out," I cried. "That's the thing moving."

Then came Drummond's voice, sharp and insistent.

"Light. Give me light. My God! what is it?"

And never to my dying day shall I forget the spectacle we saw when Darrell's torch focussed and steadied on Drummond. The thing was on him – clawing at him: a thing that looked like a black sack. Its hands were fastened on his throat, and it was by his throat that it was supporting itself. Because it had no legs – only two stumps. It was mouthing and gibbering, and altogether dreadful. Some faint luminosity still remained on its face, but in the light of the torch it was hardly noticeable. And then I forgot everything in watching that ghastly struggle.

The dust was rising in little eddies as Drummond moved, carrying the thing with him. Of its almost superhuman strength no one knew better than I, and in a few seconds the veins were standing out on Drummond's forehead. Then he braced himself against the wall, and gripped its wrists with his hands. I could see the muscles taut and bulging under the sleeves of his coat, as he tried to wrench the thing's hands away from his throat. But in spite of his enormous strength, he told me afterwards that but for the knowledge of a certain ju-jitsu grip by which a man's fingers can be forced open, the thing would have throttled him unless we had helped. As it was, help was unnecessary: the murderous hold relaxed, and, with a heave, Drummond flung the thing away from him. It landed on the floor with a thud, and for a space it stood there balancing itself on its hands and glaring at us. Then, like some great misshapen ape, it disappeared up the passage, moving on its hands and stumps.

"Good Lord!" grunted Drummond, "what a little pet."

"Where's the gun, Hugh?" said Darrell curtly.

His torch was flashing on the empty passage.

"Put it out, Peter," snapped Drummond. "I'm thinking that gun belonged to the other bloke. We'll follow up in darkness."

And then, before we had gone two steps, there came from in front of us a loud crash, followed by a terrible scream. The scream was not repeated: only a low moaning noise could be heard, and after a while that also ceased. Once again the silence was absolute.

"For the love of Heaven," came Drummond's hoarse whisper. "Keep your eyes skinned. Who is the last man?"

"I am," said Jerningham. "Don't worry about this end."

We crept forward, guided by momentary flashes of Drummond's torch. The trail was easy to follow. It led along the passage for about fifteen yards, and then turned to the right through an open door.

"Stop here," said Drummond quietly. "I'm going in alone."

And just as little details about him had struck me before, so on this occasion did the almost incredible swiftness and silence of his movements impress my mind. One instant he was there: the next he was not, but no sound had marked his going.

We clustered round the open door waiting. Once a board creaked inside, and then suddenly we heard a startled exclamation, and Drummond rejoined us.

"There's something pretty grim happened," he muttered. "Stand well away from the door. I'm going to switch on the torch."

The beam flashed on, and outlined against it was the ominous silhouette of a revolver held in his other hand. And for a space the two remained motionless: then the revolver fell to his side.

"Great Scott!" he muttered. "Poor brute!"

The crash and the scream were accounted for: also the silence that had followed.

Lying motionless on the floor close to the further wall was the thing that had attacked him. And it needed no second glance to see that it was dead. There was a dreadful wound in the head; in fact, it was split completely open. And further details are unnecessary.

For a while we stared at it stupidly – the same thought in all our minds. How had it happened? Because save for the motionless figure on the floor the room was empty. What was it that had struck the poor brute this ghastly blow in the darkness. Nothing had come out of the door, and the only window was boarded up.

It was a peculiar room with stone walls and a stone ceiling, and what it could have been used for in the past completely defeated me. Let into the wall near which the body was lying were six iron rings: except for them, the walls were absolutely bare. They were fixed in a straight line about a yard from the floor, and were three or four feet apart. And below each ring the boarding was worn away as if it had been gnawed by rats. "Didn't the landlord say that the farmer who was murdered kept savage dogs!" said Darrell. "He probably used those staples to chain them up."

"Maybe he did," said Drummond grimly. "But there ain't any dogs here now, Peter, and what I want to know is what killed that poor brute."

Once again we fell silent, staring at the twisted body.

"He looks as if he had been bashed over the head with a steam-hammer," said Jerningham at length. "That crash we heard was it."

"Yes, damn it!" cried Drummond. "But what caused the crash."

He took a step or two towards the body, and even as he did so there came to me, out of the blue so to speak, an idea. What made me think of it I don't know: what made me suddenly remember my conversation with the old gentleman that afternoon, I can't say. But the fact remains that mercifully I did.

It was the remark he had made to me that had first caused me to suspect him. I could see him, even as I stood there, giving me that strange, penetrating stare and saying – "Was it fifth or sixth? It might make a lot of difference." And the dead thing was lying between the fifth and sixth ring.

"I think I've got it," I said slowly. "It's part of the clue I was given this afternoon, and up till now I'd forgotten it."

They listened while I told them, and when I'd finished, Drummond nodded his head thoughtfully.

"You're probably right," he said. "Let's work on the assumption, at any rate."

"That's all very fine and large," grunted Darrell. "But we don't want the same result, old boy. And it strikes me that if you make a mistake you won't make a second."

"I've got to chance it, Peter," answered Drummond doggedly. "If Dixon is right, we're on the track of the next clue. And nothing matters except getting that. Let's think for a moment. What's the natural thing to do when you see a ring in a wall? Pull the blamed thing, isn't it?"

"Probably what that poor brute was doing when he was killed," said Sinclair.

"Then I will pull it, too," announced Drummond calmly.

"For Heaven's sake, man," cried Jerningham. "What's the use?"

"That remains to be seen," said Drummond. "But we're going to pull those rings – and we're going to pull 'em now. Toby, go back to the car with Algy. Keep close together going through the house. In the tool-box you'll find my tow-rope. Bring it. And don't forget that there is at least one unconsidered little trifle loose in the house."

"If I'm right," he went on as they left the room, "the danger must lie close to the wall. That thing never moved with a wound like that in his head: he died on the spot where he was hit. Anyway, one must take a chance."

And his hand as he lit a cigarette was as steady as a rock.

# CHAPTER 8

*In which we explore the Mere*

It is nervy work waiting. I know that my feelings were strongly reminiscent of those that I had experienced in France when the latest reports from the seats of the mighty indicated that enemy mining was proceeding underneath one's trench. To dangers seen and heard one can get tolerably used, but the unseen, silent horror of this room was making me jumpy. I felt I almost preferred my fight in the darkness with the thing that now lay dead.

At last, after what seemed an interminable time, Sinclair and Longworth returned with the rope.

"See anyone?" said Drummond casually.

"Not a soul. But I thought I saw a gleam of light from one of the top rooms," said Sinclair.

"Probably our friend of the gun. Give me the rope, and let's get on with it."

"Look here, old man," said Darrell, "let's toss."

"Go to hell," remarked Drummond tersely. "It's good of you, Peter, old lad, but this is my show. The only point is that in case anything happens I rely on you to carry on the good work."

He walked across to the fifth ring and slipped the rope through it. Then he stepped back, and we breathed again. Nothing had happened so far.

"Stand clear," he said. "I'm going to pull."

He gave a tug on the rope, and the next instant it was wrenched out of his hand. Some huge object had flashed downwards through the beam of his torch and landed with a sickening thud on the dead man, tearing the rope out of his grasp as it fell. Instinctively he turned the light upwards. In the ceiling was a square, black hole, and we had a momentary glimpse of a face peering at us through it. Then it was gone, and we were left staring upwards foolishly.

It was Drummond who recovered himself first.

"A booby-trap that I like not the smell of," he said savagely. "Keep that hole in the ceiling covered, Ted, and shoot on sight."

It must have weighed a couple of hundredweight – the slab that had come out of the ceiling. There was a staple let into the centre of it, with a wire rope attached, by which it had evidently been hoisted back into position the first time. One could see the faint outline of some sort of winding gear above the opening, but of the man who had operated it there was no sign.

"No – I like not the smell of it," he repeated grimly. "It's murder – pure and simple. But if the swine think they're going to stop us they're wrong."

"What's the next move?" said someone shakily.

"See what happens when we pull the sixth ring," he said. "If what Dixon said is right, that's the other important one."

"Probably the floor will give way this time," remarked Algy Longworth gloomily. "I feel I should like a mother's soothing comfort."

We waited tensely while Drummond again adjusted the rope. He began to pull, and suddenly he gave a triumphant exclamation.

"It's moving."

It was: a crack was appearing in the wall. And then with a faint creak the whole block of stone swung round on a pivot, leaving an opening about three feet wide and six feet high.

"The poor brute was looking for that, I suppose," said Drummond, "and in the darkness pulled the wrong ring."

He crossed the room, and then stopped abruptly. He was staring at a piece of paper fastened to the back of the part that had moved.

"Well done, little man," he read slowly. "Any casualties yet? But you've still got a long way to go, and I've got some far better jests for you before you've finished. Incidentally the charming gentleman without any legs is an impromptu turn as far as I am concerned. I found him on the premises when I arrived, and he struck me as being quite in keeping with the general character of the house. I rather think he must be the so-called ghost and I do hope he's behaved himself. But if he hasn't don't blame me. His predilections seem quite delightfully murderous, and he resents any intrusion terribly. But doubtless somebody loves him. Phyllis is still quite well, though just a leetle bit off her food. Isn't this fun?"

"Damn the woman," said Drummond angrily. Then he began to laugh. "Though, 'pon my soul," he went on, "if it wasn't for Phyllis, I think I should agree with her."

"Time enough for that, old boy, when we're through," said Jerningham. "Hasn't it struck you that at the moment we're in a rather bad strategical position? It's a sitting shot either from the ceiling or through that opening."

"You've said a mouthful, Ted," agreed Drummond. "Back into the passage, and we'll have a council of war."

The moon had risen, and an eerie half-light was filtering through the dirty windows, making the place seem, if possible, more ghostly than before.

"Now then," said Drummond, "let's get down to the meat juice. I should think that what our one and only Irma says is right, and that the poor devil dead in there has been responsible for all the stories about this place. Probably used that phosphorous trick to frighten people. Anyway, he's out."

"Next man in is the bloke with the hands who let drive with his bundook," said Darrell thoughtfully.

"And any other little pals of his who may be lying about," went on Drummond.

"But the thing to decide is where is the next clue?"

"The betting is a pony to a dried pea that it's down that secret passage," said Jerningham.

"Then down the passage we go, old son. But not all of us. If this was an ordinary house I wouldn't mind. But that booby-trap in there was specially prepared, and there are probably others. The question is how many of us go. I think three are enough. That leaves three to guard this end. You five do fingers out for it: two of you to come."

"Let's all come in," said Sinclair. "You too, Hugh."

"No," said Drummond decisively. "I'm going, anyway. Get a move on."

"What are fingers out?" I asked mildly.

"Laddie," said Drummond, "you may be a whale at conundrums, and I take off my hat to you over this evening's show, but your education is a bit deficient. At the word go, extend as many fingers as you like in front of you. One hand only: thumbs don't count. Go."

I extended two: a complicated mathematical proceeding took place, and the winner appeared to be Sinclair.

"Once again," said Drummond. "Only the four of you. Go."

This time I extended three, and hoped for the best.

"Thirteen in all, and we start with Dixon."

"Splendid," I murmured: I didn't mind who he started with. The passage, in spite of the dust, was comfortable: and, as far as I could see, the ceiling was ordinary lath and plaster.

"Come on then," said Drummond. "I'll go first, then Dixon, then Toby."

I opened my eyes abruptly: I suppose I'm not very clever at that game. I appeared to have won, anyway, which was frightfully jolly and all that.

"Just guard this end, you three," said Drummond. "And you'd better give us a couple of hours at least."

He stepped back into the room, and flashed his torch up at the hole in the ceiling. No sign of anyone, and he led the way across the floor to the opening in the wall.

"Don't forget," he whispered urgently, "that anything may happen."

"I won't," I assured him, and wondered if a ton of masonry on one's head was a comparatively painless death.

The passage led downwards, and the walls and ceiling gradually grew damper and damper, until large drops of water splashed on my head at each step I took forward. Drummond was in front with his torch, and progress was slow, as he tested every foothold he took before advancing. At length he paused, and waited for us to come up with him.

"I believe we're under the mere," he announced.

"Hooray!" I cried enthusiastically. "I've always wanted to drown."

And suddenly he began to shake with laughter.

"You priceless bird," he remarked. "Look here – you go back – you've done your fair share for tonight – and Toby and I will go on."

"Be blowed for a yarn," I said. "Let's get on with it."

Once more we crept forward, and at length the passage started to rise again. It seemed to be bending right-handed the whole time, and was getting drier and drier. Suddenly Drummond paused; we had come to a fork. To the right a flight of stone steps led upwards: to the left it continued on the level.

"Shall we try the steps first," whispered Drummond, and the next instant he switched off his torch. For quite distinctly and from close to had come the sound of a woman's voice.

"It can't be possible that we've found her," he breathed.

"What – your wife?" I muttered.

"No – the other," he answered. "Supposing she didn't expect us to track her so quickly, and as a result we've caught her up."

Once again came the voice, and this time a man spoke too.

"It's up the steps," said Drummond. "Toby – you wait here: we may be putting our heads straight into it. If anything happens, sprint back to the others and tell them. Dixon – you come half-way up as far as the bend."

I crept up behind him, feeling with my fingers on the walls. And suddenly I found Drummond's hand on my arm.

"Stay there," he whispered. "I'm going on alone."

Not two yards in front of us a beam of light shone out from under a closed door.

I waited tensely, crouched against the wall: could it be possible that we had run this woman to earth – that she was on the other side of the door? And, if so, how many men were likely to be with her? True, we had only heard one voice, but that meant nothing.

With a crash Drummond flung open the door and stepped into the room. A man and a woman were sitting at a table, on which the remains of a meal were lying. Two candles guttered in the sudden draught, and with a cry of fear the woman rose to her feet.

"Keep your hands on the table – both of you," snapped Drummond.

"Who are you?" said the man in a surly voice, his eyes fixed on the revolver. "And what d'you want?"

"A little conversation, my friend," said Drummond. "In the first place – who are you? And who is the lady?"

He flashed his torch on her face, and stared at her intently. She was a haggard, unkempt woman. Her face was lined and wrinkled: her hair streaked with grey. And she looked most desperately ill.

"Never you mind who we are," said the man angrily. "It ain't no blasted business of yours, is it? What are you doing in this house, anyway?"

"I admit," answered Drummond pleasantly, "that under normal circumstances you would have a certain amount of justification for your question. But you can hardly call this house normal, can you?"

"Are you the police, mister?" said the woman, speaking for the first time.

"I am not," said Drummond. "I've got nothing to do with them."

"Well, what do you want?" said the man again. "Are you one of the bunch who have been fooling round this house for the last few weeks?"

"We get warm," remarked Drummond. "No – I am not one of the bunch. At the same time, though not of them – I am after them, if you get me. But for them I should not be here. Am I to take it, then, that you disown them also."

The man cursed foully.

"Disown them," he snarled. "For two pins I'd have murdered the lot."

"Then it was not you who rigged up that pleasant little booby-trap?"

"What booby-trap? Look here, mister, I'm getting fair sick of this. For God's sake clear out."

The woman put a restraining hand on his arm, and whispered something in his ear. She seemed to be trying to pacify him, and after a time he shrugged his shoulders and stood up.

"Sorry, sir, if I lost my temper. But if you ain't the police, and you ain't one of that bunch, then what do you want?"

"One moment," said Drummond. "Dixon," he called over his shoulder.

"Look here," he whispered as I joined him, "would you recognise the hands of the man who dragged that thing away from you?"

"I certainly should," I answered. "And it's not this bloke."

He nodded. "Good. That's one thing settled, anyway. Now," he resumed, "I'll tell you what we want. Hidden somewhere in this charming country mansion is a piece of paper or a letter or a message of some sort which I am looking for. Do you know where it is?"

The man looked at the woman, and she looked at him.

"I reckon I do," he said. "And it's in a place you'd never find if you looked for ten years."

Drummond's eyes never left his face.

"How do you know where it is?" he said quietly.

"Because I saw one of them people put it there," answered the man.

"Will you show me where it is?" continued Drummond.

Once again the woman bent and whispered to him.

"All right," he said. "Look here, sir, I'll show you where it is, if you'll give me your word that you won't tell a living soul you've seen us here."

And suddenly the truth dawned on me.

"I believe," I whispered to Drummond, "that this is the man who murdered the farmer ten years ago. They've been hiding here ever since."

"Are you the man who murdered Farmer Jesson?" shot out Drummond abruptly.

The women gave a little scream, and clutched his shoulders.

"Never you mind who I am," he said angrily. "You've forced your way in here, and I've got to trust you. But unless you give me your word to say nothing, you can damned well look for that envelope yourself."

"I give you my word," said Drummond quietly.

"What about your friend?"

"I speak for all of us," said Drummond. "Now lead on. But you'd better understand one thing, my friend. Any monkey tricks, and you'll be for it good and strong."

The man looked straight at him.

"Why should there be any monkey tricks?" he remarked quietly. "All I want is to see the last of you as soon as possible. Follow me."

He took a lantern off a nail in the wall and lit the candle inside. Then he led the way down the stairs.

"Who's this?" He stopped suspiciously as the light showed up Toby Sinclair still waiting in the passage.

"A friend of mine," said Drummond. "My promise covers him."

"There's someone else about here, Hugh," said Toby in a low voice. "While you've been up there I've seen a gleam of light along the passage to the left, and I'm almost certain I heard movement."

Drummond turned to the man.

"Do you hear that?" he said curtly. "Who is it?"

The man shrugged his shoulders.

"Ask me another. This place has been like a rabbit warren lately."

"Which way do we go?"

"Along there," he pointed, "where your friend says he saw the light. Don't you want to go? It doesn't matter to me."

He stood there swinging his lantern. By its light I could see Drummond staring at him intently: was it or was it not a trap? The man's face was expressionless: he seemed completely indifferent as to whether we went or whether we didn't. And at last Drummond made up his mind.

"Lead on," he ordered. "But don't forget I'm just behind you, and there will be no soft music to herald the hitting."

Certainly there was no further gleam of light from in front, and the feeble flicker of the candle only seemed to intensify the surrounding darkness. The passage itself was opening out a little, and the roof was higher, so that walking was easy. And we must have gone about thirty yards when we came to a heavy wooden door. It was open, and our guide passed through without any hesitation.

"The note is in this room," he said, holding the lantern above his head. By its light we could see it was of a similar type to the one we had just left. There was a table and a couple of chairs, and the whole place smelt of disuse, and reeked of damp. Water dripped from the ceiling and the walls, and it struck me that wherever we had been before, we were now most certainly under the mere.

"Well, get it," snapped Drummond. "This place stinks worse than a seaside boarding-house."

"It isn't quite so easy to get it," said the man, and even as he spoke, I knew we were trapped. A sudden look in his eyes; a scowl that was half a sneer – and then darkness. He had blown out the candle.

"Hell!" roared Drummond, and from the door the man laughed.

"You poor boobs," came his mocking voice. "You don't know enough to come in out of the wet."

Well – perhaps that remark was worth it to him: perhaps it was not. It just gave Drummond time to switch on his torch. By its light we saw the door closing, and the fingers of the man's hand round it. And the next instant a shot rang out. For quickness of shooting combined with accuracy I would never have believed it possible: Drummond had plugged him through the fingers. A torrent of blasphemy came from the other side of the door as we sprang towards it: but we were just too late. The bolt clanged home as we got there: we were shut in. And from the other side of the door the blasphemy continued.

At last it ceased, and Drummond bent and picked something off the floor.

"I have here," he said, "the top joint of one of your fingers. The next time I see you, my friend, you shall have it served up as a savoury."

We listened to the retreating footsteps, and he gave a short laugh.

"On balance I think we win," he remarked. "Peter and Co. are bound to find us, and until they do we can think out a few choice methods of cooking fingers."

He lit a cigarette thoughtfully, and then he laughed. "Damn the fellow! And that fish-faced woman was in it, too, I suppose. They certainly fooled us all right."

He flashed his torch round the room: there was no trace of a window. But of one thing there was more than a trace. It stared us straight in the face – a sheet of notepaper pinned in the centre of the wall opposite the door. We crowded round it, and in silence we read the message written in the handwriting we were getting to know so well.

"Will you walk into my parlour said the spider to the fly? My dear friend, I grieve for you. This is not the old form at all. But then I always thought, little one, that your resemblance to a bull in a china shop was just a little too pronounced. And this time you've done it. Honestly I never thought the chase would end quite yet. In some ways I'm sorry: I had one or two beauties left for you. In fact the next clue is in tomorrow's *Times*, which I now fear you will never see.

"How many of you are there in here, I wonder? That will be reported to me naturally in due course, but my woman's curiosity prompts me to put down the question now. Because I have taken steps to cover all tracks, and I fear your bodies will never be recovered.

"Goodbye, *mon ami*. What I shall do with Phyllis remains to be seen. Play with her a little longer, anyway, I think."

We stared at one another speechlessly; what on earth did the woman mean? – "Bodies never recovered".

"That's where she's made her blooming error," grunted Drummond.

But his voice didn't carry much conviction.

"Let's have a look at that door," he went on. "There must be some way out."

But there wasn't; the door was as solid as the wall. And it was while we were examining the bolt that a faint hissing noise became audible. Drummond straightened up and stood listening.

"What the deuce is that?" he muttered. "And where does it come from?"

Once again his torch flashed round the room. The noise was increasing till it was almost a shrill whistle, and we located it at once. It came from a small circular metal pipe that stuck out about three inches from the wall close by the door. I put my finger over it: the pressure was too great to keep it there. Some gas was being pumped into the room, and the same thought struck us all. There was no ventilation.

"She would seem," said Drummond calmly, "to have won. Unless Peter arrives in time. Sorry, you chaps."

"What's the gas?" cried Toby Sinclair. "I used to know something about chemistry."

"Well, I didn't," said Drummond. "And whatever it is it's not likely to be for the benefit of our health."

"Keep the torch on the pipe, Hugh," said Toby quietly.

He, too, put his finger on the end, then he tasted it and smelt it.

"I wonder," he muttered, and his voice was shaking a little. "No smell: practically no taste. Do you fellows mind if I take a chance?"

"We mind strongly if you don't," said Drummond calmly. "And do it darned quickly."

Sinclair struck a match: came a sudden little pop and from the end of the pipe there shot out a long blue flame.

"I was right," he said, wiping his forehead. "It's carbon monoxide. Another five minutes and she would have won. As it is if we take turns at breathing through the keyhole we ought to escape with only a head like the morning after."

"Mother's bright boy," said Drummond lightly, but I saw his hand rest for a moment on Sinclair's shoulder. "Explain."

"Carbon monoxide, old boy. Don't taste, or smell, and you can't see it. One of the most deadly poisonous gases known to science. If you light it it forms carbon dioxide which isn't poisonous, but only suffocates. So if as I say we breathe through the keyhole in turn, and Peter isn't too long, we ought to get away with it."

It was a weird scene – almost fantastic. I remember thinking at the time that it simply couldn't be true: that it was some incredible nightmare from which I should shortly wake up. In turn we solemnly stooped down, put our mouths to the keyhole and sucked in the pure air from the other side of the door. One, two, three; one, two, three – for all the world like performing marionettes.

It was Sinclair who noticed it first, and nudged us both to draw our attention because speaking was ill-advised. The flame was decreasing in size. Now it was burning fitfully: at times it shot out to its original length – at others it almost died away. And then suddenly it went out altogether.

He took a piece of paper from his pocket and a pencil.

"Go on at the keyhole," he wrote. "Don't speak unless it's essential. Room full of carbon dioxide, but no more coming now."

One, two, three – suck; one, two, three – suck, till my back was aching and I cursed Darrell and the others for not coming. Surely to Heaven it must be at least three hours by now since we had left them. And then another ghastly thought struck me. Even when they did come how were they going to open the door without a key? And there was no key in the keyhole.

One, two, three – suck. Damn this confounded woman and all her works. I felt that I would willingly have given the whole of my extremely modest fortune and then some to have had the privilege of putting her in the room, and laughing at her from the other side of the door.

One, two, three – suck: it was becoming utterly intolerable. Once I chanced it and took a breath in the room, and it felt as if an eiderdown had been pressed over my mouth. Carbon dioxide – used up air. Old tags of chemistry came back to me in the intervals of one, two, three – suck.

Suddenly we all of us paused instinctively: a key had been put in the keyhole. The bolt was turning, and with our heads feeling as if iron bands were fastened round them we stood and watched. Trying not to breathe, and with our lungs bursting for air we watched the door open. A hand came round the edge – a hand with a curious red scar on the middle finger. It was the man who had dragged the thing away from me earlier in the evening.

I signed furiously to Drummond, but as he said afterwards it was a matter of complete indifference to him whose hand it was. All he wanted was air, and a grip on somebody's throat. He got both, and he was not feeling amused.

He was a big man – the owner of the hand, and he was wearing some form of respirator. He was also a powerful man, but as I have said Drummond was not feeling amused. He shot across the room, did the owner of the hand, as if he'd been kicked from close quarters by a mule – whilst we shot into the passage. Then having locked the door and removed the key we sat down and just breathed. And if anybody is ever in doubt as to what is the most marvellous sensation in the world, they may take it from me that it consists of just breathing – under certain circumstances.

From the other side of the door came the sound of furious blows. He seemed to be hurling himself against it with the whole weight of his body.

"What about it, Hugh?" said Toby. "The respirator he has on is only of use against carbon monoxide."

"Then let him have a whack at breathing through the keyhole," said Drummond grimly. "Gosh! I wouldn't go through that last half-hour again for twenty thousand quid. Besides I want my other little pal, and if I can find him he'll eat his finger here and now."

But of neither the woman nor him was there any trace. The room was empty; the birds had flown. And as we stood in the passage at the foot of the stairs that led to the room they had been in, the only sound that broke the silence was the hoarse shouting of the man who was caught in the trap that had been laid for us.

"I think we'll let the swab out," remarked Drummond thoughtfully. "We might get something out of him."

And it is possible we might have, had not the last little effort in that pleasing country mansion taken place. It was purely accidental, and I was responsible for it. About a yard along the passage beyond the fork a steel bar was sticking out from the wall. It looked strong: it looked quite capable of bearing my weight. So I sat on it, and found it was not capable of bearing my weight. It collapsed under me, and I found myself on the floor. And even as I picked myself up there came from the room we had left a frenzied scream of fear, and a strange rushing noise.

Stupidly we stared at the door, focussing our torches on it. From underneath it water was pouring through. From each side, getting higher and higher, it came trickling out, until it shot like a jet from a fountain through the keyhole.

"Run," roared Drummond. "Run like hell. If that door gives we're done. We've let the lake in."

It was true: the meaning of the phrase about the bodies not being recovered was clear at last. We raced wildly along the passage back towards the house. Would the door hold long enough? And it did – by about five seconds. We heard the crash as it gave when we were in the lowest part, and we pounded on up the rise. Behind us came the swish of the water now pouring unchecked through the open doorway. It came in a wall six feet high along the passage, and like a huge wave breaking on the shore it hurled itself after us two feet above the level of the mere, and then, angry and swirling, receded to its proper height.

In front of us we could see the opening into the house: behind us black and evil-looking the water still eddied and heaved. A chair which had been swept along by the torrent bobbed up and down on the surface and then gradually became still. But of the man who had been in the room there was no trace. Hidden somewhere in that underground labyrinth his body still remains, and the waters of the mere have sealed his tomb.

Slowly we climbed the last bit of the passage and stepped into the room.

"Thank the Lord," said Jerningham, "you're all right. We were just coming to find you, when the most extraordinary upheaval took place in the lake."

Dawn had come, and we followed him to the window outside.

"It's almost died away now," he went on. "But about five minutes ago, right out there in the centre the water began to heave. Almost like a whirlpool. What's happened?"

"An airy nothing," remarked Drummond. "They've tried to gas us, and they've tried to drown us, and – "

He broke off suddenly staring across the mere.

"It's a difficult light to see in," he said," but isn't there some-one moving over there in the undergrowth?"

Personally I could see nothing, but after a moment or two he nodded.

"There is. I see 'em. Two. Back from the window, boys: this matter requires thought. No one has come out this way, I take it?"

"Not a soul," said Darrell.

"Then," said Drummond to Sinclair and me, "those two on the other side are fish-faced Lizzie and her gentleman friend."

"Shall we round 'em up?" remarked Toby.

Drummond lit a cigarette thoughtfully.

"I think not," he said at length. "Look here – let us consider this matter, because it seems to me that we have come to the parting of the ways. I suppose nobody has a bottle of Bass? Bad staff work. However, let us pull ourselves together, and get the grey matter to function."

He sighed profoundly.

"A ghastly hour to do so, but I have the glimmerings of an idea. Now first of all there were in this house four individuals that we know of. First, the legless bird who got a brick on his head. Now it's possible that what she said in her note was right, and that he wasn't one of the party, but just went with the house. Anyway it doesn't matter, he is out of it."

He held out an enormous finger.

"That's one. Secondly, there's the bloke who pulled him off Dixon, and whose face we saw through the hole in the ceiling. He, dear little chap, is very dead down below there. He's drowned."

Another finger joined the first.

"And short of sending down a diver his body can never be recovered. Nor any other body that might be down there. Do you get me?"

"Not the slightest," said Jerningham cheerfully. "Are there any more down below?"

"No – and at the same time, yes," remarked Drummond.

"Lucid as ever," murmured Peter Darrell. "Hasn't anybody got any beer to give him?"

Drummond grinned gently.

"It does sound a bit involved," he agreed. "But it isn't really. The passage we went down runs under the mere. Moreover, since the good-looking lady and gentleman whom we called did not come out this way they must either still be below, or they got out some other. If they are below they also are drowned, if, on the other hand, they got out..."

"Then they're not," said Algy brightly.

"Sit on his head," remarked Darrell.

"There were two people moving on the other side of the mere," pursued Drummond. "So let us assume that the passage continues under the water and comes out in the undergrowth opposite. Further, that those two escaped. What then, my brave hearts – what then? What message of fun and laughter are they going to give to our little Irma?"

He paused triumphantly, and Algy scratched his head.

"Dashed if I know," he burbled.

"Sit on his head," repeated Darrell morosely.

"The last thing they saw of us," went on Drummond, "was when we were locked in that confounded room with carbon something or other pouring into it. And if old Toby hadn't had a brain storm, that is the last that anyone would ever have seen of us. Do you get me now? For the purposes of this little affair that is the last that anyone will see of us."

We sat staring at him, realising at length what he was driving at.

"But look here," said Toby doubtfully, "if we're going on with the chase they're bound to find out."

"Why?" demanded Drummond. "We've disguised ourselves pretty often before. Peter, Ted and Algy will carry on as before: you, Dixon and I are dead. Drowned, laddie, in the cold, dark waters of the mere."

"By Jove! Hugh," said Darrell thoughtfully, "I believe that is a thundering good idea."

"I'm certain it is," said Drummond. "Look here," he went on gravely, "we've seen enough tonight to realise that this isn't a game of Kiss in the Ring. I confess that I hadn't thought that she would go to quite the lengths she has done. It is by a sheer piece of luck only that one or all of us are not dead now. Don't let there be any mistake about that. She meant to kill us – or some of us. And that gives us a foretaste of what is to come. If she has gone to these lengths in the earlier stages of the hunt, we're going to have the devil's own time later. Well – what's she going to say to herself? She knows us of old. She knows that if we three had been killed, you three would not give up. She'll expect you after her."

Darrell nodded. "Quite right."

"So we'll have the hunter hunted," went on Drummond cheerfully. "You'll be chasing clues; they'll be chasing you and we'll be chasing them."

"There's one small flaw in your otherwise excellent scheme," I put in. "How are they to know that the next clue is contained in this morning's *Times*? Only we three saw her message to that effect, and we're dead."

"Damn the man," said Drummond. "He's quite right."

"Let's wait until we see the message," remarked Jerningham. "It may be obviously intended for you, in which case we should naturally spot it. Or it may prove necessary for us all six to cover our traces. Let's leave that for a bit. The thing that must be done at once is for you three to go to ground here somewhere, and for us three to register alarm and despondency. We'll go and search the grounds, and if by any chance we run into your two pals, we'll pretend we're looking for you. Ask them to help, or if they've seen you."

"You're right, Ted," said Drummond. "Go to it. We'll lie up here."

# CHAPTER 9

*In which we get the second clue*

And so began the second phase in this strange game. I know that I was feeling most infernally tired and yet sleep would not come. My brain was too busy with the amazing happenings of the previous night. Once again I saw that luminous face being dragged away from me through the darkness, and I fell to wondering what the poor brute had really been. Was the woman right in what she had written: had this hideous, demented creature been the sole occupant of the house for years, and thus given it its bad reputation? Living by day in the secret passage under the mere, and coming out at night if it thought intruders were about. With a shudder I glanced through the open door where it still lay with the stone on top of it; anyway, death had been quick.

And then my thoughts turned to the amazing brain that had planned it all. What manner of woman could this be who dealt out flippant notes and death alternately? The labour of preparing the mechanism for dropping that heavy stone and then pulling it up again must have been enormous.

And suddenly Drummond spoke half to himself and half to me.

"She means to get us all: nab the whole bunch. She won't rest till she does." Then he smiled a little grimly. "And you thought it was a joke."

"Guilty," I acknowledged. "You must admit though that it's a little unusual."

He laughed shortly, and then he began to frown.

"I can stand anything on two legs or on four," he grunted, "but these mechanical devices don't give a fellow a chance. And I'm uneasy about those other three. Seems to me we're letting them bear the brunt from now on. She'll concentrate on them."

He relapsed into a moody silence, and I said nothing. There seemed to be nothing to say. What he feared was quite correct, or so it appeared to me. Only the merest luck had saved several of our lives that night, and luck could not be expected to continue indefinitely. Any one of us might have pulled that fifth bolt instead of the wretched creature who now lay dead underneath it. And then, had there been time to wind it up, another might have been bagged as well.

That was the devil of it all: we weren't confronting ordinary dangers and risks – but specially and cunningly prepared ones. It was a case of the German booby-traps over again, where the most harmless-looking objects hid delay-action mines.

"What the dickens are we going to do with that body?" said Drummond suddenly.

"Why not put it into the water," said Sinclair, "and then close the passage up?"

"Not a bad idea. Stoop as you pass the window, in case those two are still outside."

And so we lifted the stone sufficiently to extricate it, and carried it down the passage to the water's edge. More wreckage had appeared to join the chair: the place smelt and felt like a charnel-house. We toppled the poor brute in, and beat it for the house: anything was better than that dank death-trap. And then we pushed on the sixth ring and the secret door slipped back into position.

"Thank the Lord that's over," said Toby with a sigh of relief. "And all I can say is that I hope in future she confines her activities to the open air."

Footsteps on the stairs made us step back hurriedly, but it proved to be only the other three returning.

"What luck?" cried Drummond.

"I think we've done the trick, old boy," said Darrell. "We ran into them on the other side – a woman of repulsive aspect and a man with his hand bound up. We were running round in small circles pretending to look for you. Incidentally, what you thought was right: that passage comes out near a broken-down old ruin on the other side. There was a rusty iron door which they had presumably opened. And when we saw them we told 'em the tale. Asked them if they'd noticed the extraordinary upheaval in the lake, and enquired with the utmost agitation if they'd seen three men anywhere about. Said we'd been ghost-hunting. I don't know if they believed us or not, but I don't see that it matters very much if they did. We never let on by the quiver of an eyelid that we suspected them."

"What did they say?" said Drummond.

" 'If your friends have been ghost-hunting,' the man said, 'I fear they've found a very substantial one. My wife and I were out for an early morning stroll, when we suddenly saw the upheaval in the lake. And if you will look down that passage' – he pointed through the opening – 'you will see the water. I fear that your friends must have inadvertently found a most dangerous piece of mechanism, which I have heard of often but never believed to be really existent. Nothing more nor less, in fact, than a diabolical arrangement for flooding the whole of this underwater passage which comes out into the house on the other side. Doubtless you found the opening there.'

" 'We did,' I saw…registering horror and despondency.

"'Then if your friends have not come out that end, I very much fear they must all be drowned. For they certainly haven't come out this.'

"'How dreadful!' said the woman, and Algy made hoarse noises presumably meant to indicate grief."

"They were damned good," said Algy plaintively.

"My dear man, you sounded like a cow with an alcoholic stomach cough," said Jerningham.

"But what happened finally?" demanded Drummond.

"They drifted off, and it seemed to us they were still on the look-out for something. And then it suddenly struck us what it was. It's the other bloke: the one who is drowned down below. So we sprinted back here, in order to prevent them coming at any rate yet. As there seem to be only the two openings they're almost bound to come and examine this end as soon as we are gone. And it was going to mess things up a bit if they found all you three here. So what I suggest is this. You three must go to ground in real earnest somewhere. And you must wait until we give you the all clear – in a day or two or perhaps a week."

"Go to blazes," said Drummond.

"We in the meanwhile will go and drown our sorrows in beer, and later on we'll bring you the corks to smell. We'll also get a copy of *The Times*, and then will come the problem of smuggling you out of this house unseen. We'll have to discuss that later."

"Right you are, Peter," said Drummond. "You've about hit it. Incidentally, where shall we go to ground?"

He glanced round, and finally stared at the ceiling.

"That seems to me to be the best spot," he remarked thoughtfully. "We know it can be inhabited because that bird was up there. And if those two come we might be able to hear something. Only how the deuce do we get up there? A chair on the top of the table and I might reach."

He could – just, and in an instant he had swung himself through the hole and disappeared from view.

"Splendid." His face reappeared through the hole. "Plenty of room for all three of us. Come along, Dixon – I'll pull you up."

He got me by the wrists, and heaved me up beside him as easily as I would lift a child. And then Toby Sinclair followed.

"Take away the chair and the table, Peter," he said. "And for the love of Allah bring back a dozen with you in your pockets. My mouth is like an asbestos washer."

"We'll come back, old boy, as soon as we possibly can," said Darrell. "I'll drive your car, and take Dixon's bicycle. And we shall say that you have been suddenly summoned to London for failing to pay the poor girl her weekly postal order if any questions are asked."

"Say what you like," said Drummond resignedly. "But bring me beer."

And so commenced a weary vigil. A passage, evidently communicating with the rest of the network, led out of our hiding-place, but there was no longer any incentive to explore. All we could do was to sit and wait until the others came back and told us the coast was clear. And that might not be for hours. In fact it seemed to me that anyway it would be unsafe to go before night, if we were to succeed in getting away unseen. Which left us with the joyful prospect of spending fourteen or fifteen hours in the most acute discomfort.

Suddenly Drummond sat up and put a finger to his lips. I had heard nothing myself, but as I had already discovered all his senses seemed twice as keenly developed as my own. And after a while I too heard a creak on the stairs outside, and then another.

"Not a sound," he breathed. "But if they find us we've got to sock 'em. Keep back from the opening or they may see us."

We drew back so that we could only just see the doorway, and waited. There was someone coming along the passage now, and a moment or two later our friend of the damaged hand put his head cautiously round the corner. Then he spoke to someone behind him.

"All right," he called out. "Come on."

The woman joined him.

"What's the use?" she said peevishly. "You're not going to find him here."

"Cut it out," he snarled. "If Jim was in the passage when the door gave with the water he may have escaped up this end, and be waiting inside."

He tugged on the sixth ring, and the secret door swung open once more. Then he disappeared down the passage while the woman leaned against the wall.

"Not a sign." He came back into the room and closed the door. "But those three guys have bunged that madman's body into the water."

He stood in the centre of the room gnawing his fingers.

"I wonder how much they knew?" he muttered.

"What does it matter what they knew," said the woman. "Let's get out of this – I'm fed up."

"You'll get a clip under the jaw in a minute," he remarked. "We're getting a couple of hundred of the best for this job, and you ain't likely ever to earn a couple of hundred pence with a face like yours."

"Well, what is it you want to know?" cried the woman irritably.

"Whether those other three guys – the ones that came down to us – are really below there."

"Heaven save the man, where else can they be?" She stamped her foot. "You got 'em in the room, didn't you? And you locked 'em in the room, didn't you? And you turned on the gas, didn't you? And they were still in the room twenty minutes after. Where else can they be now?"

"I'd like to have seen 'em," he muttered.

"Well, since you ain't a ruddy fish, you can't," she remarked. "I'm going. I want some sleep."

She paused in the doorway.

"Come on, Bill," she said in a milder voice. "It's clear enough what happened. When Jim pulled the lever he didn't get out quick enough. He got caught by the water, poor old stiff – and he's down there himself now. And so are the other three."

"I suppose you're right," he answered. "We'll push off."

And then he glanced up towards the ceiling.

"What about putting that stone back?"

"Leave it," said the woman. "If anyone gets into trouble it's going to be those three who were fooling around outside. Nobody knows we've been here, and nobody ever will if you'll only get a move on instead of standing there like a dummy. Besides, you ought to have that hand of yours looked at."

"Blast that big fellow," said the man venomously. "I'd give something to have a once over with him."

The woman laughed shortly.

"You would," she said. "From what I saw of him you'd give up every hope of ever being recognised again. He'd eat you – with one hand. Come on – or I'll fall asleep where I stand. The telegraph-office won't be open till nine, and there's nothing to be done till then. You've got her address, haven't you?"

"I've got the usual one," he answered, following her from the room.

Their voices died away as they went along the passage, and I thought the unfortunate Drummond was going to have an apoplectic fit.

"Just as we were getting something useful," he groaned. "An address. *The* address."

"Probably only an accommodation one," said Toby sleepily. "Wake me if I snore, chaps, but I must have a bit of shut eye."

And still sleep would not come to me. I got into every conceivable position I could think of – I counted innumerable sheep going through a gate: but at the end of an hour I was wider awake than ever. The other two were peacefully unconscious, and at last I gave up trying. It was as well, in any case, that one of us should remain on guard, and so I settled myself as comfortably as I could and waited for the time to pass. From below came the occasional crack of a board as the sun's warmth began to penetrate into the house, but except for that no sound broke the silence. Seven o'clock came – eight: in my imagination I could smell the smell of hot coffee and bacon and eggs. I could see racks of toast and marmalade disappearing down the throats of the other three thugs at the *Angler's Rest*. And I wondered why Heaven was treating me so. To the best of my belief I was no worse than other men. Within reasonable limits I had paid my just whack of Income Tax: I had, only recently, registered enjoyment over the acidulated beverage which my Aunt Jane fondly imagined to be port. And as a reward I found myself sitting in an attic, several inches of dust and a bad smell on a beautiful summer's morning. Moreover when I gazed into the vista of the future all I could see was myself disguised as a German tourist, or the hind legs of a cow having fun and games in even more damnable spots than the one in which I was at present. Emphatically not what the doctor had ordered...

I shifted my position so as to distribute the cramp more evenly throughout my anatomy, and in doing so I saw into the room below. Just the same except that the shadow thrown by the open door had moved as the sun got higher. A simple little problem in trigonometry, I reflected. If the door was eight feet high and the shadow was nine feet long what was the height of the sun above the horizon? Door over shadow was tangent of the angle. Or was it cosine? Anyway one would want a book of logarithms... One would want...

My tongue grew suddenly dry. The height of the sun above the horizon had nothing to do with the sudden eddy of dust that swirled up in the passage outside. Nor had it anything to do with another shadow that had just appeared – the shadow of a human being. Someone was outside: someone whom I could not see – yet.

I glanced round at the other two. They were six or seven feet away: to wake them up would cause noise. Moreover they were sleeping silently, so it was best to leave them as they were.

Once more I turned back to the room: the shadow had materialised. Standing in the doorway was a woman – one of the most beautiful women I have ever seen in my life. I put her age at about thirty, though it may have been two or three years more. She was, as far as my masculine eye could judge, perfectly dressed – but it was her face, or rather her expression, that held me spellbound. There was contempt in it, and hatred – and yet, mingled with them, a sort of pity and regret. Once her eyes travelled to the bolts in the wall, and she smiled – a lazy, almost Oriental smile. And then she did an extraordinary thing. Still standing motionless she glanced upwards. Not at me, not at the hole in the ceiling, but as a woman looks up in prayer. The whole expression of her face had changed: there was in it now a wonderful triumph. Her eyes were half-closed: her whole body seemed to relax into utter surrender. And suddenly she spoke: "I would have kept him till last, my loved one – but it was not to be. But there are still the other three – and her. After I will come to you."

And then it seemed to me that she took in her arms a head I could not see – and kissed lips that to her were real. Lingeringly, passionately – as a woman kisses her lover. Gradually her arms fell to her side, and for a while she stood with her face transfigured and her eyes closed. Then she drew herself up: the vision had vanished. She gave one more glance round the room and was gone, leaving no trace of her visit save a faint, elusive scent. Jasmine – and yet not quite jasmine, something I had never smelt before – something I could never mistake in the future. Something unique, something in keeping with the woman herself. For she had seemed to me in that moment of self-revelation, when she spoke to the unseen, to be of the type for whom men will sacrifice their honour and even their lives.

118

Stiffly, like a man waking from a dream, I moved over to Drummond and shook him by the shoulder.

"What is it?" he said, instantly awake.

"Your friend Irma has been here," I answered quietly.

"What!" he almost shouted. "Then why in hell…"

He was standing up in his excitement, but with an effort he pulled himself together. "How do you know it was her? Tell me about it."

He listened in perfect silence whilst I told him what I had seen.

"I couldn't wake you without making a noise," I said when I had finished. "And I don't know," I added candidly, "that I could have wakened you anyway. I watched that woman almost as if I had been in a trance. But one thing is certain – she thinks you are dead. Another thing is certain – she is going for the other three. And your wife. And then she will commit suicide."

"You think she's mad," said Drummond.

"No, I don't think that she's mad. I think she's more dangerous even than that. She's a woman with an obsession – a mission in life. That man she spoke to was real to her – as real as you are to me. He is still her lover – though he is dead. And her mission is to revenge his death. She's got foreign blood in her, and if I wanted any more proof then I have had already as to the seriousness of this show I've got it now. This is a vendetta – and only your deaths will finish it."

"Perhaps it's as well he didn't wake you up, Hugh," said Toby thoughtfully. "You can bet she's covered her traces pretty effectually, and what could you have done if you had caught her? It wouldn't have helped you to find Phyllis. In addition you'd have given away the fact that you're not dead."

"You may be right," agreed Drummond at length. "But, by Jove! I'd like to have seen her. You'd recognise her again, Dixon?"

"In a million," I said. "And I'd recognise that scent."

"Which is less likely to change than her appearance," he remarked shortly. And then he frowned suddenly. "You're quite certain, aren't you, that it was genuine – this performance of hers? I mean you don't think that she knew we were here and did it to bluff us."

"If that show wasn't genuine," I said, "she is the most marvellous actress the world has ever seen. No: I'm certain it was pukka."

He grunted thoughtfully and sat down again.

"Perhaps so," he said after a while.

"Besides," I went on, "what could be her object in doing it if she knew we were here?"

"When you know the lady as well as I do," he answered, "you'll realise that she doesn't conform to ordinary rules."

He relapsed into silence, his chin sunk on his chest, and for the first time the full realisation of what we were engaged in came to me. Before, this woman had been a legendary figure: a writer of would-be flippant letters – a maker of skilfully devised death-traps. Dangerous certainly – more than dangerous – but with at any rate some idea of making a sporting game of it. I had believed that if we did pull through, if we did follow the clues successfully, she intended to play the game and restore Drummond's wife to him. And I had believed that she proposed to give us a sporting chance of so doing. Now I believed it no longer.

However much Drummond might doubt it I *knew* that what I had seen was genuine. The woman had ceased to be a legend and had become a reality – a reality ten times more dangerous than any legend. Gone was any hope of a sporting chance: she meant and always had meant to kill the lot of us. What strange jink in her brain had made her decide on this particular method of doing so was beside the point – probably the same jink that makes a cat play with a mouse before finishing it off. The cruelty that lies latent in the female. And she was gratifying that whilst pursuing her inexorable purpose. Letting us think we were playing a game, whilst all the time she had no intention of playing herself. Letting us think we had a chance of success, whilst all the time we had none.

For what chance had we? True by the most marvellous fluke we had escaped the night before – but flukes cannot continue indefinitely. Sooner or later she would have us, as she had always meant to have us. And the cellar below showed exactly the amount of mercy we should receive.

What chance had Drummond against such an antagonist? I glanced at him, sunk in thought, his great fists clenched by his side. Let him get his hands on anything on two legs – well and good. God help the thing! But this wasn't a question of brute strength: this was a question of cunning and brain. This wasn't man to man: this was a human being against mechanical traps. Strength was of no avail against poison gas and specially prepared devices.

I wondered if he was even now thinking out some plan of campaign. To meet guile with guile was our only hope, and somehow he didn't strike me as being the right man for that. Something to hit hard and often and he won in a canter: but first find the thing to hit.

"Gosh! I hope they've brought the beer."

I sighed a little wearily: such was our leader's mentality.

"Doubtless they will when they come," I assured him.

"When they come!" he grunted. "You wouldn't hear a howitzer going off in the next room, laddie. They have come. That flat-footed blighter Algy has fallen over his own feet twice already. Cultivate the old ears, Dixon: in the dark they're worth more to you than your eyes."

"Damn the man," I reflected, but a suitable reply eluded me. For I could hear absolutely nothing even then.

"I wonder if they butted into little Pansy?"

He got up and yawned prodigiously, and as he did so I heard cautious footsteps coming along the passage. The next moment Peter Darrell appeared in the door followed by the other two.

"All right, Hugh?"

"Thirsty, Peter – darned thirsty. Where's the ale?"

He lowered himself through the hole and dropped to the floor.

"We've got a dozen, old boy. Is that enough?"

"Do you drink beer, Dixon?" asked Drummond, looking up.

"Not usually at this hour of the morning," I answered.

"Thank God for that," he said in a relieved voice. "It's a most deplorable habit, and I'm glad you don't suffer from it. Incidentally, chaps, you haven't run into Irma by any chance, have you?"

"Well I'm damned!" Jerningham glanced at Darrell. "Why do you ask, Hugh?"

"Because according to Dixon the poppet has been here, holding spiritual converse with our late lamented Carl. Of course he doesn't know the darling by sight, and Toby and I were both asleep. But from his account of the interview it must have been her."

He paused with his glass half-way to his mouth.

"Have you seen her?"

"As we were leaving the village, old boy," said Jerningham, "a closed car, going fast, met us. And as we passed it a woman looked out of the window. Peter was driving, and Algy was in his usual condition of comatose imbecility, so it was only I who saw her. I just got a fleeting glimpse, but I thought it was Irma myself. I wasn't sure: but from what you say it must have been. I tried to get the number of the car, but the road is dusty and I couldn't see it. And then just as I was telling Peter, we went and punctured. Otherwise we could have followed. What did she come here for?"

"To gloat over my corpse, Ted, and to assure Carl that you three weren't forgotten," said Drummond. "She's out for the lot of us."

"Bless her little heart," remarked Peter. "But she'll have to be a bit more explicit as far as I'm concerned."

He produced a copy of *The Times* from his pocket.

"Here's the invitation to the party: but Allah alone knows what it means."

He pointed to two verses in the Personal Column. They were headed – "To dear Hugh."

> "A lily with the plural put before
> A thing of beauty, but in this case, more
> Like the fair lady whom you met last night.
> When found, at any rate, you'll start quite right.
> Dipped in the river Styx one part alone stayed dry.
> Leave out the next, but take the cry
> Of every schoolboy. That should give a man.
> And now, you poor fish, find it if you can."

"Does anyone know the story of the girl who went to a fancy dress ball dressed as a lily," said Algy hopefully.

"Sit on his head," groaned Peter. "What the hell does it mean?"

# CHAPTER 10

*In which the third clue is solved*

I have said earlier that this is my first essay in writing, but I should imagine that one of the rules must be to refrain as far as possible from boring the misguided optimists who are endeavouring to wade through the completed effort. And, therefore, I will refrain from giving any description of the rest of that day. It had been unanimously decided that it would be unsafe for Drummond, Sinclair and me to leave before nightfall if we were to avoid any risk of being spotted. And so beyond mentioning that the beer expired shortly after midday, that Toby Sinclair revoked twice at bridge and was soundly beaten by Drummond for his pains, and that I got an acute attack of the hiccoughs due to ale on an empty stomach, I will draw a veil over our doings. Quiet reigned on the Western Front, broken only by the curses of the particular individual who was, at the moment, wrestling with the doggerel in *The Times*.

Drummond from the outset gave it up. With a graceful movement of the hand he waved it from him, as a child might wave a plate of prunes and semolina pudding. Algy Longworth having at last got his story about the lily off his chest was found guilty of telling the world's hoariest chestnut, and having been thrown into the passage refused to play any more. So it was left to the rest of us to try and solve it. And honesty compels me to admit that we failed – utterly. It seemed completely meaningless.

"A lily with the plural put before."

That seemed to give Slily. Toby Sinclair insisted that there was a loch of that name somewhere in the Hebrides, but on being pressed was not quite sure it wasn't an island off the coast of Cork. And that was about as far as we got. Except for Achilles: I got that.

"Dipped in the river Styx one part alone stayed dry."

That seemed to point to the Achilles Statue, an unsuitable spot, as Drummond pointed out moodily, for erecting a booby-trap. And we were all somewhat moody when we left at ten that night for his house in London. Concealment was necessary and personally I was hidden under a rug at the back of the first car. Before that I had always felt a certain contempt for individuals who endeavour to evade paying for a railway ticket by travelling under the seat. Now I regard them with nothing short of admiration. To walk is a far, far better thing.

But we arrived at length, and having got Algy Longworth's shoe out of my mouth we crept through two dust-bins to the back door. It was a risk coming to his house at all but it had to be run, since all his props for make-up were there. And after a short pause the door was opened by a manservant, who evinced not the slightest surprise at the sight of the procession.

"Have you seen any one loitering about the house, Denny?" said Drummond, as the door closed behind us.

"No, sir. But a man called this afternoon and asked for you."

"What sort of a man?"

"A stranger, sir. And I am inclined to think, not an Englishman."

"What did you say?"

"The truth, sir. I said you were away from home."

Drummond looked thoughtful.

"Look here, Peter – we've got to try and ride them off. I'm tolerably certain we weren't spotted coming in here, but it looks as if they were watching the front. Go with Ted and drive up openly to the house. Ring the bell. When Denny comes – tell him the news in a voice broken with grief. Tell him I'm dead. Tell him twice if you think the blighter outside hasn't heard. Denny – you will clutch the door, turn pale with anguish and sob out – 'No man had ever a better master.' And for God's sake don't breathe port all over the street. After that, Peter, you three go off to your rooms and wait for further orders. Somehow or other we've got to solve this confounded thing."

"Right-ho, old boy, I'll pitch Denny the tale. And then we'll wait to hear further from you."

And it was while we were waiting for them to come that I had an idea. Old Tom Jenkinson. If any man in London could solve it he could. A former schoolmaster of mine now retired, and a member of my club, he still appeared to regard me as a dirty and ink-stained schoolboy. But over acrostics, riddles or cross-words he was a perfect genius. I said as much to Drummond.

"Splendid," he remarked. "Is he likely to be at the club now?"

"Never leaves it before midnight."

"Then go and scribble a line to him, old boy, explaining what we want – and I'll send it round by Denny. You'll find paper in that room up there, but see that the curtains are pulled tight before you switch on the light."

DEAR MR JENKINSON, – *I wrote* –

I would be deeply obliged to you if you would send me the solution of the enclosed rhyme. It represents a town or locality or place of some sort, presumably in the British Isles. It is a matter of urgent importance that I should get the answer as soon as possible. Knowing you I feel sure that you can solve it at once, and the bearer of this note will

wait for a reply. I hope Mrs Jenkinson is in the best of
health.

Yours sincerely,

JOE DIXON.

"Splendid," said Drummond. "Peter has been, and according
to Denny there was a man loitering by the railings who
overheard what was said. Moreover, he's gone now, so it may
have done some good. Anyway we'll send Denny round with
that note at once.

"Go out by the back door," he said as his servant came in,
"and take this to the Junior Reform. Wait for an answer. And
don't forget – if anyone asks you – I'm dead."

"Very good, sir," said the man impassively. "There is a new
cask, sir, behind the door."

"A good fellow," remarked Drummond. "And improved
considerably since the death of his wife. She was a muscular
woman and a martyr to indigestion, and the result left much to
be desired."

He lit a cigarette, and began pacing up and down the room.

"Lord! but I hope this old buster of yours solves it," he said
once or twice.

"If he doesn't, it's unsolvable," I assured him. "But there's just
a chance, of course, that he may not be in London."

And the instant I'd said it I regretted having spoken. His face
fell, and he stared at me blankly.

"If so," I hastened to add, "we can always get him through the
club. Letters will be forwarded."

"But it means delay," he muttered. "More hanging about."

An hour passed, and two, and suddenly he lifted his head
listening.

"Denny's back," he said. "Now we shall know."

His voice was quiet, but there was a strained look in his eyes
as he watched the door. Should we have the answer, or did it

mean further waiting? And mercifully it was the former; his servant had brought an answer. I opened it, and the others listened breathlessly.

DEAR DIXON, – *it ran* –

Before giving you the solution of your ridiculous little problem there are one or two points to which I would draw your attention. In days gone by, when you went, if memory serves me aright, by the name of Stinkhound, I endeavoured, for my sins, to teach you the rudiments of English composition. Why then do you offend my eyes, and give me further proof, if such were needed, of my complete failure, by using the word would twice in the first sentence? 'I should be', not 'I would be', is the correct opening to your ill-written missive. Again, if the matter is of urgent importance, obviously you require the answer as soon as possible – a clear case of tautology. Lastly, your interest in Mrs Jenkinson's health, though doubtless well meant, is a little tardy. She died some five years ago.

However – to your problem. My opinion of your intellect was always microscopic: even so, it is incredible that anyone out of an asylum could have failed to solve it at sight – knowing that it was meant to represent a place. Let us take the first stanza. Clearly the last line has nothing to do with it: it is put in to cheer you on when you have interpreted the other three. Now, of course, I do not know the nature of the lady you met last night: your repellent habits are, I am glad to say, a closed book to me. But in this case she was obviously not a thing of beauty. *Ergo* – she was ugly or plain. But few places contain the letters UGLY: whereas there are many Plains in the British Isles. One in particular leaps to the mind – Salisbury Plain.

You may at this point ask what relation Salisbury has to a lily with the plural put before. Knowing your abysmal ignorance of everything remotely approaching to culture you probably will. The ancient name for Salisbury, my dear Dixon, was Sarum. To this day you will see the word written on many of the milestones around the town. Well, I suppose even you have heard of an Arum Lily. And therefore the first stanza is solved and gives us – Salisbury Plain.

A large area – comprising as it does a considerable portion of the county of Wiltshire. The second stanza is clearly designed to narrow our field. It does – to a remarkable degree. The first line could, of course, be solved by a child of six. But as Ruff's Guide to the Turf is doubtless more familiar to you than Homer's Iliad I shall assume that your mind has not even reached that infantile standard. Achilles was the son of Peleus by Thetis, one of the Nereids. And ancient mythology tells us that to make him invulnerable she dipped him in the Styx, holding him by the heel. Hence the phrase, the heel of Achilles – which was the only part that remained dry. The first line therefore gives us Heel.

"The cry of every schoolboy."

What the repulsive little horrors call it now, I do not know – but when you were one of them, what word rose most often to your lips? What was your moan – your everlasting bleat? Tuck. You gorged your bellies on tuck, and slept, as a result, in school – making disgusting noises. Tuck, Stinkhound – tuck.

"That should give a man."

Have you never read 'Ivanhoe'? Have you never heard of Robin Hood, and the fat and jovial Friar Tuck, his constant companion and father confessor?

And so we have Heel, Tuck and Friar. A glance at the verse will show us that Tuck is to be left out – and that reduces us to Heel and Friar.

On Salisbury Plain is an ancient Druidical temple known as Stonehenge. Outside the main circle is a great stone – the sun-stone. This is the point where a spectator, centrally placed within the temple, would see the sun rise on Midsummer Day. And the common name for the sun-stone is the Friar's Heel.

Wherefore, the solution of your childish effusion is the monolith known as the Friar's Heel at Stonehenge on Salisbury Plain. And in conclusion I can only endorse most wholeheartedly the terse and apt description of you given in the middle of the last line.

Faithfully yours,

THOMAS JENKINSON.

P.S. – I have often wanted to know one thing. Were you or were you not the miserable little boy who first nicknamed me Wart Hog? and the late Mrs Jenkinson Slab Face? A nickname – like a caricature – should bear some relation to the truth, Dixon, if it is to be considered clever. And to call me a Wart Hog is positively stupid.

"I got Achilles at any rate, confound the old ass," I remarked, as I put the letter down. "Well – there you are. Now we know."

"Stonehenge," said Drummond. "Close to Amesbury."

"With cantonments all round it," put in Toby Sinclair. "I motored past it last summer."

"How far away?" Drummond looked at him thoughtfully. "I haven't been there since I was a kid, and there was nothing built then."

"I suppose about a mile to the nearest," said Sinclair. "Perhaps less. And there's another thing, too. By day there are hordes of trippers all over the place – guides and all that sort of stunt. You've got to pay to go in."

"So nothing can happen by day. And by night – with troops as close as that – they will have to be careful."

He went to the telephone, and gave a number.

"Peter," he said as soon as he got through, "come round at once – all of you. Back door, as before."

He sat down and stared at me.

"I wonder what is the best rig for you," he pondered. "In a way, you're the least important, as only the man and the woman of last night know you."

"And our venerable friend of the *Angler's Rest*," I reminded him.

"True. I'd forgotten him. Still a moustache, a pair of spectacles and the earnest air of a tourist should meet the case. And if you see any of those three, efface yourself. Toby – I've got a very good line in elderly professors for you. Butterflies, I think. You can gambol lightly over Salisbury Plain making a noise like a killing-bottle."

"Thanks, dear old boy," said Sinclair. "What are you going to be?"

"That remains to be seen," answered Drummond with an enigmatic smile. "I've got two or three half-formed ideas."

The smile faded slowly from his face.

"But whatever it is, I'm thinking that the sooner we begin to put the fear of God into this bunch the better."

And I realised suddenly how he had earned the sobriquet of Bulldog.

A minute or so later Peter Darrell and the other two came in.

"You've solved it?" asked Jerningham eagerly.

"A pal of Dixon's has," said Drummond. "A stone called the Friar's Heel at Stonehenge. You can read the letter later."

"And you can read this one now," said Darrell. "Delivered by hand."

It consisted of one line.

Read today's *Times*. Personal column.

"So she really does think we're dead, Peter." Drummond rubbed his hands together. "Excellent. However, let's get down to it. In the first place, from now on you three have got to run this show alone. Officially, that's to say. And, dash it all, I don't like it."

"Cut it out, you ass," laughed Jerningham.

"It's all very fine and large, Ted – but they mean business. And I don't want any casualties. I believe that what Dixon said is absolutely right. Whether she is insane or not is beside the point: there's not much sign of insanity about her plans up to date. But from what he heard her say this morning we are all for it, and Phyllis as well, before she goes to join Peterson. She was never remarkable, was she, for the quality of mercy. And now that she's obsessed with this idea, she will be utterly merciless. It's revenge run mad. So for the love of Heaven be careful. I'd never forgive myself if one of you took it in the neck."

"We'll be careful all right, old boy," said Darrell quietly. "But Phyllis has got to be found, hasn't she?"

"I know that. But I'm wondering if it wouldn't be better for you three to chuck it and leave it to me."

"We have but little desire for a rough house," said Jerningham, "but there's going to be one in a moment unless you cease talking tripe."

"Well, well; so be it," grinned Drummond. "But I thought I'd just mention it. So as I said before – let's get down to it. From what Toby says, the place is stiff with people all the day. So by day there can't be any risk. Now, it's possible that all we are going to get there is another clue – in fact, it's probable. I really don't see how they can rig up anything in a public place like that, which can be dangerous – even at night. And so as I see it – there's just one thing to fear, and that can only happen at night."

"What's that?" said Darrell.

"Common or garden murder, Peter," said Drummond gravely. "There may be a clue; on the other hand, it may be a trap."

"Murder," I said doubtfully. "In a place like that."

"Why not?" said Drummond coolly. "What leads in nine cases out of ten to the discovery of a murder? Motive. And what possible known motive is there for killing any of them. We know the motive: who else does? If we told this story to the police we'd be laughed out of court."

"And Phyllis would pay the price," said Jerningham gravely.

"We know they are utterly unscrupulous: we know that they intend to kill them. What more likely than that they'll have a dip at it at the Friar's Heel? And that is a thing I do not propose to risk unless it is absolutely essential. No. Peter, my mind is made up, old boy – so there's no use your looking like that. I promise you that when it is necessary, I'll send for you."

"What is your suggestion, Hugh?" said Jerningham after a while.

"This, Ted. From what Dixon overheard Irma say, this little show will not be concluded until they've got you – all three. I may be wrong, but I don't think they will try for you in London: in her own distorted way she is going to play this game through to the end in the way she intended. And, therefore, nothing further will take place until you come to the Friar's Heel. Now my proposal is this. But for this freak pal of Dixon's, Heaven alone knows when we should have solved that last clue. So there will be nothing surprising about it if you take at least a couple of days over finding the answer. And during those two days – or until I wire for you – you will remain in London, ready to leave the instant you hear from me."

"And you three?" asked Darrell.

"We'll go down in disguise and spy out the land. Maybe we shall find nothing; maybe the clue, if there is one at the Friar's Heel, will only be given to one of you. If so, I'll wire you. But it's possible that we shall find the clue, and get a short cut to what we want."

"I don't like it, Hugh," said Jerningham.

"Ted, old boy, it's best from every point of view. I don't want one of you killed – or the lot. And, my dear old lad, they mean business. Supposing you were all killed, from another point of view altogether – where should we be? Ignorant of where Phyllis is, with the game over as far as they are concerned. The whole bunch of us wiped out. The only person left then to finish off is Phyllis. There are such things as silencers for guns, laddie, as we know only too well. No, no: it's absolutely obvious. We will go first and see what we can find out. If we find out nothing – then you come in. If, on the contrary, we get on their tracks – then you still come in, but in a far sounder strategical position than if you went down now. Because when you arrive they will think the Friar's Heel is your objective, whereas in reality it won't be. They will lie up for you there, and you will short-circuit them."

"He's right, Ted; perfectly right," said Darrell unwillingly. "I wish he wasn't; but he is."

"So I shall rig up Toby and Dixon tomorrow, and they will go to some pub in Amesbury."

"What's your own game, Hugh?" said Algy.

"That, old boy, you will know in due course. For the time being I think it's best that none of you should know. It's going to be touch and go – this show – and I'd sooner have an absolutely free hand. And, finally, don't forget the old Froth Blower's dirge. Twice for danger."

"Froth Blower's?" I asked. "Is that the thing I've heard you singing?"

"Laddie," laughed Drummond, "you can't be real. When peace comes your education shall be taken in hand. Now is all clear?"

"Absolutely," said Darrell.

"Then a long night in, chaps. We'll want all we can get in the sleep line. And one other thing. If you want to get me, drop a line to John Bright at the Post Office, Amesbury."

They went casually with a nod and a grin – did the other three; demonstrativeness was not a characteristic of this crowd. But when they'd gone, Drummond sat for some time staring in front of him with his beer untasted on the table at his side. And at last he rose with a grunt.

"Come on; bed. I hope to Heaven they'll be all right in London."

He showed me to my room, where a pair of his pyjamas had been laid out.

"Hope they won't be too small," he said with a grin. Then he paused by the door. "Deuced good of you and all that, Dixon, to mix yourself up in this show. Though, 'pon my soul, I don't know what we'd have done without you."

And, astounding though it may seem, I can recall no remark made to me in my life that has occasioned me greater pleasure. Whether it had anything to do with it, I don't know, but certain it is that no sooner had my head touched the pillow than I was asleep. And the next thing I knew was his servant shaking me by the shoulder the next morning.

"Nine o'clock, sir," he said. "And the Captain would like you to come along to the music-room as soon as you've had your bath."

The music-room appeared to be so-called because there was no trace of any musical instrument in it. It resembled nothing so much as an old-clothes shop. Suits of all sorts and descriptions littered the floor; wigs, false hair and the usual make-up appliances were on the table.

Drummond was standing in the middle with two complete strangers by him. One of them was obviously of the hairdresser type; the other was an elderly man of scholastic appearance.

"Morning, Dixon," said Drummond. "Now, Albert, there you are. What are we to do with him? A minimum on his face, because he's not used to it."

The hairdresser man eyed me critically.

"I thought a moustache," went on Drummond. "And glasses. For Mr Seymour. Don't forget Dixon – Fred Seymour."

"Can't we dispense with the moustache?" I said. "It's certain to fall off at the wrong moment."

"Not as I shall fix it, sir," said the hairdresser in a pained voice. "Will you kindly take a seat here?"

"Who is the old bloke?" I whispered to Drummond as I passed him.

"My dear fellow," he cried, "excuse me. I quite forgot. This is a very old friend of mine – Professor Stanton – Mr Dixon. He's come to give Toby some advice on butterflies."

"A fascinating hobby, Mr Dixon," remarked the Professor, and I stared at him in amazement. Surely I knew that voice.

"Great Scott," I muttered. "It's you, Sinclair."

They all laughed.

"What an amazing disguise," I cried. "But for your voice I'd never have known you."

"And under the ministrations of the excellent Albert the result will be the same in your case," remarked Drummond. "The whole essence of disguise, Dixon, is to make it as simple as possible, and therefore as unnoticeable."

He was watching Albert's efforts as he spoke.

"Most people are extraordinarily unobservant," he went on. "If you wear different clothes from usual, alter your walk a little, and put on a pair of dark spectacles, you'll pass nine people out of ten that you know in the street without being recognised. Whereas if you wear a large red nose and fungus all over your face, you may not be recognised, but you'll certainly be noticed. And once you're noticed the danger begins. Albert, I think a respectable bank clerk of about thirty-five is what we want."

He began rummaging in the pile of clothes.

"We'll give you a rather badly cut suit of plus fours, and a cap. Horn-rimmed spectacles, Albert. Now let's have a look at him."

The three of them stared at me critically.

"Get into these clothes," said Drummond. "I can't be sure till you're out of that dressing-gown."

I contemplated the garments with distaste.

"I suppose there are people who wear things like that," I remarked, "or nobody would make them."

"It's a misfit," he said. "I bought a dozen of 'em once, and that's about the last. Don't mind if your stockings come down a bit; it helps the effect. Yes, Albert: that will do."

"I think so, sir," said Albert complacently, and at that moment I saw myself in the glass.

The shock was ghastly, but at the same time I was forced to admit that the result was amazing. I do not look at my face more often than necessary as a general rule, it shakes me too badly to see it. But the reflection that confronted me as I stood there was that of a complete stranger. Moreover, it was true to type. I had seen hundreds of similar examples at the seaside during August, or on char-à-banc trips.

"Then that's finished," said Drummond. "Now the only pub, as far as I can make out, is the *Amesbury Castle*. I think you'd better arrive separately, and you can strike up an acquaintance afterwards."

He smiled suddenly and held out his hand.

"Thank you, Dixon; I'll take charge of that."

"Charge of what?" I said blankly.

"Blokes dressed like you, old boy, do not use expensive gold and platinum cigarette-cases with Asprey written all over 'em. We'll put that in my safe, and here is a tasty little thing in leather. Nor, laddie, do most bank clerks smoke Balkan Sobranis, I suggest the perfectly good yellow packet..."

"I loathe Virginian cigarettes," I groaned.

"Well," he conceded, "you may smoke cheap Turkish if you like. But a Balkan Sobrani would shout aloud to heaven. Anything more, Toby?"

"Nothing, I think, Hugh. We aren't to know you, are we?"

Drummond smiled.

"You *won't* know me, Toby," he said quietly. "All you've got to do is to keep your mouths shut, and your eyes open – and if you want me, John Bright at the Post Office finds me. If I want you I'll let you know."

He grinned again.

"So long, boys. Leave the house by the back door separately, and for Heaven's sake, Dixon, try not to appear self-conscious. Be a city clerk: don't only look it."

Which was a policy of excellence, but not quite so easy as it sounded. As I walked along Berkeley Street, I felt that everybody was looking at me. And when I ran straight into a woman I knew opposite the *Ritz*, I instinctively lifted my cap. She stared at me in blank surprise, and I dodged down Arlington Street to recover. Ass that I was – giving myself away at the very first moment. But after a while confidence began to return. I realised that though Joe Dixon would have caused a mild sensation garbed as I was – Fred Seymour caused none at all. And I further realised that if I as Joe Dixon had met me as Fred Seymour, I should have paid no attention to me. Fred Seymour was just one of a numerous type – no more conspicuous than any other individual of that type. The truth of Drummond's remark about the red nose was obvious. I was just an inconspicuous unit amongst thousands of others.

And so, as I say, gradually my confidence returned. I walked normally, and to test myself I determined to pass the commissionaire outside my club. I looked him straight in the face: he returned the look without a sign of recognition. And he on an average must see me five hundred times a year.

A sudden thought struck me: I had no baggage. For a while I debated between the rival merits of a rucksack and a hand-bag, deciding finally on the former. Then I bought a couple of shirts and some socks, and thus equipped, I made my way to Paddington. The last phase of the game, though I little knew it, had begun.

# CHAPTER 11

*In which I go to Friar's Heel by day*

Up to this point the telling of my story has been easy, even if the manner of the telling has been crude and poor. But from now on it becomes more difficult. Things happened quickly, and we were all of us scattered in a way we had not been before. In fact, for the greater part of the time, the only member of the bunch who I was able to talk to was Toby Sinclair. But I will do my best to make clear the happenings that led up to that last astounding denouement, which even now seems like some fantastic nightmare to me. And if some of those happenings are boring, I can only crave pardon, and assure my readers that it is necessary to write of them, for the proper understanding of what is to follow.

I arrived then, at the *Amesbury Castle* in time for a late lunch. It was a typical hotel of the English country town, relying more, I should imagine, on lunches and dinners to pay its way, than on people taking a bed. The food was of that grim nature which one associates with hotels of the type – plain and tough. An aged waiter, with most of yesterday's ration on his shirt front, presided over the dining-room, and looked at me in a pained way as I came in.

"Very late, sir," he remarked.

"And I am very hungry," I answered cheerfully.

He polished a menu card morosely on his trousers.

"Mutton hoff," he said. "Beef, 'am, tongue – and pertaters. Been a run on the mutton today," he added confidentially.

I gazed at the flies making a run on the beef and decided on ham and tongue.

"Many people staying here?" I asked.

"Full up for lunch," he said. "And the hotel be fairly full, too. A bunch of people came last night. Lumme! 'ere's another."

I glanced at the door to see Toby Sinclair coming in.

"Splendid," he cried, in a high voice that nearly made me laugh. "Food, waiter, for the inner man, and then to resume my search. Tell me, have you seen a *Bragmatobia fuliginosa*?"

The waiter recoiled a step.

"A'ow much?" he demanded. "There's beef, 'am, tongue and pertaters."

"And only this morning," went on Toby, "I am convinced I perceived a *Psecadia pusiella*. Members, my dear sir," he said to me, "of the great family of *lepidoptera*. In other words butter-flies."

"Beef, 'am or tongue," said the waiter resignedly. "The mutton's hoff."

"Ham, waiter, with a fragment of chutney. You are, sir," he turned again to me, "on a walking tour perhaps?"

"That is my idea," I said. "But I propose to make this hotel my headquarters."

"You may possibly care to come out with me once or twice. My name is Stanton – Professor Stanton."

"Mine is Seymour," I told him.

"Well, Mr Seymour –" He broke off suddenly. "Waiter, I asked for ham and chutney, not the mummified sole of a shoe covered with glue."

"The tongue is worse," said the waiter drearily. "And that there chutney has been here two years to my certain knowledge."

"As far as I am concerned it will remain for another two years. Give me some bread and cheese. Dixon," he said to me urgently, as the waiter left the room, "there's a man in the lounge outside I want you to have a look at. I only got a glimpse of him that night at the Mere, but I believe it's the bloke who was with the woman. Anyway he's got his hand bandaged up. No, Mr Seymour, a life-time is all too short for my entrancing hobby. Bless me! waiter, I think this cheese must have been here for two years also. Get me a pint of ale, will you. Yes, sir – a life-time is too short. Nevertheless I hope to capture the *Cyligramma fluctuosa* before I die. Are you doing anything this afternoon?"

"I thought of going over to Stonehenge," I remarked.

He nodded.

"We'll go over to Stonehenge. I wonder if one can hire a car."

And at that moment a man passed through the lounge. He looked in at the door, gave us both a casual glance and then disappeared.

"It is certainly our friend of the Mere," I said. "I'd know him anywhere. Now what the devil is he doing here?"

"Why shouldn't he be here?" said Toby. "This is the centre of activity at the moment."

"It may be," I agreed. "But don't forget that Darrell and Co. know him just as well as we do, and they might come at any moment, as far as the enemy knows."

"That's true," he said. "Still, their intelligence work is probably good. We've got to watch him, Dixon. Waiter," he called out, "is it possible to hire a motorcar? Mr Seymour and I were thinking of visiting Stonehenge."

"There be a Ford down at the garage," answered the waiter. "You might be able to get 'old of that if no one else ain't already. Be you staying 'ere or do you want the bill?"

"Staying," said Toby. "Room 23. Well, Mr Seymour, shall we go and see about this Ford? I have an idea that I might perhaps

see a *Cerostoma asperella* if my luck is in. Ah! pardon, sir –
pardon."

He had bumped into a man just outside the door – the man we
had both recognised.

"I trust I have not hurt your hand at all," he went on earnestly.
"So clumsy of me."

The man muttered something and sheered off, whilst I
followed Sinclair into the street.

"The gentleman was suspiciously close to the door, Dixon,"
he said quietly.

"Still, I don't think he suspected us," I answered.

"Not as us, perhaps. But I think the whole bunch of them
suspect everybody. When you boil down to it, they're tackling a
pretty dangerous proposition. If the police did get hold of them,
abduction and attempted murder form a nasty charge."

"That is the very point that has occurred once or twice to me,"
I said. "One can understand the lady risking it: she has the best
of motives – revenge. But I'm blowed if I see where these other
fellows come in. There's no question of revenge with them. So
what the devil are they doing it for?"

He shrugged his shoulders.

"Money. I'm told that in Chicago you can hire a gunman for
a dollar. And I haven't the very smallest doubt that you can do
the same in England, if you know where to look. We heard that
bloke at the Mere mention two hundred pounds. And there are
scores of swine who would murder their mothers for that. Good
Lord!"

His voice changed suddenly to that of the Professor.

"And so, my dear Seymour, if we can get this car I will try and
show you some of those beauties of nature which I feel sure are
as yet quite unsuspected by you."

A man brushed past, favouring us both with a penetrating
stare.

"What's the matter?" I said, when he was out of earshot.

"Just for a moment I thought the dead had come to life," said Sinclair. "You saw that man who passed us?"

"That thin-lipped blighter who stared? Yes: I saw him. Is he one of them?"

"I haven't a notion," he remarked. "Look here, I'm just going to drop a line to Hugh, and I'll tell you the rest when we get in the car. Here's the garage."

The Ford turned out to be available, and I got in and waited for Sinclair, who was scribbling a note in the office.

"We'll post it in some pillar-box as we go out," he said as he joined me. "Better than leaving it at the main Post Office. Stonehenge, please, driver."

"What did you say?" I asked, when we'd started.

"I told him about the man at the pub," he answered. "And also about that other bloke. Of course there may be nothing in it, but the likeness is really so astounding to a man we once had dealings with, and who was one of the leaders of this very gang, that for a moment I thought it was him."

"Is there any reason why it shouldn't be?"

"Every reason. He died most substantially three or four years ago. Hugh killed him."

He grinned suddenly.

"Of course this is all Greek to you, so I'll tell you about it. When we first bumped into Carl Peterson – now defunct, and the lady you saw at the Mere, it was at the instigation of Mrs Drummond – before she was Mrs Drummond. It's altogether too long a story to tell you the whole thing; but in a nutshell, they were engaged in a foul criminal plot. Assisting them was one of the biggest swine it has ever been my misfortune to run into – a man called Henry Lakington. He was a mixture of chemist, doctor, thief, murderer and utter blackguard. But clever – damned clever. He wasn't as big a man as Peterson, because he hadn't got the vision – but he was a far more ineffable swab. Peterson, at any rate, at times had the saving sense of humour:

this man had none. And in the course of our little contest Drummond fought him and killed him. It was one or the other, and that's a bit dangerous for the other, if the one is Hugh. Now that man who passed us is the living spit of Henry Lakington; he might be – and for all I know is – his twin brother. And the coincidence struck me as so peculiar that I thought I'd mention it to Hugh. Of course, there's probably nothing in it."

"You are convinced," I said, "that this man Lakington was killed."

"Absolutely certain of it," he answered. "On that point there's not a shadow of doubt. But if there's anything in the theory that certain types of mentality have certain types of faces, that man would steal the bird seed from a pet canary's beak. Hullo! here we are."

It was years since I had been to Stonehenge, and emphatically the impressiveness of the ruin had not been increased by the military buildings that had sprung up around it. Equally emphatically the difficulty of playing any monkey tricks there, either by day or night, had considerably increased.

At the time we arrived several empty char-à-bancs were standing on the road, and crowds of trippers were wandering round the huge stones escorted by guides. And having paid our modest entrance fee we joined a group.

"There, ladies and gentlemen, you have the slaughter stone on which the victim was sacrificed as the first rays of the sun, rising over the Friar's Heel, touched his body. Inside you perceive the altar stone…"

The guide droned on, but I paid scant attention. My thoughts were concerned with the present, and not with the past. Was Drummond right in his surmise, was this place – the scene of so much death in the dawn of history – to be the setting for murder as merciless as anything of old? What he had said was correct in one respect certainly; if Darrell, or any of them, were done to death it would be, to the world at large, a crime without motive.

And the instant those three were disposed of, the end would come for Mrs Drummond.

It had been sound generalship on his part, leaving them in London. But the crux of the whole matter was whether, if there really was a clue to be obtained, we should get it. True, that we saved them the risk of being murdered, but did we not also prevent any possibility of getting information? Granted that our disguises held, what reason was there for us being told anything? To get a short cut to our goal, as Drummond hoped, presupposed our obtaining the necessary clue. And as far as I could see at the moment, the only connecting link we possessed was the man with the wounded hand.

To the other who, Toby Sinclair said, was like this dead man Lakington, I attached no importance whatever. Chance likenesses are frequent, and the mere fact that he bore a striking resemblance to a dead criminal was no proof that he was a criminal himself. No, the man with the damaged finger was our only link, and I began to wonder if we hadn't been foolish in losing sight of him.

I glanced round: Toby Sinclair had wandered off and joined another group. And it suddenly occurred to me that it could do no harm to make a closer inspection of the Friar's Heel. It was a perfectly ordinary and normal thing to do, and would not cause any suspicion, even if our opponents had spies in the crowd. And there was always the bare possibility of finding a clue.

I wandered over to it, to find a big man in rough seafaring clothes staring at it curiously.

"Rum old pile this, guv'nor, ain't it? I've seen the same sort of thing at Stornoway up in Lewis. Though I reckons the stones there ain't as big. This Friar's Heel as they call it is a big 'un all right."

"You've been to the Hebrides," I said casually.

"Been there! Lor' bless you, there's not many parts of this little old globe that I ain't been to. And with it all I guess there are as curious things and as beautiful things in England as anywhere else. Only people don't know it, or else they're too lazy to go and look."

I looked at him curiously, out of the corner of my eye. Could this be another clue? If it was it meant we had been spotted. And then I took a pull at myself: I was beginning to suspect everybody and everything.

"Stopping in these parts?" he went on.

"For a few days," I said.

"Funny sort of country," he remarked. "Good for the soldiers, I suppose, but it's a bit too bare for me. I like it with a few more woods and trees. Still – it's fine, especially at night. I reckon that these pebbles would look grand with the moonlight shining on them."

Once again I stared at him thoughtfully.

"Yes, one could imagine all sorts of terrible things happening here at night," I said quietly. "Ghosts of old Britons who had been sacrificed: and violent deaths, and – murder."

He laughed.

"You ain't half got an imagination, guv'nor, have you? But I take it you're one of the town-bred lot – meaning no offence. Put you down in the country at night, and you begin to see things that ain't there – and hear things that ain't real. Murder! Who's going to murder anyone here?"

He laughed again.

"I don't suppose anyone ever comes to a place like this at night," he went on. "And yet it's a rum thing. I was bicycling along that road late last night – been seeing some friends of mine – and it seemed to me as if there was something moving about the place. Round this very stone. Of course it was dark, and I may have been mistaken, but there ain't generally much wrong with my sight."

Last night, I reflected. Had the clue been guessed at once, Darrell and the other two could have been at the Friar's Heel by then. Had there been someone here in readiness? To give them a further clue, or to deal with them – otherwise.

"You didn't investigate?" I asked casually. "See if you were right?"

"Not me, guv'nor. None o' my business. And one of Ben Harker's rules in life has always been to mind his own business."

He produced a well-used old briar from his pocket, and proceeded to fill it from a weather-beaten leather pouch.

"Have a fill?" he said. "Ship's tobacco; the best in the world."

"A bit strong for me, I'm afraid, Mr Harker," I thanked him. "We miserable city clerks are hardly used to that sort of smoke."

"You prefer them damned fags, I suppose," he grunted. "Ah! well, everyone to his own taste. Personally…"

He paused, and I glanced at him. His fingers had ceased filling his pipe, and he was standing absolutely motionless staring over my shoulder. Only for the briefest fraction of time did it last, and then he continued his interrupted sentence.

"Personally, I can't ever get any taste out of a cigarette."

As I say the pause was only for a fraction of a second – a pause which I might quite easily have missed, had I not happened to have been watching his hands. But I hadn't missed it, and I knew that he had seen somebody or something behind me that had caused it.

"A match at any rate, I can offer you," I said, and as I spoke I turned round casually. Coming slowly towards us was the thin-lipped man who resembled Lakington.

"Thanks," he answered, lighting his pipe in the unmistakable method of a man used to the wind. Then he handed me back the box.

"Well, good day to you," he said. "Maybe if you're staying in these parts we shall meet again."

He strolled off with the slight roll of the seaman, and I lit a cigarette. Certainly nothing he had done or said connected him in the slightest degree with the game, and yet I wasn't quite sure.

Why that sudden pause in the middle of a sentence? And then it struck me that there was nothing to connect the man who had caused it with the game either, except a resemblance to a dead criminal.

I sat down on the ground, and proceeded to study the huge stone, acutely conscious that the thin-lipped man was standing just behind me.

"You are interested in this sort of thing?" he remarked politely.

"As much as a bank clerk who knows nothing about it can be," I answered.

"It has always been a hobby of mine," he said. "The past is so infinitely more interesting than the present. One admits of imagination; the other is bare and brutal fact. These motorcars; this crowd of terrible people peering in their asinine way at the scene of age-old mysteries. Doing the place at high pressure, instead of steeping themselves in the romance of it."

He talked on, and there was no denying that he could talk. His voice was pleasant and well modulated, and after a while I began to listen entranced. Evidently a widely travelled and well-read man, with the rare gift of imparting information, without becoming a bore. And after a while I began to keep up my end of the conversation.

It was when he happened to mention the Zimbabwe Ruins in Mashonaland, ruins that I had broken my journey at Fort Victoria in order to see; ruins, as many believe, of a vanished civilisation, which had fascinated me at the time, that I became really interested.

He, too, knew them, and we started an argument. I maintained that they were an ancient legacy from some civilised people dating back, perhaps, to before the days of Solomon: he inclined to the theory that they were only the work of local natives, and at most mediaeval.

"Evidently," he said at length, "you have studied the matter more closely than I have. Did you spend long there?"

"I was actually in South Africa for about six months," I told him. "And I used to collect opinions from those qualified to express them."

"A fascinating country. Though perhaps for any big scheme of emigration which would cover all classes of our countrymen, Australia is more suitable."

"I've never been there," I said. "As a matter of fact I'm thinking of going next year. And to New Zealand."

"By the way," he said affably, after we had chatted for another ten minutes or so, "if you are staying in this neighbourhood you might care to have a look at my collection of curios. Though I say it myself I think I may say there are few finer in the country. And a man of taste like yourself would appreciate them."

"It is very good of you," I remarked, "and I should greatly like to see them."

He had risen, and I stood up also.

"Where is your house?"

He glanced at his watch thoughtfully.

"I have my car here," he said, "and if you can spare an hour I could run you over and show them to you. Then my car can take you back to your hotel."

"There is only one small difficulty," I said. "I came over from Amesbury with a gentleman I happened to meet at lunch. I see him over there – Professor Stanton. An enthusiast on butterflies."

"Professor Stanton," he cried. "Not *the* Professor Stanton."

"I really don't know," I murmured. "I met him quite by chance at lunch today."

"But," he exclaimed excitedly, "if it's Professor John Stanton his reputation is world-wide."

I suppressed a slight smile; whatever Toby Sinclair's reputation might be in certain purlieus of London, it could hardly be described as world-wide.

"He's coming to join us," I remarked, "and you can ask him."

"But it is him," he cried, as Toby approached. "What stupendous luck. My dear Professor," he advanced with outstretched hand, "you remember me. What a fool I was not to recognise you in Amesbury when I passed you."

Sinclair stared at him blankly.

"I fear you have the advantage of me, sir," he remarked.

The other waved a deprecating hand.

"Ah! but, of course, you would not recall me. I am merely one of the thousands who have sat at your feet. It was presumption on my part to imagine that my face would be familiar to you. But how entranced I was at that lecture you gave on the habits of *Pieris rapae*."

"You must be making some mistake, sir," said Toby coldly. "I am not the gentleman you think."

"Modesty, Professor – modesty. Tell me have you discovered a specimen of it yet? You told us, if you remember, that it was to be your life work."

"Though you are making a mistake, sir, as to my identity – yet I can well imagine that it would have been the life work of the man I resemble. The rarest of all the species, perhaps. But I have seen today a marvellous specimen of the *Opsiphianes syme*."

"Stupendous," said the other admiringly. "What eyesight: what wonderful eyesight. Well, I mustn't detain a public character. Good day, sir, good day. And if you care to join your friend in a little visit he has promised to make to my humble abode, I shall be delighted to show you my amateur collection."

He bowed courteously and walked off, leaving Sinclair and me staring at one another.

"I say, old boy," said Sinclair, "I hope this is all right. I wonder who the hell Professor Stanton really is. Hugh's made a bit of a bloomer there. He oughtn't to have given me the name of a pukka character. Anyway, I think I pulled the jargon on him all right. I must consult my list of names again."

And it was as he was pulling it out of his pocket that a strange noise close by drew our attention. It appeared to come from a little man of astonishing aspect, whose false teeth were clicking together in his excitement. He also seemed to be trying to speak. We waited: by this time I was prepared for anything.

"Are you acting for the films?" he spluttered at length. "Or are you being more stupid than you look for some purpose?"

"Explain yourself, little man," said Toby with interest.

"Lying, sir – lying offensively on a subject which is sacred to some of us." His teeth nearly fell out, but he pushed them back with the care of long practice. "Using words, sir, which betray you as an impostor. How, sir, did you see a specimen of *Opsiphanes syme*?"

"With the jolly old peepers, laddie," said Toby soothingly.

"Bah!" cried the little man. "Are you so profoundly ignorant of the subject you desecrate that you do not know that only in the swamps of Brazil is that beautiful butterfly found?"

"No wonder he said my eyesight was good," said Toby thoughtfully.

"And further, sir – do you see that?"

He pointed a shaking finger at two Cabbage Whites chasing one another near-by.

"The rarest of all the species, you called them. *Pieris rapae*, sir. Bah! you make me sick. You should be prosecuted, sir; you should be prosecuted."

"Look here, you'll swallow your teeth in a minute," said Toby, but the astounding little creature had already departed, waving his fists in the air.

"Takes all sorts to make a world, gents," came a laughing voice from behind us. "But you do certainly seem to have said the wrong thing."

We swung round: the man who looked like a sailor was standing there.

"Don't you know anything about butterflies – or is he talking through his hat?"

He gave Toby a penetrating stare.

"Dangerous thing, sir, pretending to know more than you do. Or be what you ain't."

He strolled away, and once again we looked at one another.

"He's one of 'em," I said. "For a certainty. That's torn it."

"Hell," he remarked. "And again, hell. What about Lakington the second? Is he one, too?"

# CHAPTER 12

*In which I write my mind to Drummond*

Toby Sinclair was thoroughly despondent.

"I looked up a bunch of Latin names in an Encyclopaedia," he said morosely. "How the dickens was I to know that the damned thing only lived in Brazil?"

We were sitting in his room at the hotel.

"And the devil of it is, Dixon," he went on, "that even if Lakington is not one of them we've still given the show away to that sailor bloke. You could see his suspicions sticking out a yard."

"Hold hard a moment," I said. "You say we've given it away."

"Well then – I have, if you like that better," he said sulkily.

"Don't get huffy, old man," I laughed. "I'm not trying to pretend that I should have done any better than you if I'd been the Professor. But as luck would have it I was only a clerk."

"What are you driving at?" He looked at me curiously.

"Simply this. Up to date I have not given myself away – either to the sailor or to the man you call Lakington. I think I may say that I have been the bank clerk on holiday to the life."

"Yes – but they know you know me," he objected.

"They know – and if they choose to take the trouble to ask it will be corroborated – that you and I met casually in the coffee-room at lunch today. If you are an impostor, which unfortun-

154

ately they must know by now – there is still no reason whatever why I should have known it earlier."

"But you know it now as well as they do."

"Now – yes," I agreed. "But the fact that I went to Stonehenge with you throws no suspicion on me. I didn't know it then."

"I'm hanged if I get you," he said.

"You've got to clear out," I remarked. "Vamoose. Hop it. Disappear from this place for good."

"I'm blowed if I do," he said.

"My dear fellow – you must. If we're to do any good, and help Drummond in any way, it's impossible that you should stay on. They know you're an impostor; they know I know you're an impostor. Well, how can we both stop on here? Am I to cut you dead? Or am I to continue talking to you realising that you are an impostor? Don't you see that it's sufficient to bring suspicion on me at once? Besides – I'm going to speak quite frankly. Your value to the side at the moment is *nil*. In fact, old man, you're a positive source of weakness."

"I suppose you're right," he agreed reluctantly. "Well – what do you suggest?"

"That you tell them downstairs that you've changed your mind and will not require your room. Then you hop it, and I'm sorry to say, as far as I can see you fade out of the picture. I shall stay on, and without being blatant about it, I shall drop an occasional remark about your extraordinary idea of a holiday. The strange sort of kink that makes a man pretend to be what he isn't – that line of gup. Form of conceit – you know. I can easily cough it up. And by doing that I shall remove any small half-formed suspicion they may have about me. I am just an ordinary bank clerk taken in by you, as anyone else might have been."

He grunted and rose to his feet.

"You're right. I'll go. Drop a note to Hugh explaining things – and tell him I'm eating mud."

And then he suddenly paused.

"But, good Lord! Dixon – it's no good. The damage is done. If they've got a line on me they'll know Hugh and you and I aren't dead."

"They haven't got a line on you as yourself," I said. "You might be somebody else rigged out like that – Algy Longworth for instance. Clear out and clear out quick. For unless you do, if I'm not greatly mistaken you'll be for it. They will think you're just another member of Drummond's bunch, and as such require to be exterminated. I'm going down now into the bar; if I happen to see you before you go I shall be pretty terse in my remarks."

"What sickening luck," he muttered. "Damn that blinking butterfly."

"It's bad luck," I said, "but I'm sure it's the only thing to do. Look out into the passage and see if there's anyone about. Then I'll make a bolt for it."

He opened his door, and gave me the all clear. And a few moments later I strolled into the bar. A little to my surprise, the seafaring man was there, seated in a corner. He was talking earnestly to someone, and as I saw who his companion was, my pulse beat a little quicker. It was our friend of the Mere, the man with the damaged hand. Proof – absolute and definite.

I ordered a pint of ale and sat down near them. And the instant he saw me the sailor leaned across and beckoned me to join them.

"Draw up, mate," he cried. "You know it's none o' my business, but what was your friend's great idea this afternoon? I've just been telling this gentleman about it. Your butterfly pal, I mean, who knew nothing about butterflies."

"I assure you," I said a little stiffly, "he's no friend of mine. He's the most casual acquaintance. He happened to be lunching late at the same time as I was, and I gathered that he was a Professor Stanton, and an authority on butterflies. And he suggested we should go to Stonehenge together."

"Can't understand it," said the sailor man. "Now, if one of you started to talk to me about seafaring matters, I guess I'd spot in two shakes how much you know about the sea. And what's the good, anyway, of pretending you know what you don't know? You look such a blazing fool when you're found out."

"I think the explanation is very simple," I remarked. "It's merely a peculiar form of conceit. That man probably knows a smattering about butterflies, and for some reason or other likes to pose as an expert. He got it in the neck all right from that little man with the false teeth."

The sailor slapped his thigh with a blow like a pistol-shot and roared with laughter.

"Got it in the neck! Not half he didn't. Well, it will teach him a lesson. And butterflies – of all things. Look out – here he is."

Toby Sinclair came fussing in, and as soon as he saw me he crossed to our table.

"Ah! Mr Seymour," he said, "our little trip tomorrow must be cancelled, I fear. I have been unexpectedly called back to London, to my annoyance."

"I am sorry to hear that – er – Professor," I said a little stiffly.

"Going to catch *Opsi* – whatever it was – in Trafalgar Square," chuckled the sailor.

"I quite fail to understand you, sir," said Toby, drawing himself up. "Well – goodbye." He turned to me and held out his hand. "I trust you will enjoy the remainder of your holiday."

He went out into the lounge, and I watched him paying his bill.

"Really an extraordinary case," I said thoughtfully. "He's the last man in the world I should have thought would do anything so foolish. Even now I can't help thinking there must be some explanation. Though I suppose it's really a very unimportant matter."

"You never can tell," said the sailor darkly. "It may be that you're well clear of him, mate. Blokes don't masquerade like that unless they've got to. And they haven't got to unless there's something wrong somewhere."

"I quite agree," said the man with the damaged finger, speaking for the first time. "And as I happen to be a member of the police, I think I'll just keep an eye on the gentleman."

He finished his drink and left the room, and the sailor whistled under his breath.

"I wonder what the bloke has done," he said. "Or whether it's what you said – just a form of conceit. Anyway – have another."

For a moment or two I sat there undecided. Only too well did I know that the man with the damaged hand was not a member of the police; only too well did I know what he was a member of.

"Thanks," I said perfunctorily. "The same again, please."

Should I, too, follow and tell Toby? But if I did, the sailor would in all probability begin to suspect me. He was a member of the gang, too, and it was vital that I should be thought genuine. At the same time, how could I possibly let Sinclair run into some trap? He'd been a fool to come over and speak to me, seeing who I was with. Still, I couldn't let him down. He must be warned.

"I think, after all, I won't have another at the moment," I said. "I shall go out for a bit of a stroll. I'll go on up and get my hat."

"Right ho! mate. You might see the Professor getting more butterflies."

I left the bar and went upstairs to my room. Was I doing the right thing or was I not? After all, nothing much could happen in Amesbury in the middle of the afternoon, and Toby was quite capable of tackling the man with the damaged finger single-handed. If he knew about him – that was the point.

I went down slowly into the lounge, trying to decide. The sailor was still sitting in his corner of the bar: he evidently regarded the rest of the half-section as preferable to a walk.

"A note for you, sir."

The girl called to me out of the office.

"For me?" I said, staring at her.

She was holding it out, and I glanced at it. It was addressed to F Seymour, and the unfamiliar name almost caught me napping.

"That's not – " I began, and then I remembered and took it. "Thank you," I said. "Who left it?"

"I really don't know, sir," she said. "I've been out of the office for a few minutes and I found it lying here when I got back."

Who on earth could it be from? No one knew me: and then, of course, I got it. Toby had left it on his way out. I slit open the envelope, and for a moment I stared at the contents uncomprehendingly.

"Do not follow Toby – H D."

H D Drummond! But where was he? How on earth did he know I had intended to follow Toby? And even as I racked my brains for an answer, a thickset man in plus-fours crossed the lounge and entered the bar. He had a short, clipped beard, flecked with grey, and his hair was thinning a little over the temples.

With an immense feeling of relief I followed him. Thank Heaven! he had arrived on the scene. Naturally I was not going to pretend to know him, but I couldn't resist throwing him a casual glance as I passed. By the mere fact that I was there he would know that I had carried out his orders, so that it was unnecessary for me to do more. And I had the satisfaction of getting a quick look of approval.

"Changed your mind, mate, after all," called out the sailor. "However, better late than never, and good beer tastes none the worse for the waiting."

"It looked so infernally hot in the street," I said. "And even the chance of seeing our butterfly expert arrested for bigamy wasn't a sufficient inducement to go out."

I purposely spoke in a loud voice, so that Drummond should hear.

"Bigamy; that's good," chuckled the sailor. "With a face like his, I should think he'd be lucky to get one. Say" – he lowered his voice confidentially – "what do you make of the bloke in the corner? The one with the grouse moor on his face."

"Nothing much," I said. "Why? You don't think he's another criminal, do you? Seems a perfectly ordinary sort of bird."

And then it suddenly occurred to me that it would be a good thing to let Drummond know that this man I was talking to was one of the enemy.

"By the way," I said casually, "seeing that you're a beer drinker, I suppose you're a Froth Blower."

The sailor shook his head.

"I've heard of it," he remarked. "But I ain't a member. What's the idea?"

"Well, they've got a sort of anthem," I said, conscious that Drummond was looking in our direction, "by which they recognise one another. It goes something like this."

"Great Scott!" said the sailor, after I'd finished. "Does it? You've got a funny sort of voice, haven't you, mate? Or is that really the tune?"

"It should under certain circumstances be sung twice," I remarked. "This is one of them."

"I'll take your word for it," he said urgently. "I don't want to be rude, guv'nor, but your voice is one of them things when a little goes a long way. Have another gargle?"

I declined his offer, and a little later I made my way into the lounge. Drummond had left the hotel, and it was fairly obvious that the only interest that the seafaring gentleman could have in me was one of curiosity. Though we had done our best to allay suspicion, Toby Sinclair's mistake had greatly increased my difficulties. To be associated, however innocently, with a man who has been found out as a fraud is bound to make one conspicuous. And that is exactly what I had no desire to be.

The saving point in the situation up to date had been – though I said it myself – my own acting. And as I sat in the lounge, idly scanning a local paper, I confess I felt a little amused. Drummond's absolute assurance that we should not recognise him struck me as being distinctly funny. Seldom had I seen a more obvious disguise than the one he had adopted. Of course, I realised that he had definitely given himself away to me by writing the note, but even without that I should have known him anywhere. The beard was so very obviously false. In fact, I made up my mind that when I dropped him a line to tell him exactly what had happened over Toby Sinclair I would warn him about that beard. It looked the sort that might fall off in the soup. And one thing was certain. If any of the enemy who had known him in days gone by – the woman herself, for instance – should chance to see him, he would be spotted for a certainty.

It surprised me, I confess. In one way and another I had heard so much of his resource and daring, that it seemed all the more amazing that he should be so crude. To do him justice, the results he had obtained with Sinclair and myself were extremely good. Why, then, did he fail so dismally over himself? Could it be that he was so self-confident that he had become careless ? Or was it merely that he was relying absolutely on the fact that the other side thought we were dead?

A very strong asset, doubtless – immensely strong – for just so long as they continued to think so. And that was where the great danger of Toby Sinclair's mistake lay. Supposing they got him and stripped off his disguise. He had been a member of Drummond's gang all through: he would be recognised at once by the woman. And the instant he was recognised it would be obvious to the meanest capacity that we had not been drowned. If he had escaped, we must all have escaped. And once that fact was known, suspicion would be bound to fall on me, in spite of anything I might do. As for Drummond with his beard, a child would spot him at the other end of the street. Had not the sailor himself been suspicious the instant he saw him? And did it not prove, if further proof was necessary, that up to date I was entirely unsuspected? Otherwise would he have spoken as he did to me?

It certainly gave me a feeling of confidence, but just as certainly it increased my responsibility. As far as I could make out, I was the only person who with any degree of safety could carry on. Sinclair was out of it; and I found myself hoping to Heaven that Drummond would stop out, too. Of course, I knew he wouldn't, but with his extremely conspicuous appearance he would do far more harm than good. In fact, as I continued to think over it, I began to feel thoroughly irritable. This wasn't a game of Hunt the Slipper, or Kiss in the Ring. It was a game in which, as we knew to our cost, any false step might prove fatal. And it wasn't playing fair to any of us to come into the thick of it with an appearance that called to high Heaven – this is a disguise. Toby Sinclair's mistake had been foolish, perhaps, but that I had managed to rectify by acting promptly. But nothing I could do would rectify Drummond's. He, once he was seen, was beyond hope.

I crossed to a writing-table: something must be done. He might be our leader and all that, but I failed to see the slightest reason why I should run a considerably increased risk of getting it in the neck.

"Surely," I began, "it is nothing short of insane to come here with such a blatantly false beard on. The thing shrieks at one. The man who looks like a sailor, and who, as I told you by signal in the bar, is one of them, suspected you at once. I rode him off, of course – but if the woman should see you, you're done for. We all are. Would it not be wiser, in view especially of Sinclair's bad mistake this afternoon, for you to leave this thing in my hands for the moment? I am the only one who is unknown to the other side. I obeyed your instructions, and did not go after him when he left the hotel, but are you aware that he was followed *by the man whose finger you shot off*? What is going to happen if they catch him? Don't you see that the whole show is up? They will realise at once that none of us were drowned. And what then? Once that occurs, you will forgive my blunt speaking – but you won't last a minute. You will be spotted immediately. And because of my association with Sinclair they will even suspect me.

"Would it not, therefore, be better if, as I said before, you lay low for a bit? I will keep my eyes open, and find out what I can – notifying you at once of any developments. My principal hope lies in the sailor, and in the man with the damaged hand. The latter we *know* is one of them: the former I am equally certain is one also. Not, of course, absolutely so: but his whole demeanour at Stonehenge this afternoon was *most suspicious*. In fact, only the certainty of my perfect disguise prevents me from thinking that he was giving me the next clue. And if he was, it is Stornoway, in the island of Lewis. But of this I am not sure. Why should he waste a clue on an inoffensive bank clerk? Let us hope, at any rate, that I am wrong. Our difficulties in crossing undiscovered to such a sparsely populated locality as the Hebrides will be great.

"Then there is another man, about whom I think Sinclair wrote to you. He resembles apparently a man you killed some years ago called Lakington. We met him in the street here, before starting for Stonehenge; and we again met him at the Friar's Heel itself. I had a long talk with him first, and found him a most delightful and cultivated individual. In fact, I cannot believe that he is one of the enemy. Then Sinclair joined us, and committed his terrible gaff. He told him he had actually seen a butterfly which, as we subsequently gathered, only lives in Brazil! Now whether this man, who for purposes of reference I will call Lakington, actually spotted this mistake, or whether he didn't, I cannot say with any degree of certainty. But the point is really immaterial. Because the man who looks like a sailor most certainly did. After Lakington had left us, an odd little man, who obviously knew what he was talking about, though he acted as if he wasn't all there, told Sinclair to his face that he was an impostor. And the sailor, *who was close by, heard*. Now do you see the danger we are in? Sinclair is spotted: you, I'm afraid, are spotted also, so that only I am left. And if by any chance they begin to suspect me – which is not likely, but at the same time is a possibility we must reckon with – the coincidence would be too marked to escape their notice. One newcomer in disguise might be anybody: three – one of whom is a big man – tapes us unerringly. We shall have lost the priceless asset of secrecy.

"Wherefore I beg of you lie low. Hide, if necessary, in whatever room you may have taken, and *wait for information from me*. I am repeating myself, I know, but frankly, my dear fellow, it never even dawned on me that you would appear quite as you are. I venture to think it would almost have been better if you had come as yourself. However, the mischief is done now – and all that we can try to do is to rectify it.

"You may rely implicitly on me; but please do not make my task any harder than it is already."

I read through what I had written. Strong, perhaps – but not one whit too strong. He must be made to understand the enormity of his offence. And if he didn't: if he persisted in going about the place as he was, I should have to consider very seriously whether or not I would throw the thing up. Where would they have been without me up to date? I had more than half-solved the first clue: I had completely solved the second: and, through old Jenkinson, I had given them the answer to the third. Which entitled me to express my opinion pretty tersely. And if Drummond didn't like it, he could damned well lump it.

I addressed an envelope to John Bright, and called for a stamp. And it was while I was waiting for it to be brought that a trick of memory brought to my mind an incident in some detective story I had read years ago. A man had given himself away by leaving behind him a piece of blotting-paper, which he had just used. And the blotting-paper, when held up to a looking-glass, revealed exactly what he had written.

Just one of those little things, I reflected, where brain counts. One of those small details where the blundering type of fellow is apt to get caught. So I took the blotting-paper, tore it into small pieces, and dropped them in the paper-basket.

"Bit extravagant, aren't you, mate?"

With a feeling of annoyance, I turned round in my chair. Standing by the door of the bar was the sailor, and with him was the man with the damaged hand. And they were both staring at me.

For a moment I was tempted to ask him angrily what the devil it had to do with him, but I instantly suppressed the impulse. After all, it was a very harmless remark – one, moreover, which I was quick enough to see gave me an excellent opportunity of consolidating my position.

"A habit we clerks get into in a bank," I said. "Clean blotting-paper always after finishing a job."

"Is that so?" he remarked. "What a good idea."

I rose and crossed to the front door – I had no wish to post the letter in the hotel. And it was as I was actually stepping on to the pavement that a sudden awful thought struck me. Supposing they suspected me – just supposing – what was to prevent them, as soon as I was gone, from getting the torn-up pieces out of the basket and fitting them together.

At all costs I must prevent that, and the question was how. The sailor was still by the door, though the other man had disappeared. There was only one thing to be done: get back to the table, write another letter, and in some way or other retrieve those incriminating pieces.

I wrote another letter, and still he stood there. But at last he went, and I made a dive for the basket. The bits were all together, but mixed up to a certain extent with old cigarette ends and two

165

used pipe-cleaners. However, there was no time to worry over trifles: it was imperative that I should get that blotting-paper. I grabbed the lot, including the pipe-cleaners, and some soft, wet object, and crammed everything into my pocket. Then, breathing freely, I once more stood up, only to see that confounded sailor pop out again like a jack-in-the-box from the bar.

"Lumme, mate!" he cried, "what have you got on your coat? It looks like something out of a dust-bin."

I glanced down, just as the soft, wet object fell with a flop on the carpet.

"'Why," he said with interest, "that's the rotten plum I threw away an hour ago. You don't half have funny habits at your bank, old man, do you?"

The situation was undeniably difficult, and the only thing to do was to carry it off lightly.

"I threw away an important paper by mistake," I laughed.

"Well, you must have had St Vitus' dance in your fingers when you picked it up again," he said. "You've got an old bootlace and two toothpicks on your coat, sticking in the plum juice."

He retired into the bar again, leaving me fuming inwardly. The man was absolutely ubiquitous: it seemed impossible to get rid of him. Moreover, it was one of those stupid little things that have the power of irritating one profoundly. To be seen by anybody grabbing rotten plums out of a wastepaper-basket is annoying: in this case it might have been worse but for the cool way I had ridden him off.

However, there was only one thing to be done – dismiss the matter as unimportant. I had retrieved the blotting-paper which was the main point: the next item on the programme was to post my letter to Drummond. And then the real business would begin.

I strolled along the street, thinking out the best means of tackling the problem. The whole thing boiled down to a question of subtlety and brain: of meeting cunning with cunning. Once I had obtained the next clue, or located our opponents' main even if only temporary headquarters – strength would doubtless be required. And then Drummond could shed his ridiculous beard and emerge from seclusion. But until then – well, my letter was concise on that point.

My eyes suddenly narrowed: surely there was Drummond himself – beard and all – going into the Post Office. I quickened my steps: I felt that my letter was so vitally important that it would be worth while running some small risk to obtain immediate delivery. Every additional moment that he was at large in that absurd and obvious get-up increased our danger.

He was leaning over the counter as I entered, and I went and stood next to him.

"Are there any letters here for Bright?" he asked the girl. "John Bright."

She turned round to look, and I nudged his arm gently, showing him at the same time the letter I held in my hand. Then I dropped it on the floor.

"One just come," said the girl handing over Toby Sinclair's note.

Drummond took it, and then, as she attended to me, he stooped down and picked up mine. I bought some stamps, and stayed chatting with the girl for a few moments to give him time to get away. Then with a feeling of relief that my warning had reached him safely I followed at a reasonable distance. That vital matter was settled anyway.

Once more I returned to the problem. Two main lines of action presented themselves, so it seemed to me. The first lay in shadowing the sailor, or the man with the damaged finger, or possibly both: the second entailed a further visit or visits to the Friar's Heel, and both courses involved certain obvious difficulties.

It was true that up till now I had successfully avoided suspicion, but if I proceeded to attach myself permanently to either of the two men, how long should I continue avoiding it? If I tried to stalk them at a distance I was at once confronted with the fact that Salisbury Plain is not a very populous spot, and that I was almost certain to be discovered. On the other hand, if I went to the Friar's Heel, what chance should I have of obtaining any clue? Why should anything be said to an inoffensive bank clerk?

The best course I decided would probably be a mixture of the two. I would cultivate the sailor's acquaintance, and if I kept my ears open I might learn something of value either from him or the man with the damaged hand. But I would confine my dealings with them to the bar, or at any rate the hotel, unless some opportunity presented itself to accompany them anywhere outside. In addition I would pay a further visit to the Friar's Heel, and see if I could pick up anything there.

And that was the conclusion I had reached as I turned into the lounge. Prudent, and at the same time calculated to give the maximum of result. The sailor was in his usual corner of the bar, and he waved a cheerful hand at me as I entered.

"Been picking up any more plums?" he enquired. "Anyway, what about that gargle you wouldn't have before?"

"My shout this time," I said genially, as I sat down. "Just been having a stroll through the town. What is it?"

He was leaning towards me, and signing me to put my head close.

"I believe," he said in a hoarse whisper, "that that man's beard is false."

"What man?" I asked bewildered.

And then, to my rage and fury I saw that Drummond had just entered the bar. For a moment or two I could scarcely speak, so angry did I feel. After my urgent letter, after my imperative warning, for the triple distilled fool to parade himself again in the hotel of all places was too maddening.

"I don't think so," I managed to get out after a while. "Why should a man wear a false beard?"

"Why should a man pretend to know about butterflies when he doesn't?" he remarked. "Why should a man pick rotten plums and toothpicks out of a wastepaper-basket?"

"I trust," I said stiffly, "that you don't think there is anything mysterious about me."

"Lumme! no, mate," he laughed. "There ain't nothing mysterious about you."

He was staring covertly at Drummond all the time.

"It is false," he affirmed. "It waggles."

"Confound him and his beard," I cried. "Let's have that drink."

And even as I beckoned to the waiter, what little self-control that I still had after Drummond's colossal idiocy very nearly left me. Who should be crossing the lounge and heading straight for the bar but Algy Longworth?

He came drifting in and I stared at him speechlessly. Had everybody gone mad I wondered. That he should come here at all must be due to Drummond. And that Drummond should have sent him knowing that the man with the damaged hand was in the hotel could only be explained by the fact that our much vaunted leader's brain had failed.

True they took no notice of one another, and, after a time Longworth came over and sat down at the next table to ours. He, of course, did not know me, and I therefore judged it safe to address a casual remark to him. It might perhaps enable me later to warn him of what had happened and tell him to clear out.

"Motoring through?" I said casually.

He nodded.

"Jolly place, isn't it?" he remarked. "I always love dear old Salisbury Plain, ever since I spent six months on it at the beginning of the war. But I don't know this end very well: I was up Ludgershall way. Is it far from here to Stonehenge?"

169

"Stonehenge," repeated the sailor. "About three miles, I suppose. This gentleman and I were there this afternoon."

"I thought of going tonight," said Algy, and I felt I could have cheerfully murdered him.

"Did you?" remarked the sailor, staring at him thoughtfully. "Well, it's an interesting place, ain't it, mate?"

He turned to me.

"What did they call that stone where we were talking? The Friar's Heel, wasn't it?" And as he said it he deliberately raised his voice. I had a momentary glimpse of the man with the damaged hand standing in the door staring at Algy. Then he disappeared, and I saw him leave the hotel quickly. The damage was done: the message had been given.

# CHAPTER 13

*In which I go to Friar's Heel by night*

I don't mind confessing that I very nearly chucked in my hand. The whole thing was too disheartening. It was worse than disheartening – it was suicidal. I realised, of course, that my letter had not reached Drummond in time for him to warn Longworth that the sailor was one of the other side, but even so Algy should have known better than to discuss his plans with two complete strangers. And now the thing was what to do.

Drummond had left the bar shortly after, and up till dinner time I had no chance of a private word with Longworth. I made him one or two covert signs, when the sailor was not looking, but he missed them all. In fact he seemed to me to be wilfully dense. He must know that I was about somewhere, even if he didn't actually recognise me.

At dinner it was just the same. I came in to find him sitting at the long table between an elderly lady and a man who looked like a prosperous farmer. And not once did he even glance in my direction though I tried to catch his eye on several occasions.

The sailor had beckoned to me as I came in to sit at his table, but I had pretended not to see. I wanted peace and quiet to think out this new development. If Algy went to the Friar's Heel that night he was for it. That much was obvious. Unless, of course, Drummond proposed to be there, too, and bring the matter down to brute force. But even if he did, surely he must realise that it was very unlikely it would help us to find his wife's hiding-place.

Or did Drummond intend to lie hidden in the hope of getting a clue, and to use Longworth as a decoy without whom the clue would not be given? That, of course, was possible. But what the damned fool seemed to fail utterly to realise, even now, was the folly of doing such a thing in his present disguise. Already the sailor suspected him: once let him be discovered at the Friar's Heel, even if his great strength did enable him to get away, suspicion would become certainty. Then they would either move Mrs Drummond, or finish her off right away, and we should be in a far worse position than we were now.

If only he would leave the thing to me. It seemed such an obvious solution to the whole matter. Instead of which, here they were blundering round, suspected by everybody and finding out nothing.

At length I finished my dinner, and went into the lounge. I had seen Longworth go out previously, but there was no sign of him as I sat down. And as I tried to drink some of the concoction that passes in the average English hotel for coffee, the sailor went by towards the door.

"Good night, mate," he called out.

"Where are you off to?" I asked carelessly.

"Going to see some friends out Netheravon way," he answered with a wink. "At least – a friend."

He went out under the pleasing delusion that he had deceived me, and I sat on. Where was Algy?

A quarter of an hour passed: a half, and at length I could stand it no longer. I would chance it and go to his room. I got up and strolled over casually to the office. There was the entry in the book right enough – "A Longworth, Room 15." I went upstairs; the room was facing me. And after a quick glance round to see that no one was about I opened the door and went in.

The room was empty, and I stood there wondering what to do next. It seemed obvious that he must have left the hotel, and if so he was probably on his way to Stonehenge by now. And the only thing to do as far as I could see was to follow him. After all, who knew what he might be up against, and even if Drummond was there a third person would do no harm.

I decided that I would walk. The night was fine though dark, and an hour, I calculated, would just about see me there. Then I would lie concealed unless my help was wanted, and find out what I could.

It was just about eleven that I reached the slight hill that passes the monument. I was walking on the grass beside the road to deaden the sound of my footsteps, and when I got level with the great stones, I sat down for a while to reconnoitre. I could see them dimly outlined in the darkness some hundred yards away, and I craned my eyes to see if I could make out any sign of movement. There was nothing: all was silent and motionless, until after a while I began to imagine things.

I recalled that vigil of the other night by the stranded motorcar, and realised that unless I did something soon my nerves would begin to go. And one thing was obvious: if I did want to find out anything I would have to go nearer.

I put a leg through the wire fence, and even as I did so I heard a sound that froze me into immobility and brought me out in a cold sweat. It was a shrill scream of fear, and the voice was the voice of a man.

It came from the direction of Stonehenge, and I crouched there listening with every sense alert. The scream was not repeated, though it seemed to me that I heard a hoarse worrying noise for a time. Then utter silence.

Suddenly I became aware of something else. I was still standing half straddled over the fence, when I felt by the faintest movement of my legs that someone else was touching the wires. And not very far away either.

I peered into the darkness: was that the dark outline of a man – or was it only a little mound? It was moving, I could swear it was moving. But it was moving away from the road and towards Stonehenge.

Then came the next unexpected development. This time there was no mistake about it: someone was scrambling through the fence without taking any precautions whatever. The wires literally twanged, and once again I crouched down waiting. Well for me that I did so: well for me that I was not still in the place where I had sat down first.

For a moment later a man, bent almost double, came swiftly past right over the spot from which I had only just moved. The fence was between us but even so, he was so close that I could have touched him, and how he missed seeing me I do not know. But I saw him, and long after he had vanished into the darkness I sat there motionless trying to puzzle out this new development. Even without the momentary glimpse I had got of his face, another sense would have proclaimed the truth. The man was a coal-black Negro.

I looked round again: the mound was no longer there, and after a little hesitation, I too started to crawl cautiously towards Stonehenge. Whether I liked it or not the reason of that dreadful scream had got to be discovered.

Foot by foot I wormed my way forward, peering ahead at every step to try and see the other man who I knew must be somewhere in front of me. Suddenly from about twenty yards away came the faint glow of a screened electric torch. I stopped instantly: without realising it I had almost reached one of the great stones. And for a space I stared at the terrible spectacle the light revealed.

Lying on his back, his legs sprawling drunkenly, was a man, and it only needed one glance to see that he was dead. There were ghastly marks round his throat, and his head lolled sideways.

The poor brute had been throttled by a man of immense strength, and it looked to me as if his neck had been broken.

It was not Algy Longworth: the dead man was a complete stranger. But who was the man who held the torch? His face was in shadow: I could not see the outline of his body. Was it the sailor? Or was it the man with the damaged hand? I craned forward, and as I did so the torch was extinguished. I had a blurred impression of movement, and then silence. The man, whoever he was, had gone. I was alone with the dead body. And even as I realised it, and began to wonder what I should do next, I heard the faint thrumming of a motorcar from the road. Then came the slight squeak of a brake, and the sound of a door being opened. I looked round. Whoever it was was running without lights.

Very cautiously I backed away from the murdered man. An unlighted car stopping where this one had, seemed too suspicious for my liking. And having gone what I thought was a safe distance I lay down and waited: waited until the next thing happened, a thing which almost made me throw caution to the winds.

"To the right," came the voice of a man, speaking low.

"You have your torch?" came the answer, and the man grunted assent.

And the second speaker was a woman. I could see them dimly outlined against the darkness not five yards away. But it wasn't that that filled me with a wild excitement: it was the smell of a scent like jasmine – and yet not quite jasmine. It was the woman herself – Irma – our arch-enemy.

They moved away, and I wormed after them.

"Here he is," said the man's voice. "I'll switch on the torch for a second."

Once more came the faint glow, and then a sharp exclamation from her.

"This isn't one of them. I've never seen this man before in my life."

The torch was extinguished.

"Darling – are you sure?"

"Of course I'm sure," she said fiercely. "I know the whole brood by sight. That is no more Longworth than you are."

"Then what on earth was he doing here?" muttered the man.

"How should I know?" she answered. "That fool Pedro has killed the wrong man."

"Unless this man is a new member of their gang," said her companion.

She almost spat at him.

"I'm not concerned with new members. I want the old lot."

"My beloved," came his voice, vibrant with love and passion, "can't you chuck it? This is all such a ghastly risk. Drummond is dead already: you've got his wife. Isn't that enough?"

"It is not," she said coldly.

"Well, what are we going to do about this body?" he asked wearily. "Every moment we're here increases our danger."

"Are those sheds over there empty?"

"But the risk, *cherie*. It is bound to be discovered."

"Not until we have finished," she said in a peculiar voice. "Send Pedro back from the car to carry it there."

They were moving away, back towards the road. And to my mind there returned those strange words of hers – "After, I will come to you." And her voice as she said the word "Finished", had been the same. What was in this strange woman's brain? What dark, hideous plan had she conceived? Because the conviction was growing on me that she was not only a woman obsessed with an idea – she was mad.

And who was this man, her companion, who evidently loved her? Where did he come in? Did he hope for reward after her plans were fulfilled – did he hope for her? What wouldn't I have given for the clue to the events of the night. Who was the dead man? Who was the man who had first examined him and then disappeared into the darkness?

And then the noise of the car starting recalled me to the present. Pedro must be the black man I had seen dodging past me down the road, and I had no wish to meet Pedro whatever. Crouching low, I dodged away from the place where the body lay: I had seen enough. I would go back to the hotel, and think things over tomorrow.

I reached the railings, and cautiously crawled through them. Then I started on my three-mile walk. From behind me came the harsh cry of a night bird, and once I paused and listened. It seemed to me that I heard a strange, worrying noise, followed by a sharp shout that was instantly suppressed. With an involuntary shudder I walked on, till the dim outline of the giant stones were hidden by the hill. Nothing would have induced me to return to the place again. But I couldn't help wondering what further horror had happened there. Had the Negro suddenly encountered the other wanderer by night? And who was it who had shouted?

One ray of light, and one ray only shone in the general fog. They had intended to kill Algy Longworth that night: they therefore intended to kill Darrell and Jerningham. The last lingering doubt that this woman intended to play the game had been dispelled. And it was therefore imperative that they should be warned. They must at all costs be kept away from the place. Once they were caught, the end would come at once: nothing could save Drummond's wife. This woman Irma would imagine that we were all accounted for, and no further reason would exist for delay. So Algy would have to be sent away as soon as possible, and told to stop away until, at any rate, I had discovered the headquarters of our enemy.

It ought not to be difficult, I reflected. Surely someone in the neighbourhood must have seen the Negro. He would be a conspicuous figure in a locality like this. And once he was identified, the house was identified. And once that was done, there was one thing on which I was absolutely determined. The police must be informed. If Drummond wouldn't do it, then I would. It was essential: the house must be completely surrounded by a cordon of men. The time for fooling with matters was past: things were altogether too serious. We were up against a mad woman and a man who was infatuated with her. And they would have to be put under restraint, or else exterminated.

Then another thought struck me. What if I informed the police at once, or first thing next morning, of what I had seen? Told them that in one of those old disused military sheds they would find the dead body of a man, and that the murderer was a Negro. That would take them direct to the place and settle things. As a foreigner, I took it, he would have to be registered: his address would, therefore, be known. The only trouble was that my own doings might require a little explanation. Why was I masquerading about in a disguise? Why had I entered my name in the hotel books as Seymour when it was really Dixon? Well – I should have to tell them everything, that was all, though I frankly did not relish the idea of trying to make a stolid local police-officer believe me. The whole thing sounded too much like a nightmare induced by a surfeit of lobster.

I paused to light a cigarette, and as I did so I saw a red light on the road ahead of me. It was the tail-light of a car, and it was stationary. It seemed to be about a hundred yards away, and for a moment or two I stared at it thoughtfully. True, there was nothing inherently suspicious about a stationary motorcar, but tonight I was in a mood to suspect anything.

I crept cautiously a little nearer. Something had evidently gone wrong: I could see the outline of the chauffeur as he peered into the bonnet. Another man was standing beside him holding an electric torch in his hands, and the chauffeur was tinkering with a spanner.

Suddenly the man holding the light turned it for a moment on to the chauffeur's face, and I stopped abruptly. For the chauffeur was the man who had sprung at me out of the ditch three nights before, and whose hands I could still feel on my throat. No doubt about it now: the car in front of me belonged to the enemy. And, surely, unless it was a very amazing coincidence, it must be the same car that had stopped by Stonehenge earlier.

I crawled into the hedge and tried to decide on a line of action. There in front of me lay the means of running the gang to earth if only I could seize it. But how? Once the defect was put right, the car would be off, and manifestly I couldn't follow it on foot. I cursed myself for not having come on a bicycle: then I might have had some chance. Now it was hopeless. And yet I knew that if I could but track that car to its destination our problem was solved.

I crept a little nearer, and suddenly an idea dawned on me. The luggage grid was down at the back. Suppose I managed to get on that! It would have to be done with the utmost care: the exact psychological moment would have to be seized. Just as he let in his gear would be the time. And if I was spotted, I would pretend that I was trying to jump a ride. Disguised as I was, the chauffeur would not recognise me: the woman, anyway, did not know me, and the only danger was the other man, of whose identity I was still in ignorance. Still, it was worth the risk: the information, if I could get it, would be so invaluable.

The chauffeur was closing the bonnet: the man who had been holding the light opened the door and got in. The moment had come. Stooping low, I ran the few yards to the back of the car, just as I heard the noise of the self-starter. Then the engine was raced for a few seconds, and I gripped the grid with both hands, and swung myself on to it. We were off.

A wild feeling of triumph swept over me: so far, I had not been spotted. But it didn't last long, and if the road had not been good, it would have lasted an even shorter time. For sheer discomfort, commend me to a ride on the luggage grid of a fast car. Several times I was nearly shot off as we went over bumps. In addition, the car was over lubricated, and emitted a dense cloud of blue smoke from just underneath me. But for all that, I felt it was worth it: I'd done the trick. I'd succeeded where, at any rate, up to date the others had failed. All that was necessary now was to hang on until we reached our destination – drop off as the car slowed down, and escape into the darkness. And in spite of my extreme agony, I almost laughed as I pictured Drummond's face the next morning when he heard the news.

I felt the brakes being applied, and heaved a sigh of relief. And then the car swung right-handed, and turned through a gate. I could tell by the scrunch of gravel under the tyres that we were in a drive, and suddenly a light inside the car was switched on. That was a complication I had not thought of, for now the ground behind the car was illuminated through the back window. And if either of the occupants happened to look out, they were bound to see me when I dropped off. I hesitated, squeezing myself as close as possible to the car. Should I chance it? And while I was trying to make up my mind, the car stopped at the front door.

Now I thought detection was certain, but still my luck held. The man and the woman passed into the house: the door closed behind them. And the next instant the car moved on. Once again did I get ready to jump off, when the noise of the gravel ceased, and I realised we were in the garage. Moreover, it was a big garage, and the chauffeur had driven the car in as far as it would go so that I had at least ten yards to cover before reaching the door. I heard him get down and start fiddling with some tools on a bench. Should I make a dart for it now? Then the lights were switched off, and he yawned prodigiously. He had evidently finished for the night, and I only just had time to dodge to one side of the car as he came by on the other.

He heaved on the sliding doors, and they met with a clang. A key turned: his footsteps died away. And I couldn't help it – I laughed. The situation really had its humorous side. Without doubt I had successfully tracked the tiger to its lair – so successfully that I was inside while the tiger was out. And as my position came home to me I stopped laughing: the humour of the situation lay with the tiger.

I started to make a tour of inspection. The main doors were locked: there was nothing to be hoped for in that quarter. And a brief survey of the windows showed that none of them were made to open. Cautiously I felt my way along to the further end. A wooden bench littered with spanners and things filled three-quarters of it: in the other quarter, and my hopes rose as I saw it, was a second door. I tried the handle: it was locked. That finished it: I was caught like a rat in a trap. With the arrival of the chauffeur next morning I must be discovered. Nothing could prevent it.

What a drivelling idiot I had been! I had accomplished absolutely nothing. I didn't even know where I was, which would have been some recompense. Then, even if they kept me a prisoner, I might have found an opportunity of communicating with Drummond. As it was, all that I had succeeded in doing was to get locked up in an unknown place.

What about breaking one of the windows? It gave me a possibility of escape, whereas if I waited there was none. But I soon realised the difficulty of the idea. The panes were small – far too small for me to squeeze through. It would mean smashing wood and everything, and there, not ten yards away, was the house. Still, it *was* a possibility. I was bound to be heard, but in the general confusion I might escape. And even as I was turning the matter over in my mind I stiffened into sudden rigidity. A light was shining below the bottom of the second door, and I could hear footsteps approaching.

The key turned, and I dodged behind the car. A man came in, and I could hear him cursing under his breath. He had an electric torch in his hand, and he appeared to be searching for some tool on the bench. His back was towards me, and for a moment I had the wild idea of hurling myself on him and taking him unawares. I think if I had had any weapon in my hand I would have done so and chanced it.

He found what he wanted, and left the garage. My opportunity, if it ever really had been an opportunity, had gone. But had it? For he had left the door wide open.

Light streamed in, and I crept a little nearer. He was walking along a short passage, and a further door at the other end was open. It led into a room, and it was from the room that the light came. The passage was evidently to enable one to reach the garage from the house under cover, but it was not of such prosaic details that I was thinking. It was the brief glimpse I had obtained of the interior of the room, that made me rub my eyes and wonder if I was dreaming.

The entire furniture appeared to consist of big stones. I had seen no chair – no table, only square and oblong stones. At least, I thought they were stones: they certainly looked like stones – stones about three or four feet long and a foot thick. And if they were stones, what in the name of fortune were they there for? Had I come to a private lunatic asylum? Was the whole place bughouse?

He had half-closed the second door behind him, so that I could no longer see anything from the garage. But I could still hear, and the noise was the noise a stone-mason makes when chipping with a cold chisel.

I crept even nearer. Confound the risk, I thought; I was caught, anyway. And by this time my curiosity was so intense that it banished fear. At last I got near enough to see into the room, or, rather, into a part of it. And what I saw confirmed my opinion. They were bughouse: the whole darned lot of them.

The room was a big one, and the first impression that it gave was that it had been specially prepared for some mystical religious ceremony. The walls were completely concealed with black curtains, and a thick black carpet covered the floor. On this carpet, in the portion of the room that I could see, big greyish-white stones were lying about apparently haphazard. Some were on their sides: others stood endways. Some lay isolated: others were arranged as a child might arrange bricks. One particular group that I could see consisted of four stones on end and spaced at intervals of about a foot, with a fifth laid flat across their tops. In short, the whole effect was that of a stone-mason's yard arranged by its owner when under the influence of alcohol.

Through the black curtains the lights stuck out – big, white, frosted lights that seemed to hang unsupported in the air. And after a while, as I looked at the one opposite me, it began to have the most extraordinary effect on my brain. First it would diminish in size, receding into the distance until it was only the size of a pin's head; then it would come rushing towards me, blazing bigger and bigger, till it seemed to fill the whole room. I found myself swaying, and with a monstrous effort I looked away. Almost had I walked towards that light, self-hypnotised.

I forced myself to think of other things, and after a while the influence waned. What on earth was this extraordinary room? What was the man doing on the other side of the door? I could not see him, but steadily, monotonously, the chip, chip, chip went on. And then it suddenly stopped.

I glanced up, only to shrink back against the wall of the passage. Where she had come from I did not know, but there, standing in the middle of the room, was the woman. It was the first time I had seen her without a hat, and for a while I could only gaze at her speechlessly.

She was dressed in some sort of loose white robe, and as she stood there outlined against the black background, a hand resting lightly on one of the big stones, she seemed like the priestess of some ancient cult. Her beauty was almost unearthly: her whole appearance utterly virginal. In her eyes there glowed a strange light – a light such as might have shone in the eyes of a martyr. And I felt that her soul was all the depth and height of space away.

It was incredible to think ill of such a woman – to believe her capable of evil. Almost did I believe that she was someone else – someone I had not seen before. To think that it was she who had planned the death trap at the Mere; to think it was her I had heard talking coarsely and brutally at Stonehenge not two hours ago seemed unbelievable. And then it came once more, that faint scent like jasmine – and yet not quite jasmine.

"Have you finished?"

She spoke quietly, and now her voice was a delight to hear. And then she stiffened and drew herself up. Into her face there came a look of disgusted contempt. But the poor fool kneeling at her feet, with his arms round her knees, was oblivious of it. He was stammering wild words of love, was the man who looked like Lakington; and so engrossed was I in the scene that the fact of my unknown man being the man who looked like Lakington seemed almost trivial. What did it matter who he was, poor devil: he was just an actor in the game that is age-old.

"When, my beloved, are you coming to me?"

Again and again he said it, his voice shaking, his hands trembling. And she just stood there, utterly aloof: to her he was non-existent. Her eyes were fixed in front of her, and once her lips moved as if she was speaking to someone no earthly vision could see. Even as I had seen her speak at the Mere.

"Have you finished?"

With a sigh of utter weariness the man rose to his feet.

"Yes," he said. "I have."

She smiled, and held out her hand.

"Good. For now there must be no delay, my friend. Pedro's mistake has forced our hand. By the way, is he back?"

The man shrugged his shoulders.

"I don't know. Probably by this time."

"Anyway, I have written a letter which must be delivered to one of the three tomorrow morning. We know that Longworth is here, so he will therefore be the one. Listen, I will read it to you.

"'My friends, the game has begun to pall. My revenge is sufficient. If you will follow the bearer of this you will come to your destination. And the widow shall be handed over to you. If you don't: if you are afraid to come, you will still be quite safe. No further steps will be taken against you. You will not be worth it. But Phyllis Drummond will die. So take your choice. Her life lies in your hands.

"'But let me repeat the warning given to your late lamented leader. My information is good, so no police. Otherwise Phyllis Drummond will die before you get here.'"

"But, *carissima*," cried the man, "will they come on that? It seems such an obvious trap."

"Quite clearly, Paul," she said, "you have much to learn concerning the mentality of Englishmen of their type. They will come, even if a cordon of machine-gunners stood in their way. And we shall be ready for them."

"And then? After it is over?"

He stared at her hungrily, as if trying to read her very soul.

"After it is over," she repeated coolly. "Why, then, my dear Paul, we shall see."

"But you promised," he muttered. "You promised by all you held sacred. Beloved" – his voice grew urgent and pleading – "for nearly a year I have worked unceasingly to give you your revenge. Worked without reward: at times without thanks. Only hope has kept me going, *carissima* – the hope that when all was over you would come to me. And now, you say, 'We shall see.' Never have I kissed your lips during all these long months. Irma – say to me, promise me again – that I have not worked in vain."

"No, *mon ami*," she said. "You have not worked in vain."

With a cry of joy he snatched one of her hands and smothered it with kisses. And over his bent head I saw her face. She was shaking with a hideous, silent laughter. I craned forward fascinated: that such a change could take place in any human being's expression seemed impossible. No longer a priestess of unearthly beauty, but evil incarnate that made one shudder to look at.

Suddenly the man straightened up, and instantly her face became a mask. Even did she go so far as to smile encouragingly at the poor fish.

"No, Paul," she repeated. "You have not worked in vain. Tomorrow night…"

The sentence was never finished; too late I realised that in my absorption I had stepped into the light. For a moment or two she stared at me in silence. Then – "Who is that man?"

Like a flash her companion swung round.

"Why," he said softly, "it's the bank clerk. Have you come to see my collection?"

He was moving towards me as he spoke, and in his right hand there gleamed a wicked-looking automatic.

"Come in, bank clerk," he said, still in the same deadly soft voice. "I am honoured indeed, even if the hour is a little unconventional."

# CHAPTER 14

*In which I meet Mrs Drummond*

The situation was undeniably awkward. The fact that I had realised all along that detection was inevitable, made it none the less unpleasant when it came. And I liked neither the look of the automatic nor that on the man's face. I stepped into the room.

"I fear it must seem a little strange," I began, making a valiant endeavour to keep my voice steady.

"It does," he agreed suavely. "May we be favoured with an explanation?"

I plunged desperately.

"To tell you the truth," I said, "I lost my way. I went out for a long walk tonight, and after taking one or two turnings I realised I hadn't the faintest idea where I was. Passing along the road, I saw this house, and I came up to see if someone could put me right. I couldn't get any answer, but I saw your garage door was open. So I went in, meaning to ask when the car returned. And I suppose I must have fallen asleep, for when I woke up, the car was back and the door locked."

"I see," said the man. "It seems a pity that such a big discrepancy exists between the first few words of your explanation and the rest."

"I don't understand what you mean," I remarked, uncomfortably conscious that a pulse was hammering in my throat.

"You prefaced your interesting little story," he explained, "by the five words, 'To tell you the truth'. Why not do so?"

With a faint feeling of relief, I saw that the automatic was no longer in his hand.

"I am not accustomed – " I began haughtily.

"Be silent," said the woman imperiously. "Do I understand you know this man, Paul?"

"I met him at Stonehenge yesterday afternoon, my dear," he remarked. "A bank clerk with lengthy holidays. South Africa last year; Australia next. I must apply for a position in that bank."

His eyes were boring into me, and I could have kicked myself with mortification. I, who had thought that my playing of the part had been perfect – that I alone was unsuspected. I tried another bluff.

"You are very clever, sir," I said coldly. "But not quite clever enough. My father keeps one of the few remaining private banks, in which I am a clerk. But, as you will understand, not an ordinary clerk. And to broaden my mind he has allowed me to travel extensively."

"Most interesting," he answered. "And most considerate of your father. Anyway, that's better than the one before. You're improving."

"Stop all this nonsense," said the woman harshly. "Why wasn't I told about this man?"

"My dear," he said pleadingly, "what was the use?"

"On your own showing," she snapped, "you suspected him. Why wasn't I told?" Her voice was vibrating with anger. She swung round on me. "Who are you, you little rat?"

"My name is Seymour," I stammered.

Suddenly her mood changed, and she lit a cigarette.

"Put him in one of the seats," she ordered quietly.

"This way, Mr Seymour," said the man.

"And what if I refuse," I blustered.

For a moment he stared at me – thin lipped and motionless.

"Just this," he said gently, "I will blow out your brains where you stand."

"A messy proceeding." I strove to speak jauntily. "But may I ask – "

He whipped out his revolver and covered me.

"Move," he snarled. "And move damned quick. Come here."

He crossed to one of the stones, so did I. The more I saw of that man, the less I liked him.

I found that the stone at which he was pointing had been fashioned into a sort of rough seat.

"Sit down, and put your arms where I tell you. There – and there."

I obeyed: there didn't seem anything else to do. And then there came a sudden click, and I felt two thin steel bars close over my wrists. I tugged and he laughed quietly.

"I wouldn't waste your time," he remarked. "You're as much a part of the furniture now as the stone you are sitting on."

"Look here, sir," I said, "this is going beyond a joke. I admit that I had no right whatever to be in your garage, but that doesn't afford you any justification for treating me like this."

He took no notice: he was speaking in low tones to the woman. And suddenly she nodded and came towards me. For a time she stood in front of me staring into my eyes, and then she spoke.

"Do you know Hugh Drummond?"

Now subconsciously, I suppose, I had been expecting that question, and on that one little effort of mine I do flatter myself.

"Hugh Drummond." I looked at her blankly. "I've never heard of the man in my life."

Still she stared at me, but my face gave nothing away. And at last she turned and spoke to the man.

"Well," I heard him say, "we might try." She crossed to a door hidden in the curtains and disappeared, leaving me alone with the man.

189

"What has happened," he said suddenly, "to that egregious fraud who was pretending to collect butterflies?"

"I haven't an idea," I answered. "He left the hotel before dinner."

"Say nothing about him," he said curtly. "It will pay you not to."

"I wasn't proposing to," I remarked. "I fail to see the slightest reason for discussing a casual hotel acquaintance, or what bearing he has on my present position."

"If you hadn't been a damned fool you wouldn't be in your present position. Now the truth, my friend. Who are you, and how did you come here?"

"I have nothing to add to what I have already said," I answered.

He stared at me moodily, and I grew more and more puzzled. Try as I would I couldn't get a line on his mental attitude. If, as I now knew, he had spotted Toby Sinclair as a fraud, and me also, one would have expected him to show signs of gratification, even of triumph at having caught one of us so easily. Instead of which he seemed positively annoyed at my presence. True I had interrupted him in the middle of his love-making, but I felt that didn't account for it.

"You must be one of them," he said half to himself. "And that butterfly fool as well. Damn it! you swarm like rabbits."

I said nothing: light was beginning to dawn on the situation. Our thin-lipped friend wanted the lady, and wanted her quickly. But before he got her, he had in the vernacular, to do a job of work. And that job had consisted up till now of disposing of the six of us. He believed that three were accounted for: the others were to be settled in the near future. And now he was confronted as he thought with further additions to the party, and therefore further delay in obtaining his purpose.

"How the devil did you get here?" he repeated angrily.

"I have nothing to add to what I have already said," I repeated with a smile.

"Damn you," he snarled. "You'll smile the other side of your face before long. It may amuse you to know that you'll never leave this room alive."

"That," I remarked with a confidence I was very far from feeling, "remains to be seen."

He took out his cigarette-case savagely and started pacing up and down. And I for the first time since I had come into the room, began to examine it more thoroughly. And the more I examined it the more amazing did it become. The whole of it was in keeping with the part I had seen from the passage. Stones – and yet more stones, placed apparently indiscriminately. And yet, were they? Was there not some definite design? And as I stared round trying to find the solution, I noticed a thing which gave me a queer little thrill. There were other roughly shaped seats beside the one I was sitting in – five others, making six in all. And each one was fitted with the same steel bars that encircled my own wrists. Six chairs, and six of us. What fantastic scheme had been evolved in that woman's deranged brain? Time, I reflected grimly and time alone would tell.

The sound of a door opening made me turn my head: Irma had returned. But now another woman was with her – a woman who was blindfolded. And with a sudden quickening of my pulse I realised that this must be Phyllis Drummond herself.

She had evidently been awakened from sleep. Her bare feet were thrust into slippers: and she had slipped a *peignoir* over her pyjamas. Her face under the handkerchief that covered her eyes was pale, but absolutely determined: guided by her captor's hand on her arm she walked firmly and without hesitation until she was halted in front of my chair.

"What new foolery is this?" she asked scornfully, and I metaphorically took off my hat to her. Captivity had not broken her spirit.

"No foolery at all, my dear, but a very pleasant surprise for you."

Mrs Drummond's hands clenched convulsively.

"You don't mean that Hugh has found me?"

A faint smile passed over Irma's face; the news of Drummond's supposed death had evidently been suppressed.

"Not quite that," answered the other, "but one of his friends has."

"Then," said Mrs Drummond breathlessly, "he has succeeded. And so I am free to go. Who is it? Is it you, Peter?"

With a quick movement Irma whipped off the handkerchief, and for a while Drummond's wife stared at me blankly. Then she turned wearily to her captor.

"Why torment me?" she said. "What's the good? You know Hugh's friends. I've never seen this man before in my life."

And Irma who had been watching her intently relaxed and turned to the man.

"That's genuine," she said briefly.

"Is this by any chance," I remarked ponderously, "a private lunatic asylum?"

"You may well ask, sir," said Mrs Drummond. "I don't know who you are, or how you came here, but there is at any rate one mad person present. And that is this woman."

Irma laughed, and lit a cigarette.

"Dear little Phyllis," she murmured. "Always so direct and positive, aren't you? And now that you've been introduced to this room a little sooner than I had intended, tell me what you think of it?"

Mrs Drummond looked about her, a look of complete bewilderment spreading gradually over her face.

"What on earth does it all mean?" she said at length. "What are all these stones for?"

"A model, my dear," answered the other gently, "that it has taken Paul much labour and trouble to construct. A model that is accurate in every detail."

"A model of what?"

"Of Stonehenge. One or two of the stones have been left out, but all the important ones are here. There for instance you see the Friar's Heel, and that one is the altar stone. You know the legend, of course. Some authorities do not believe in it, but it's a very pretty fairy story anyway. It runs that when the first rays of the rising sun on Midsummer Day shining over the Friar's Heel strike this third stone, the name of which I have not yet told you, the ceremony begins."

Her voice was soft and almost caressing, nevertheless my lips were dry. For I knew what the third stone was.

"It must have been an interesting ceremony, Phyllis. Can't you see those wild-eyed priests clad in fantastic garments; can't you see that great rolling plain and the waiting multitude of savages – waiting in the hush that comes before the dawn for the first gleam of the sun above the horizon?"

I was staring at her fascinated: her eyes were glittering feverishly – her cigarette was forgotten.

"A minute more – and a sigh runs round the spectators. A few seconds, and the excitement grows. You can feel it – hear it like wind rustling in the trees.

"Inside the sacred circle stand the priests – some by the altar stone, some by this third stone here. All eyes are turned towards the east to greet the arrival of their god. This is the day on which He vouchsafes them His visible presence longest: this is the day on which it is meet and proper that He should be propitiated and thanked. An offering must be made: a sacrifice given.

"And on this third stone, waiting too, for that first ray to strike her, lies the sacrifice. For those around her, for the hushed multitude outside the moment that is just coming means life – the continuation of the benefits their God has bestowed on them since last Midsummer Day. For her it means – death: the stone on which she lies is the slaughter stone."

She fell silent, and I glanced at Mrs Drummond. She was staring at the speaker with a dawning horror in her eyes, and suddenly she bit the back of her hand to keep back a cry. She knew – and I knew. But after a moment she pulled herself together with a great effort.

"Most interesting," she remarked steadily. "And did you have all these stones put up so that you could play charades on them?"

Slowly the madness faded from the other's face, and she flicked the ash from her cigarette onto the carpet.

"That's it," she smiled. "A little game of let's pretend. We shall be playing it tomorrow, my dear – or rather tonight. What part would you like to take?"

The silence grew unbearable, and yet once again did I take off my hat to that poor girl. She was powerless: she was trapped – but she was white clean through.

"I am not very good at acting," she said indifferently.

"Yours will be a passive – even if a very important role," returned the other. "No histrionic ability will be required."

"And may I ask," I remarked politely, "if I am to be privileged with a part? I must say I don't think much of the comfort of your stalls."

For the moment at any rate my role was clear: I must remain the outsider who had blundered into a madhouse. Slowly the woman turned and stared at me.

"I think you will look nice as a dead-head," she murmured.

"Am I to understand that the rest of the audience will have paid for their seats?"

"They will at any rate have worked hard," she returned. "But I can assure you there will be no jealousy on that account. The unexpected guest is always welcome."

"Charming," I said cheerfully. "At the same time, if it is all the same to you, I would rather like to know the hour the show starts, so that until then I can enjoy my very short holiday in the manner I had intended to. Frankly this seat is giving me cramp."

I winked ostentatiously at Mrs Drummond: obviously this female must be humoured. But there was no response from her: somewhat naturally she accepted my role at its face value.

"This gentleman knows nothing about your wicked game," she burst out. "It's unfair, it's unjust to keep him here."

"To know nothing about the play is always an advantage," returned the other. "However, I grow weary. We will retire, my dear Phyllis – so that we shall both be fresh for the performance."

She led the way to the door, and I was left alone with the man.

"Look here, sir," I said angrily, "this has gone far enough. I admit that what I told you sounds a bit fishy: nevertheless it happens to be the truth. And I insist upon being allowed to go. Or if you wish to give me in charge then send for the police. But this is preposterous. You now know that I am not one of them, whoever 'they' may be."

"And you," he retorted calmly, "now know altogether too much. So for the purposes of this entertainment – positively for one night only – I fear you will have to be treated as if you were one of them."

He strolled through the door leading to the garage, and I heard the chink of metal against metal as he put the tools back on the bench. My last hope had gone, my last bluff had failed. When Mrs Drummond had failed to recognise me, and Irma herself had said "That's genuine," there had seemed for a while a possibility of escape. Now there was none. Now everything must depend on Drummond. He would follow the other three, of course, but without an idea of the strength he was walking into.

I counted them up in my mind. There was the man called Paul, the chauffeur; the man with the damaged hand; the sailor – and last but not least the Negro. So many I knew of personally; how many more there were remained to be seen. And what chance had Drummond against a bunch like that. If only I could have got away I could have warned him.

I began to tug desperately at the steel bars, until a woman's laugh made me look up suddenly. Irma had returned.

"You can save yourself the trouble, bank clerk," she said mockingly, and at the sound of her voice Paul returned.

"I suppose we had better gag him, my dear," he remarked, and she nodded carelessly.

"Yes," she said. "Gag him – and then go."

"This is an outrage," I spluttered, and the next instant he had deftly slipped a gag into my mouth, and then wrapped a handkerchief round me.

"If I hear a sound," he said quietly, "I shall come down and finish you off on the spot. *Carissima*, you must be tired." He crossed to the woman. "Won't you come to bed?"

"Go," she said curtly. "I shall come in a few minutes."

He went unwillingly, and for a while the woman stood motionless staring in front of her. The strange look had returned to her eyes: she had forgotten my existence. Noiselessly she moved about on the thick black carpet, the incarnation of grace and beauty. First to one stone, and then to another she glided, as a hostess might move round her drawing-room, giving it the finishing touches before the arrival of her guests.

And then at last she paused before the altar stone. She knelt down, and ran her fingers along underneath it searching for something. At length she found it, and pulled it out. It was the photograph of a man.

Fascinated I watched her as she kissed it passionately: then she placed it on the altar in front of her, and bowed her head as if in prayer. I heard the murmur of her voice, but the actual words I could not distinguish. And after a while, I began to feel drowsy. The gleaming white light opposite seemed to be growing bigger and bigger; my head lolled back. And on the instant I was wide awake again.

Part of the roof was glassed in, like the roof of a racquet court, and some of the panes were open for ventilation. And staring through one of the openings was a man. His eyes were fixed on the kneeling woman: his face was inscrutable. Then he glanced at me, and for a brief second our eyes met. In an instant he had disappeared, and I was left trying to fit this new development into the jigsaw. For the man who had been staring through the skylight was the sailor.

Still her voice droned on musically, but I paid no attention. It confirmed, of course, my knowledge that the sailor was one of them, but why should he be on the roof? Spying, presumably: spying on the woman. And when he realised that I had seen him he had disappeared at once for fear I might say something.

"My lover! My God!"

Her words, clear at last, came through the silent room, and once again I looked at her. With her hands clasped together, she was rocking to and fro on her knees in front of the photograph.

"Tonight, I come to you, my beloved."

And the lights shone on, gleaming like great stars against the black curtains. And the carpet seemed to glisten like some dark mountain pool deep hidden in the rocks. And the great white stones that rose from it took unto themselves life, and joined in a mighty chorus – "My beloved."

I closed my eyes: I was dreaming. It was some dreadful nightmare.

"My beloved, I come to you."

The sailor was shouting it: the man who had sprung at me out of the ditch was shouting it: Paul, his face a seething mass of black passion, was shouting it. I was shouting it, too – shouting it better than anyone – shouting it so well and so loudly that the woman herself, Irma, looked into my eyes and praised me. I could feel her fingers on my eyelids; from a great distance she nodded as if satisfied. Then came darkness: I slept.

It was daylight when I woke cramped and stiff in every limb. There was a foul taste in my mouth, and I wondered if I had been drugged. I had noticed nothing peculiar on the handkerchief, but only on that supposition could I account for my condition. My head ached: my eyes felt bleary, and I'd have given most of my worldly possessions for a cup of tea.

By a stupendous feat of contortion I twisted my head so that I could see my wrist watch, only to find that the damned thing had stopped. Not, I reflected, that it mattered very much what the time was: an odd hour or two this way or that was of little account situated as I was. And after a while I began to curse myself bitterly for having been such an utter fool. If only I hadn't shown myself in the passage: if only…

But what was the use? I hadn't slipped off the car: I had shown myself in the passage. And here I was caught without, as far as I could see, a chance of getting away. What made it more bitter still was the knowledge I possessed, the invaluable knowledge, if only I could have passed it on. Why if Hugh Drummond only knew he, with his marvellous shooting ability, could dominate the whole scene from the roof. But he didn't know, and all he would do would be to walk straight into the trap after the other three.

After a while my thoughts turned in another direction, – even less pleasant than the first. What was in store for us? Was it all some grim, fantastic jest, or was it a revenge so terrible that the mere thought of it made me almost sick? Could it be conceivably possible that this foul woman intended to kill Mrs Drummond in front of us all? And afterwards deal with us?

It seemed inconceivable, and yet the trap at the Mere was just as dastardly. It was no good judging her by ordinary standards: therein lay the crux. She was mad, and to a mad woman everything is conceivable. Anyhow the present was bad enough without worrying over the future.

Faintly through the wall I heard the self-starter being used, and then the car leave the garage. That must be the note going to Darrell and Co. Would they walk into it blindly, or would they take some rudimentary precautions? Would they believe that this woman did really intend to set Mrs Drummond free if they came?

From every angle I turned the thing over in my mind, only to arrive at the same brick wall each time. Whatever they did do or didn't do, I was out of the picture. I was powerless to help them in any way so there wasn't much use worrying.

"Have we slept well?" came a sardonic voice from the door.

Paul with a sneering smile on his thin lips was standing there looking at me. Then he came over and removed the handkerchief and the gag. For a time I could only move my jaws stiffly up and down, and make hoarse grunting noises – a thing which seemed to cause him unbounded amusement.

"Damn you," I croaked at last, "did you dope me last night?"

"A very efficacious and but little known narcotic, Mr Seymour," he remarked suavely, "was on the handkerchief I put round your mouth. Was your sleep dreamless and refreshing?"

"For God's sake," I muttered, "give me something to drink. My tongue feels like a fungoidal growth."

"A defect, I admit," he said, "in that particular drug. It leaves an unpleasant taste. And so I have much pleasure in telling you that it is on the matter of breakfast that I have come."

"Breakfast," I shuddered. "If I saw an egg I'd be sick."

There came a little click from behind my chair, and the steel bars slipped off my wrists.

"Stand up," he said. "At the moment the warning is unnecessary, I know. But bear in mind that freedom from your late position does not imply any further concession. So – no monkey tricks."

He was right: at the moment – and for a considerable number of moments – the warning was unnecessary. Both my arms had gone to sleep: and, as soon as I got up, I was attacked by the most agonising cramp in my left leg. But at last I managed to regain some semblance of normality.

"Where's that drink?" I muttered.

"All in due course," he returned. "Owing to the fact that certain small preparations have to be made here for our little entertainment tonight, we have to find other accommodation for you today. It would be a great pity if the element of surprise was lacking. And so you will come with me, Mr Seymour: and you will bear in mind that I have a revolver in my hand, Mr Seymour, and that my finger is on the trigger, Mr Seymour. And that should you give me the slightest trouble, you wretched interfering little busybody, that finger will connect with the trigger and the result will connect with you. So, hump yourself."

I could feel the muzzle of his gun in the small of my back, as he pushed me towards the door. But I didn't care: anything was better than the atrocious discomfort of that stone seat. Moreover a drink appeared to be looming in the horizon.

The door led into the hall. No one was about, and still in the same positions we reached the foot of the stairs.

"Up," he said curtly.

At a turn in the staircase stood a grandfather clock, and I saw it was half-past nine. So I reckoned I must have slept for five or six hours.

"Through that door," he ordered.

A man I had never seen before rose as we came in. But I didn't care about him: my eyes were riveted on a teapot.

"Charles will be your companion for today," he remarked. "And you had better look at Charles."

I did: then I returned to the teapot. As an object to contemplate Charles did not appeal to me.

"Charles has orders," continued the other, "to deal faithfully with you in the event of the slightest trouble. That is so, isn't it, Charles?"

"I'll deal with 'im faithfully, guv'nor," he chuckled. " 'E won't try nothing on twice, I gives yer my word. Why, I'd eat a little mess like that."

He emitted a whistling noise through a gap in his teeth.

"Paint the wall wiv 'is faice, I will," he continued morosely.

"A character is Charles," said Paul to me. "Equally handy with his fists or a knife. So be careful, Mr Seymour – very careful."

I gulped down my cup of tea and began to feel better.

"I am sure I shall find him a most entertaining companion," I murmured. "Now don't let me detain you any more, little man. Run away and have your children's hour with the bricks downstairs. Or are you going to play puffers in the passage?"

And, astounding to relate, it got home. For a moment I thought he was going to hit me. His face was white with rage: his fists were clenched – evidently a gentleman without the saving grace of humour. But he controlled himself and went out slamming the door behind him, and I began to feel better still.

Anyway my limbs were free, and I'd had something to drink. Moreover there were cigarettes in my pocket.

"Charles," I said, "will you smoke?"

Charles said – "Yus," and I began to take close stock of Charles. And one thing was quite obvious at first glance. He was perfectly capable of painting the wall with my face if it came to a trial of strength. So that if I was going to turn the change of quarters to my advantage it would have to be a question of brain and cunning and not force. And the first and most obvious method seemed bribery.

I led up to it tactfully, but diplomacy was wasted on Charles. At the mention of the word money his face became quite intelligent.

" 'Ow much 'ave you?" he demanded.

"About thirty pounds," I answered. "It's yours here and now if you'll let me go, and then there's nothing to prevent you clearing out yourself."

"Let's see the colour of it," he said, and with a wild hope surging up in me I pulled out my pocket-book. If I got away at once I'd be in time.

"There you are," I cried. "Twenty-eight pounds."

"Looks good to me," he remarked. "Though I ain't partial to fivers myself. Some suspicious blokes takes the numbers. You ain't suspicious, are you, matey?"

He slipped the bundle into his pocket, and I stood up.

"Is it safe now?" I said eagerly.

"Is wot safe now?"

"For me to go, damn it."

"Go where?"

"Out of the house, as you promised."

"Naughty, naughty," he said reproachfully. "Do you mean to say that that there money was hintended as a bribe?"

I stared at him speechlessly.

"And I thort as 'ow it was just a little return for the pleasure of be-olding my faice."

"You confounded scoundrel," I spluttered. "Give me back my notes."

Charles became convulsed with an internal upheaval that apparently indicated laughter.

"Yer know, matey," he said when he could at last speak, "I didn't know that they let things like you out of a 'ome."

Once more the convulsion seized him, and a dull over-mastering rage began to rise within me. The limit of my endurance had been reached: I felt I didn't care what happened. Damn Drummond and all his works: damn the moment I'd ever let myself in for this fool show. Above all, damn this great hulking blackguard who had pinched my money, and now sat there nearly rolling off his chair with laughter.

202

And suddenly I saw red. I sprang at him and hit him with all my force in the face. Then while he was still too surprised to move I got in a real purler with the teapot over his right eye. And after that I frankly admit I don't remember much more. I recall that he did not remain too surprised to move for long. I recall seeing something that gleamed in his hand, and feeling a searing, burning pain in my forearm. I also recall that an object which felt like a steam-hammer hit my jaw. Then – a blank.

# CHAPTER 15

*In which some of the others join me*

When I came to myself I was back in the room below, fastened to the same seat as before. The filthy taste was in my mouth again, so I guessed they had used the narcotic on me once more. But this time that wasn't my only trouble. My jaw felt as if it had been broken: and my arm, which someone had bound up roughly, ached intolerably.

For a while I sat there motionless. I was feeling dazed and drowsy: I'd almost come to the end of my tether. A sort of dull apathy had hold of me: I felt I didn't care what happened as long as it happened quickly.

The room was absolutely silent, and after a time I forced my brain to work. I was alone: I was ungagged. Supposing I shouted for help. There was a bare chance that I might be heard by some stray passer-by. Anyway it was worth trying.

"Help!" I roared at the pitch of my lungs. "Help!"

I listened: still no sound. Very good: I'd try again. I opened my mouth: I shut it. Or perhaps it would be more correct to say it shut itself.

A huge black hand had suddenly materialised from nowhere – a hand with the fingers curved like a bird's talon. I stared at it fascinated, as it moved gently towards my throat. There was no hurry, but the utmost deliberation in the whole action. And this time I nearly screamed in sheer terror.

The fingers closed round my throat, and began playing with it. Still quite gently: no force was used. But every touch of those fingers gave its own message of warning.

As suddenly as it had appeared, it went, and I sat there sweating and silent. So I was not alone: somewhere behind me, out of sight, was that cursed nigger Pedro. The hand that had closed on my throat was the actual hand that had murdered that poor devil the night before. And as if he had read my thoughts there came from above my head a hideous throaty chuckle. Then silence once again.

Gradually I grew calmer, though the thought of that great black brute lurking behind me was horrible. If only I could see the devil it would be better. But he remained out of sight, and after a time I began to think he must have gone. Into the garage perhaps – the passage leading to it was behind me. Whether he had or whether he hadn't, however, I dismissed the idea of calling for help.

To distract my mind, I studied the room with closer attention. I could see more than half, and I wondered what the small preparations were that Paul had spoken of. As far as I could see nothing was changed: the same stones, the same carpet. And then it struck me that on one of the stone seats was what looked like a block of wood. It was about the size of a box of a hundred cigarettes, and a cord stuck out from one end on to the carpet.

I looked at the other seats: a similar block was on each one of them. And by pushing myself backwards in my own, I could feel the sharp edge against my spine.

By twisting my head I could just see the cord attached to it. It was a long one, and I followed it idly with my eyes across the carpet until it disappeared behind the next stone. Part of the preparations evidently, but with what purpose was beyond me. Just as everything else was beyond me. Time alone would show.

But that fact didn't stop one thinking. Round and round in my head ran the ceaseless question – what was going to happen that night? From every angle I studied it till my brain grew muzzy with the effort. What was going to be done to us? Did that woman really mean all she had implied, or had it been a jest made to frighten Mrs Drummond?

After a while I dozed off, only to wake up sweating from an appalling dream in which two of the great stones were being used to crush my head by the nigger. Looking back now I suppose I was a little light-headed, but at the time I wasn't conscious of it. I had lost a good deal of blood from the wound in my arm though I didn't know it then. And as the day wore on, and the room gradually grew darker and darker I sank into a sort of stupor. Vaguely I heard odd sounds: the car in the garage, a man's voice in the hall, but they seemed to come from a long way off. And the only real things in my mental outlook were those cursed white stones.

They moved after a while, passing me in a ceaseless procession. They heaved and dipped and formed fours, till I cursed them foolishly. And something else moved, too – a great black form that flitted between them peering and examining. Twice did I see it, and the second time I forced myself back to reality.

It was the Negro, and he seemed intensely interested in everything – almost childishly so. He touched stone after stone with his fingers: then he picked up one of the little blocks that I had noticed and examined it closely, grunting under his breath.

Suddenly he straightened up and stood listening. Then with a quick movement he replaced the block, and vanished behind me just as the door into the hall opened and Paul came in. He crossed to my stone and stood looking down at me, while I feigned sleep. And after a time he too began to stroll round amongst the other stones.

He examined each of the blocks, and the cords that ran from them. And as I watched him out of the corner of my eye I noticed a thing I had missed before. On the altar stone was a little black box, and all the cords appeared to lead to it. He seemed particularly interested in that box, but in the bad light I couldn't see what he was doing. At length, however, he put it down, and lighting a cigarette once more came and stood in front of me. I looked up at him dully.

"You really are the most congenital ass I've ever met, Mr Seymour," he said pleasantly. "Did you honestly think Charles would let you go?"

"I've given up trying to think in this mad house," I retorted. "When is this ridiculous farce going to end?"

He made no reply for a while, but just stood staring at me thoughtfully.

"I really am rather interested in you," he said at length. "It would be most devilish funny if you really have got nothing to do with them."

"I've already told you that I don't know what you are talking about," I cried. "You're making a fearful mistake. I don't know who you mean by them."

He began to chuckle.

" 'Pon my soul," he said, "I'm almost beginning to think that you don't. Which makes the jest excessively rich."

"A positive scream," I agreed sarcastically. "Would it be too much to hope that I might be permitted to share it?"

"I fear," he answered, "that you might not quite appreciate it."

He continued to chuckle immoderately.

"You will in time, I promise you," he went on. "And then you will see how terribly funny it all is. I must say," he continued seriously, almost more to himself than to me, "I did think yesterday that you and the butterfly gentleman were mixed up in it."

"I wish to Heaven," I said wearily, "that you would realise that I haven't the remotest idea what you're talking about. And I further wish you to be under no delusions as to what I'm going to do when I do manage to get out of this place."

He started laughing again.

"What are you going to do?" he asked. "Don't, I beg of you, terrify me too much."

I stuck to it good and hard. Useless it might be, but at any rate it was better than nothing.

"I shall go straight to the police," I said, "and lodge a summons against you for assault and battery. And as for that cursed ruffian upstairs…"

"Poor Charles," he remarked. "You dotted him one with the teapot all right. Well, thank you for your kindly warning. You'll have some other privileged spectators coming to join you soon – three of them."

He strolled to the door, and looked back as he reached it.

"I can keep no secrets from you, bank clerk," he said. "You have an indefinable attraction for me. Do you see those little blocks in the seats?"

"Yes," I said.

"There is one in yours, just behind you."

"I've felt it already," I remarked.

"Well, be very careful how you feel it," he said gently. "Do nothing rough with it. Treat it as a mother treats a sickly child – gently and tenderly. Because it happens to be gun-cotton. Admittedly a safe explosive – but one never knows."

For a moment I was absolutely speechless.

"Gun-cotton," I stammered at length. "Good God! man – are you joking?"

"Far from it," he said. "But I can assure you that there's no chance of it going off – yet." He smiled genially. "The fact of the matter, is, bank clerk, that you have butted your head into some rather dirty work. I don't mind admitting that there are moments when I think it is almost too dirty. But" – he shrugged his shoulders – "when the ladies get ideas in their charming heads, who are we to gainsay them?"

"If by the ladies you allude to that partially demented female who was talking such infernal rot last night," I said grimly, "I'll tell you one idea that she has got wedged in hers. She's got about as much use for you as a Cockney has for a haggis."

"I don't understand you," he said softly, but I noticed that, of a sudden, he was standing very still.

"Then I'll make myself clearer," I remarked. "You cut no ice with her, Paul: she loathes the sight of your face. I watched her last night when you were pulling out the knee clutching business, and her expression was that of one who contemplates a bad egg from close range."

"You are pleased to be insolent, Mr Seymour."

He was still standing motionless by the door.

"I am pleased to be nothing, you flat-headed skate," I answered. It struck me that a little of Drummond's vocabulary might assist. "But if you imagine that after you've done whatever fool tricks you are going to do, you're then going to land the beauteous lady, you're making the deuce of an error. Nothing doing, Paul: you can take my word for it."

"But for the fact," he remarked after a time, "that the death you are going to die is such a particular choice one, I would strangle you here and now for those words."

"Doesn't alter the fact that she loathes the sight of your face, laddie," I mocked. "And I certainly don't blame her."

He sprang across the room towards me, and I don't think I have ever seen such a look of demoniacal rage on any man's face before. In fact but for the interruption I believe he would have carried out his threat. As it was he managed to control himself with a monstrous effort as the door opened and the woman herself came in.

"Quick, Paul," she cried. "They are coming – the three of them. Where's Pedro? Charles is here, but we want the nigger. And gag that fool of a clerk."

He stuffed a gag into my mouth, and glared at me.

209

"One sound, and I'll knife you," he muttered. "Pedro!"

He looked over my shoulder.

"Where is the damned fool?" he said irritably. "I've hardly seen him the whole day. Pedro!"

There was a guttural grunt, and then the huge nigger shambled past me. His head was down, and in the dim light he looked a terrifying sight.

"Get behind the curtains, Pedro. And don't kill. We want them alive in the chairs. Charles – get the other side of the door."

Sick with anxiety I waited. Could nothing be done to warn them? They were walking straight into the trap, and suddenly the full realisation of our position seemed to strike me. All very well to gain a little cheap satisfaction by taunting the man over his love affair, but it didn't alter the fact that once these three men were caught the odds against us were well-nigh hopeless. Drummond couldn't fight half a dozen men, especially when two of them had the strength of the Negro and the one called Charles.

The woman had left the room: the three men were hiding behind the curtains, so to all appearances except for myself it was empty. And then I heard Darrell's voice in the hall.

"So we meet again, madame," he said gravely. "As you probably know we have come without informing anyone, trusting that you will keep your side of the bargain."

"Quite like old times seeing you," she answered. "And Mr Jerningham and Mr Longworth, too."

"Shall we cut the conversation, madame?" he remarked. "At your instigation three men – one of whom was Hugh himself – have been foully murdered. So you will pardon me if I say that the sooner you hand Mrs Drummond over to us the better I shall be pleased. In your letter you said that your revenge was sufficient. Let us then be done with it."

"We seem much milder than of yore," she mocked.

"You have Mrs Drummond in your power," he said simply. "We have no alternative. Well, madame, we are waiting."

"Yes, *mes amis*, you are right," she answered after a pause. "We will be done with it. You shall have Phyllis. And believe me I am almost sorry now that I ever started it. Moods change. A few weeks ago there was nothing I desired more than the deaths of all of you. Today I regret the Mere. Come this way."

"One moment, madame. Does she know that her husband is dead?"

"No – she does not. Mr Darrell, it is easy to say, I know, but I wish he were not."

"A pity you didn't think of that a little earlier, madame," he said grimly. "Where are we to go? Why cannot Mrs Drummond be handed over to us in this hall?"

"You will soon see why," she answered, appearing in the door. "Besides I particularly want to show you all this room."

I gave an agonised guttural choke but it was no good. As she had doubtlessly anticipated they paused inside the door, completely taken off their guard by the strangeness of their surroundings.

"What on earth," began Jerningham, and even as he spoke the three hidden men sprang on them.

In a few seconds it was all over. Paul had a revolver in Jerningham's neck. Charles gave the same attention to Darrell. And poor little Algy Longworth was the Negro's share. He was merely picked up like a kicking baby and deposited in a seat. Then the steel bars were turned and he sat there glowering.

"You damned dirty nigger," he shouted angrily.

"Silence, you little rat," said Irma. "Get the other two fixed. Shoot, Paul, if they give any trouble."

But the muzzle of a revolver in the nape of a man's neck is a good preventer of trouble, and soon the four of us were sitting there like trussed birds.

"So it was a trick, was it?" said Darrell quietly.

The woman began to shake with laughter.

"You fools," she cried, "you brainless fools. Did you really imagine that I was going to hand Phyllis over to you and let you walk out of the house? You must be mad."

She turned on Charles and the nigger.

"Go: get out. But be at hand in case I want you. Paul – you can ungag the bank clerk."

Her glance roved from one to the other of us.

"Four," she said musingly. "And there should have been six. You see, Darrell, that there are six seats prepared for your reception."

Her eyes were beginning to glitter feverishly; and as she stood in the centre of the room her body swayed gracefully from side to side as if she was dancing. To me it was not unexpected, but the other three were staring at her in amazement. As yet they had not seen one of her outbursts.

"Still we must make do with four, I suppose," she went on. "Unless, Paul, we sent out for two more. No – better not. Let us keep our final meeting as intimate as possible. And we already have one stranger."

"Where is Phyllis Drummond?" said Jerningham.

She turned and looked at him dreamily.

"Phyllis is waiting," she answered. "For days she has been waiting for you to come, and now very soon she will join you."

"And what then?" snapped Darrell.

"Why then, *mon ami*, you shall all go on a journey together. A long journey. Ah! if only Hugh was here: if only my circle was complete. Then indeed the reunion would be a wonderful one."

And now the crazy glitter in her eyes grew more pronounced till I marvelled that the man called Paul could ever have hoped for any return for his love. The woman was frankly crazy, and stealing a glance at him I saw that he was staring at her with a dawning horror in his face.

"*Carissima*," he muttered. "I beseech of you, do not excite yourself."

"But as it is we shall have to make do with four." Her voice had risen. "Four instead of six. And the principal guest not here. Why – the whole lot of you could go if only Drummond was here. But I did my best, Carl – I did my best."

She had turned to the altar stone, and was speaking to it.

"I did my best, beloved – I did my best. And his end was not unworthy. Gassed – and drowned like a rat in a trap."

She threw herself across the stone, her arms outstretched, and for a space there was silence in the darkening room. Then abruptly she rose and swept to the door.

"At nine o'clock, Paul, we will begin."

"Look here," I said when she had gone, "Paul – or whatever your name is – what is the good of going on with this?"

He stared at me dully.

"The woman is clean plumb crazy. She is as mad as a hatter. So what are you going to get out of it? You can't marry a mad-woman: you can't even make love to her."

He muttered something unintelligible under his breath.

"For God's sake, man," I went on urgently, "pull yourself together. Set us free, and let us go."

"She'll be all right – after," he said at length. "Quite all right – after."

He turned towards the door, and in desperation I played my last card.

"You poor ass," I cried, "there isn't going to be an after for her. When she has finished us, she's going to commit suicide. And whatever you choose to do with a lunatic, you're stung good and strong with a corpse."

It was no good. He opened the door and went out. In fact I doubt if he even heard what I said, and with a feeling of sick despair I looked at the others.

"So they haven't spotted you, Dixon," said Darrell in a low voice.

"Not yet," I answered. "I don't think it ever dawned on them that I was one of the three they think were drowned at the Mere. But, for a while, they suspected me of being another member of the bunch – a new one. Then Mrs Drummond rode them off."

"You've seen her?" said Jerningham eagerly.

"Last night," I said. "She was brought down here blindfolded, and suddenly confronted with me. And there was no mistake about her failure to identify me being genuine. Not that it matters much," I went on gloomily. "We're hopelessly for it, unless Drummond can do something. Why in Heaven's name did you fellows walk into it so easily?"

"Because he told us to," answered Darrell calmly.

"Told you to," I echoed in amazement.

"A short note," he said. "Just – 'Follow the messenger – all three of you. Be surprised at nothing. And tell Dixon that he must not reveal my identity until he hears the anthem whistled once.'"

"He knows I'm here?" I cried. "But I don't understand."

"Frankly – no more do I," said Algy. "What's this damned stone quarry?"

"It's a model," I said, "of Stonehenge. Look here, you fellows, I'll tell you all I know. I can pretend that we are strangers if anyone comes in. But there is no reason why we shouldn't talk in view of the position we are in – its most damnably serious."

"Fire ahead," said Jerningham quietly.

I told them everything; what I knew, and what I only suspected. I told them of the dead man at Stonehenge, and the scene of the night before. And they listened with consternation growing on their faces.

"It was our last hope," I said, "trying to make that man realise she was mad. But he's wild about her – absolutely wild."

"You really think she's going to commit suicide," said Darrell doubtfully.

"I do," I answered. "Though the point is of academic interest only as far as we are concerned. She is going to do all of us in first."

"Man – but it's a fearful risk," said Jerningham.

"Don't you see," I cried, "that she doesn't care a damn about the risk. What does the risk matter to her if she's going to join Carl, as she thinks, after? And that poor fish, Paul, is so infatuated with her that he is prepared to run any risk to get her."

We argued it from every angle whilst the room grew darker and darker. To them the only thing that mattered was that Drummond had told them to come: that Drummond had something up his sleeve. But try as I would, I couldn't share their optimism. What could he do alone – or at best with Toby Sinclair to help him? The odds were altogether too heavy. Had we all been free it would have been different. Then we could have put up a good show: as it was the thing seemed hopeless to me. And yet he had deliberately told these three to walk into the trap. It was incomprehensible.

It appeared that they had not seen him, but had only received the note. And the previous night Algy Longworth had also got a note which explained his movements to me. It had contained instructions to the effect that he was to announce publicly his intention of going to Stonehenge after dinner; that as he valued his life he was not to go but was to take a walk in the opposite direction.

"If I had gone," he said, "I suppose I should have shared the fate of the poor devil you saw dead. I wonder who he was."

"Ask me another," I remarked. "He was a complete stranger to me. But he was undoubtedly murdered by that foul brute of a nigger."

Conversation became desultory: all our nerves were getting frayed. The light had almost gone; we were just vague shapes to one another as we sat there fastened to those fantastic stones, waiting for nine o'clock.

"I can't believe it," burst out Jerningham once. "Damn it – it's like a nightmare."

No one answered; only the throaty chuckle that I had heard before came from somewhere behind me.

"It's the nigger," grunted Darrell. "Get out, you filthy brute."

He chuckled again, and then like some monstrous misshapen animal he began to shamble round the room. I could just see him in the darkness peering first at one thing and then at another. He went to the two unoccupied seats and began fiddling with the mechanism that moved the two curved steel bars. He worked it several times, chuckling to himself like a child, and suddenly came Jerningham's voice strained and tense.

"Come and do that to my chair, nigger. I'll give you some cigarettes and money if you do."

But the black man took no notice. He had transferred his attentions now to the black box that lay upon the altar stone. That occupied him for a long while, and all the time the throaty chuckling continued. Every now and then came the chink of tin on stone: then, as silently as he had come, he vanished again.

It was the suspense of waiting that was so appalling, and I began to long for nine o'clock. A mood of dull resignation had come over me. I felt I simply didn't care. Anything – so long as they got on with it. And as if in answer to my thoughts the door leading into the hall slowly opened, and a clock outside began to chime.

"Nine," muttered somebody.

The final act was about to begin.

# CHAPTER 16

*In which we have a rehearsal*

I think my main feeling was one of intense curiosity. There was no light in the hall, but a faint lessening of the general darkness marked the door. For a time nothing happened, then something white appeared in the opening, and the room was flooded with light.

The woman Irma was standing there clad in the same white garment she had worn the preceding night. Behind her hovered Paul – his face more saturnine than ever, but it was on her that all our attention was concentrated. In her hands she held some largish object which was covered with a silken cloth, and after a while she advanced to the altar stone and placed it there reverently. Then she removed the wrap, and I saw that it was a full size plaster cast of a man's head.

"Dashed if it isn't our late lamented Carl," muttered Darrell.

The woman took no notice, she was staring intently at the cast. Once or twice her lips moved, but I heard no words, and for a time her hands were clasped in front of her as if in prayer. Then quite suddenly she turned her back on the altar and began to speak, whilst we watched her fascinated.

"A few months ago," she said, "I stood beside the wreckage of Wilmot's giant airship, and over the charred body of my man I swore an oath. That oath will be finally fulfilled tonight."

Her voice was quiet and conversational.

"But for an accident last night – a mistake on the part of one of my servants, I should not have sent you three the note I did. But Pedro, whom you have doubtless seen, killed a man at Stonehenge, and that necessitated a hastening in my plans. Why did you not go to Stonehenge, Longworth?"

"Got hiccoughs after dinner, darling," said Algy cheerfully. "Tell me, my poppet, is that a new line in nightdresses?"

And just as Paul became livid with rage when I had jeered at him that morning, so now did the woman turn white to the lips with passion.

"You dog," she screamed. "How dare you? Strike him, Paul – strike him across the face."

Then she controlled herself.

"Stay," she said in a calmer voice. "He is not worth it. I will continue – for there is much to say. But for that accident, I might – in fact I think I would have given you one further clue. And yet I do not know: the game in very truth had begun to pall since Drummond died. You were only the puppies that followed your master. He was the one I wanted – not you. However, it was not to be, and because the finish comes tonight, I thought that Phyllis should have you with her as she cannot have her husband. As yet she does not know that you are here: she does not even know her husband is dead. That she shall learn later – just before the end."

She paused, and I saw that Darrell was moistening his lips with his tongue, and that Jerningham's face was white. There was something far more terrifying in this calm matter-of-fact voice than if she had ranted and raved.

"This fourth man," she continued, "this bank clerk presented a conundrum. Believe me, sir," she turned to me, "I have no enmity against you. It is a sheer misfortune that you should be here, but since you are, you've got to stay."

"Please don't apologise," I said sarcastically. "Your treatment of your guest has left nothing to be desired."

But she seemed to have forgotten my existence: her real audience consisted of the other three.

"The Friar's Heel," she remarked. "You solved that quicker than I thought you would. And here you are. This gentleman has doubtless already told you that these stones form a model of Stonehenge. And you wonder why I should have taken so much trouble. I will tell you.

"Revenge is sweet, but to taste of its joys to the utmost, to extract from it the last drop of satisfaction, it must be as carefully planned as any other entertainment. That is why I regret so bitterly that it was Drummond himself who died at the Mere. I like to think of him struggling in that room – struggling to breathe – and knowing all the time that it was I who had done it. But I would far sooner have had him here; because he has escaped the supreme thing I had planned for him."

With one hand outstretched she stood facing the other three.

"He killed my man. You know it. You cannot deny it."

"If by that you mean he killed Carl Peterson, I do not deny it," said Darrell calmly. "And no man ever deserved death more richly."

"Deserved death!" Her voice rose. "Who are you, you dogs, to pronounce judgment on such a man?"

With an effort she controlled herself.

"However, we will not bandy words. He killed my man – even as I shall shortly kill his woman."

She fell silent for a while staring at the plaster cast, and I saw Darrell's anxious eyes roving round the room. They met mine for a moment, and he shrugged his shoulders helplessly. It was out now: there was no bluff about it. Death was in sight, and the manner of it seemed of but little account. Death – unless...

Feverishly I stared around. Death, unless Drummond intervened. I looked up at the roof, remembering the sailor of the night before – but this time it was empty. And all the time the man called Paul stood watching the woman with sombre eyes.

219

"It has not been very easy, Darrell." She was speaking again. "My servants have blundered: mistakes have been made. But from the moment she fell into my hands the final issue has never been in doubt. I might have had to forego this. I might even have had to forego getting the lot of you. But her life has been forfeit since that moment: I have played with her at times, letting her think that she would be free if you found her, and she, stupid little fool, has believed me. Free!" She laughed. "There have been times when only the greatest restraint has prevented me killing her with my own hands. And now I am glad, for I would like you to see her die."

"*Carissima*," said the man called Paul, "is it wise to delay? All has gone so well up to now, and I fear something may happen."

"What can happen?" she said calmly. "Who can interrupt us? The time has passed when there was danger of surprise. Your police, Darrell, are stickers. And although I did not think you would enlist their aid, there was the little matter of the blood in the ditch. I felicitated dear Phyllis on that: Paul tells me that she practically killed him with one blow of that heavy spanner – naughty girl."

"For God's sake get on with it, woman," said Jerningham harshly.

"The essence of satisfactory revenge, my friend," she remarked, "is not to hurry. The night is yet young."

I closed my eyes. The powerful gleaming lights against the black made me drowsy. It was a dream all this – it must be. In a few moments I should awake, and see my own familiar room.

"What think you of the setting of my revenge?" From a great distance her voice came to me, and I forced myself back to reality again. "Stonehenge – in miniature. Theatrical – perhaps: but the story fascinates me. And because in this year of grace the real place cannot be used it was necessary to make a model."

With brooding eyes she stared in front of her.

"We will rehearse it once, Paul. I am in the mood. Turn out the lights."

"*Carissima*," he protested, "is it wise?"

"Turn out the lights," she said curtly, and with a muttered oath he obeyed.

"I am in a strange mood tonight." Her voice – low and throbbing – came to us out of the darkness. "It is true that I have rehearsed it before, that I know exactly every effect – but I would postpone it awhile. Besides it may be that you, who will watch the real performance, can suggest something at the rehearsal. Think well, you watchers: use your imagination, for only thus will you appreciate my plan.

"Night. Darkness such as this. Around us on the grass a multitude who wait."

I sat up stiffly: was it imagination or had something passed close to my chair?

"They wait in silence, whispering perhaps, amongst themselves of what is about to happen. They have seen it before – many times, but the mystery of what they are about to see and the wonder of it never palls.

"Darkness – and then in the east the faint light that comes before the dawn. Look!"

It was clever – damnably clever. How the lights had been arranged to give the effect I cannot say, but at the end of the room behind the Friar's Heel there came a faint luminosity. It was more a general lessening of the darkness than anything else, and one could just see the outlines of the stones against it.

"A murmur like a wave beating on the shore – then silence once again. A gentle breeze, faint scented with the smell of country kisses their faces, and is gone, whilst all the time the dawn comes nearer: the tense expectancy increases."

I couldn't help it. I was fascinated in spite of myself. My reason told me that all these elaborate preparations were nothing more nor less than the preliminaries to cold-blooded murder.

And yet, theatrical though they might be, and were, they were also artistically impressive. I remember that I found myself thinking what a marvellous stage effect it would be.

Gradually the light behind the Friar's Heel increased, and then the woman began to sing. Her voice was small but true, and she sang in a tongue I did not know. It was a wild barbaric thing that sounded like one of those bizarre Magyar folk songs, and the effect was incredible. I found myself sweating with sheer excitement, all danger forgotten; and the others said after they had felt the same. The light grew brighter: her song wilder and more triumphant. And then suddenly she ceased.

"It comes," she cried. "The God comes. And as the first rays fall on the slaughter stone, and the woman who lies there, the sacrifice is made."

Out of the lessening darkness came a rim of golden light. It appeared behind the Friar's Heel, and gradually grew larger and larger, even as the sun appears above the horizon. A yellow ball of electric light being raised slowly on a winding gear: so said reason. But imagination saw the scene of countless centuries ago.

"The shadows shorten," she whispered. "Soon they will reach the slaughter stone and pass it by. This time there is no victim – but next... My God! What's that?"

Her voice rose to a sudden shrill cry, and for a while we all stared stupidly. For now the slaughter stone was bathed in light, and on its smooth surface was a gruesome object. One end was red with dried up blood, and the other had a nail.

The man called Paul moved slowly towards it.

"It's a man's finger," he muttered, and his voice was shaking.

"A man's finger," repeated the woman. "But how did it get there? How did it get there?" she screamed. "How did it get there, you fool?"

And Paul could give no answer.

"A man's finger," she said once more, and glancing at her I saw that every drop of blood had drained from her face. "Where is Grant?"

"Grant," said Paul stupidly. "Why do you want Grant?"

"Drummond shot his finger off," she answered. "In the room below the Mere. Get him. Get him, you wretched fool, at once."

"But will you be all right?" he began, and again from behind me came the throaty chuckle. "Great Scott! the butterfly man."

I turned round. Sure enough there was Toby Sinclair, powerless in the hands of the Negro. The mystery of the finger was explained.

"Damn you!" he cried, "this is an outrage."

"Put him in a seat, Pedro," said the woman, and Toby was forced into the chair next to mine.

"If it isn't Mr Seymour," he fumed angrily. "Are these people mad? Is this place a lunatic asylum?"

He subsided into angry mutterings, and I said nothing. For now I was too excited to speak: it was evident that the game was beginning in grim earnest.

"Get Grant," said the woman, and Paul left the room.

She stood motionless leaning against the altar stone whilst that damnable nigger shambled round the room and then disappeared again. Toby Sinclair still continued to curse audibly, and the other three stared in front of them with eyes bright with anticipation. What was going to happen next? Once Sinclair stole a glance at me and winked, and I must confess that wink heartened me considerably. Because even now I saw very little light in the darkness.

The door opened, and Paul came in followed by the man with the damaged hand.

"Grant," said the woman quietly, "is that your finger?"

He gave a violent start: then he picked it up with a trembling hand.

"It is," he muttered foolishly. "At least, I – I think it is, it must be."

"Do you recognise any of these men?" she went on.

"I recognise those three," he stammered, and Darrell nodded pleasantly.

"A little morning exercise by the waters of the Mere," he remarked.

"And what of the others?" she said.

He looked at Toby and me, and shook his head.

"I've seen them," he said. "At Amesbury. And I thought" – he looked sideways at Paul – "I thought. The boss," he went on sullenly, "said that I was to say nothing about them."

For a moment she stared at Paul, with a look of such concentrated cold fury that I almost felt sorry for the man. After all, swine though he was, he did love her, and had only embarked on this affair for her sake. But what she was going to say to him we shall never know, for at that moment there came a diversion.

The man with the damaged hand had suddenly come very close to me and was peering into my face. Then with a quick movement he seized my moustache and tore it off.

"God in Heaven!" he muttered, "it's one of them. One of the three that were drowned."

A dead silence settled on the room, which was at last broken by Toby.

"What about *Opsiphanes syme*?" he burbled genially.

Another dead silence, broken this time by the woman.

"So Drummond is not dead," she said softly. "How very interesting."

"I seem to recall," drawled Jerningham pleasantly, "in those dear days of long ago, that our lamented friend whose repulsive visage adorns the altar had frequent necessity to remark the same thing."

And then Paul spoke with sudden fear in his voice.

"It's a trap. An obvious trap. He's probably got the police with him."

"There wasn't a soul outside when I came in," said Grant. "There hasn't been a thing past the gate since eight o'clock."

"Go out," said the woman, "and mount guard again. Paul – fetch Phyllis."

For a moment or two he seemed on the point of arguing with her: then he thought better of it and both of them left the room.

"So you are Sinclair," she said, coming over to Toby.

"Quite right, sweet girl of mine," he answered. "And how have we been keeping since our last merry meeting?"

"All of you except Drummond." She was talking half to herself. "Helpless: at my mercy."

A triumphant smile was on her lips, and as it seemed to me with justice. It exactly expressed the situation, and now that the momentary excitement of the finger episode had worn off I began to feel gloomier than ever. It was all very well for the others to be flippant, but unless they were completely blind to obvious realities it could only be due to bravado. We were absolutely in this woman's power: there was no other way of looking at it. That their mood might be due to a blind unquestioning faith in Drummond's ability was also possible, but unless he came with four or five exceptionally powerful men to help him, this was going to be a case of the pitcher going to the well once too often. For what none of them seemed to realise was the fact that this woman was careless of her own life. There lay the incredible danger: discovery meant nothing to her provided her revenge had come first.

I came out of my reverie to find Darrell's eyes fixed on me.

"Learnt that tune yet, Dixon?" he said.

Toby Sinclair was humming the Froth Blower's anthem, and I nodded. I was free now to give Drummond away, but what earthly good it was going to be Heaven alone knew.

"A new recruit, dear Irma," went on Darrell. "You will be pleased to know that it was he who solved most of your clues."

She turned her strange brooding eyes on me. "How did you get out of the Mere?" she asked curiously.

"A little substitution," I remarked. "The gentleman you left below arrived too soon, and then I sat on the water handle by mistake."

"I am glad," she said. "The audience will now be complete."

"Think so," said Jerningham mockingly. "One seat, and a rather important one, still remains to be occupied."

"It is possible that it may remain unoccupied," she said enigmatically. "Good evening, Phyllis. Your husband's friends have all arrived, as you see."

Mrs Drummond stared round with a wan little smile.

"Hullo! chaps," she said. "Where's Hugh?"

"The Lord knows, Phyllis," answered Darrell. "We don't."

"He will come," said Mrs Drummond calmly. "Don't worry."

"You think so," answered Irma. "Good. And anyway why should you worry. Whether he comes, or whether he doesn't the result as far as you are concerned will be the same. In fact I am not sure that my revenge would not be all the sweeter if he didn't come – until too late."

Once more she was leaning against the altar stone, with one hand resting on the bust of Carl Peterson.

"Imagine his feelings for the rest of his life if he arrived to find you all dead: knowing that at last he had failed you."

"May I remind you once again of the number of times we have heard remarks of a similar nature from your late lamented – er – husband – " said Jerningham with a yawn.

"And may I remind you," she answered, "of my original little verse to Drummond concerning the Female of the Species. I shall wait a little, and then we will proceed. Should he come in the interval, I shall be delighted for him to participate in our little ceremony: should he fail to appear he will not. He will merely find the results. And should he be so injudicious as not to come alone he will encounter two locked doors, doors which will take even him some time to knock down. He will hear you screaming for help inside here – and then – "

Her voice rose: her breast heaved: she was tasting of her triumph in advance.

"Bonzo's meat cubes are highly recommended for preserving a placid disposition," said Algy brightly. "You'll split a stay lace, my angel woman, unless you're careful."

"Why do we delay, dear one?" said Paul anxiously. "Let us be done with it now, and leave him to find what he will find."

But she shook her head.

"No: we will give him half-an-hour. And if he is not here by then…"

I thought furiously: every moment gained might be an advantage.

"How is he to know anything about it?" I said. "If he is where I last saw him, he is in Amesbury. And it will take more than half-an-hour get a messenger to him, and for him to reach here."

She looked at me thoughtfully.

"Is he also disguised like you and Sinclair?"

"He is," I said shortly. "He has a large black beard…"

"You fool," howled Sinclair. "You damned treacherous fool. My God! We're done."

I stared at him stupidly, and a sudden deadly sick feeling came over me.

"But," I stammered, "I thought…"

I looked across helplessly at Darrell. What had I said? Surely the message was clear, to say who he was after I heard the anthem once.

"I could kill you where you sit, you cur," went on Sinclair icily, "if only I had my hands free."

"You seem to have said the wrong thing, Mr Dixon," said Irma pleasantly. "So dear Hugh is disguised in a large black beard, is he? I don't think I should like Hugh in a black beard. Well, well! I wonder what little amusement he has in store for us. We will certainly wait, Paul, until he arrives. I couldn't bear to miss him in a black beard."

"He had a scheme," said Sinclair furiously to the other three. "An absolute winner. But everything depended on his disguise. You fool, Dixon: you fool."

"Shut up, Toby," said Mrs Drummond peremptorily. "I'm sure Mr Dixon didn't mean to do any harm, and anyway" – she turned to me – "thank you a hundred times for all you've been through on my behalf."

I looked at her gratefully, though I was too much upset to speak. I simply couldn't understand the thing. Evidently Drummond had altered his plans since he'd sent the message through Darrell. But if so – and he didn't want me to comply with his first instructions, why hadn't he sent countermanding orders through Sinclair? And after a while I began to feel angry: the man was a damned fool. From beginning to end he had bungled every single thing. It was I who had borne the burden and heat of the whole show. And what possible hope had he got of deceiving anybody with that absurd false beard?

"And have you any idea if our friend is coming soon," pursued Irma sweetly. "Or shall we send a note to Amesbury, addressed to Mr Blackbeard?"

"You needn't worry," said Sinclair sullenly. "He's coming all right."

He glowered vindictively at me, and I glowered back at him. I was absolutely fed up – so fed up that I almost forgot what was in store for us. Of all the bungling, incompetent set of fools that I had ever known this much vaunted gang won in a canter. And their so-called leader was the worst of the lot.

My mind went back to Bill Tracey's remarks about him and the extraordinary things he had done. I'd tell Bill the truth when I next saw him. I'd put him wise. And then my stomach gave a sick heave: *I should never see Bill again.* The sweat poured down me: my anger had gone – reality had returned. In a short while this astounding farce would be over, and I should be dead.

The room swam before me. I could only see the faces of the others through a mist. Dead! We should all be dead. By a monstrous effort I bit back a wild desire to shout and rave. That would be the unforgivable sin in front of this crowd. They might lack brains, but they didn't lack courage.

I pulled myself together and stared at them. Boredom was the only emotion they displayed – boredom and contempt. This foul woman could kill them all right: she could never make them whimper.

"I'm damned sorry," I said suddenly. "But for God's sake don't think it was treachery."

For a moment no one spoke. Then –

"Sorry I said that," said Toby gruffly. "Withdraw it and all that sort of rot."

Silence fell again: the only movement was Paul's restless fidgeting. The woman still leaned gracefully against the altar stone. Mrs Drummond sat motionless, staring at the door.

"He will probably be coming soon, Paul," said Irma suddenly. "And it would be better not to give him any warning. Gag them."

"What about the girl?" he said.

"Gag her as well, and put her in the vacant chair for a time."

"Don't touch me you foul swine," said Mrs Drummond coldly. "I will go there."

"And then when dear Hugh comes," said Irma, "he shall take your place, Phyllis. Whilst you will be placed elsewhere."

She clenched her hands, and for a moment the feverish glitter returned to her eyes. Then she grew calm again.

"Now turn out all the lights except the one at the end."

And so for perhaps ten minutes we sat there waiting. Once I heard Pedro's throaty chuckle that seemed to come from the passage leading to the garage: and once I thought I heard the sound of a car on the road outside. Otherwise the silence was absolute.

Through the open skylight I could see the stars, and I began wondering what had become of the sailor. Somewhere about the house I supposed: one of the infamous gang. And then I started to wonder how Drummond would come.

Should I suddenly see his bearded face peering through at us – covering the woman with a revolver? But the stars still shone undimmed by any shadow, and after a while my brain refused to act. My arm was throbbing abominably. My thoughts began to wander.

I was back in my club, and the woman Irma was the wine steward. It was absurd that I couldn't get a drink before eleven o'clock in the morning in my own club. A fatuous war-time regulation that should be repealed. I'd write to my MP about it. Everybody ought to write to their MP about it. Here was that doddering ass old Axminster coming in. Thought he owned the place because he was a peer… What was he saying? I listened – and suddenly my thoughts ceased to wander.

It wasn't Axminster: it was the man with the damaged hand.

"A big bloke with a black beard is dodging through the bushes towards the house," he said. "What are we to do?"

The woman stretched out her arms ecstatically.

"Let him come," she cried triumphantly. "Pedro."

Came another throaty chuckle from behind me.

"Come into the room after him, Pedro. Don't let him see you. Then I leave him to you. But don't kill him."

# CHAPTER 17

*In which the curtain rings down*

So long as I live I shall never forget the tension of the next few minutes. The light was so dim that the faces of the others were only blurs. Paul had joined the woman, and they were standing side by side against the altar stone. The door in the hall was ajar, and the hall itself was in darkness so that it was impossible to see anything distinctly.

"He had a scheme: an absolute winner."

Sinclair's words came back to me, and I wondered what it was. Had I really done the whole lot of us in by my indiscretion? But at last the period of waiting was over. Drummond's voice could be heard in the hall.

"Very little light in this house."

The woman by the altar stiffened.

"His voice," she said exultingly. "Drummond at last."

And then, or was it my imagination, there seemed to come a funny sort of hissing noise from the hall. Had the Negro got him already? But no, he was speaking again.

"I am a police-inspector, and I wish to see the lady of the house on a very important matter."

In the dim light I could just see Darrell's expression of blank amazement, and I sympathised with him. Was *this* the brilliant scheme? If so, was a more utterly fatuous one ever thought of? Why, his voice gave him away.

"A very serious matter. I may say that I have two plain clothes men outside. What is that door at the end there? Don't attempt to detain me. Oh! I see – you're leading the way, are you?"

The door opened, and there stood Drummond. I could just see his black beard, but it wasn't at him that I looked for long. He took a couple of steps into the room, and like a shadow the Negro slipped in – dodging behind the curtain. I heard hoarse gurgling noises coming from the others as they strove to warn him, but Paul had done his work too well.

With a swift movement he stepped back and shut the door, so that Pedro was not more than a yard from him.

"Good evening, Inspector. Your voice is very familiar."

"A little ruse, my poppet," said Drummond pleasantly, "for getting into the august presence. May I say that I have a revolver in my hand, in case you can't see it in this light? And will you and your gentleman friend put your hands up? I've dealt with one of your myrmidons outside in the hall, and my temper is a bit ragged."

With a faint smile the woman raised her hands, and Paul followed suit.

"How are you, *mon ami*?" she said. "We only required you to complete the family circle. In fact I was desolated when I thought you'd succumbed at the Mere."

I worked madly at the handkerchief with my jaws. Why didn't he come further into the room? At any second the Negro might spring on him.

"And what is this ridiculous entertainment?" he asked.

"Specially staged for you, Hugh," she answered.

"I'm sorry you've wasted your time," he said shortly. "A truce to this fooling. I've had enough of it. You and the swine with you are for it, now."

"Are we?" she mocked.

"Yes – you are. Come here, you swab. I don't know your name, and I don't want to, but hump yourself."

232

"And if I refuse?" said Paul easily.

"I'll plug you where you stand," answered Drummond. "I don't know how my wife and friends are secured, but set them free. And no monkey tricks."

And then, with a superhuman effort I got the handkerchief half off my mouth.

"Look out behind," I croaked, and even as I spoke the gleaming white teeth of the Negro showed over his shoulder. That was all I could see at that distance, but I could hear.

There came a startled grunt from Drummond, that foul throaty chuckle from the black man, and the fight commenced. And what a fight it was in the semi-darkness. I forgot our own peril: forgot what depended on the issue in the thrill of the issue itself. Dimly I could see them swaying to and fro, each man putting forward every atom of strength he possessed, whilst Irma swayed backwards and forwards in her excitement and the man Paul went towards the struggling pair in case he was wanted.

"Leave them, Paul," she cried tensely. "Let Drummond have his last fight."

And then Darrell got his gag free.

"Go it, Hugh; go it, old man," he shouted.

I heard someone croaking hoarse sounds of encouragement, and suddenly realised it was myself. And then gradually the sounds ceased, and my mouth got strangely dry. For Drummond was losing.

From a great distance I heard Darrell muttering "My God!" over and over again to himself, and from somewhere else came pitiful little muffled cries as Mrs Drummond realised the ghastly truth. Her husband was losing.

It was impossible to see the details, but of the main broad fact there was no doubt. At long last, Drummond had met his match. The nigger's chuckles were ceaseless and triumphant, though Drummond fought mute. But slowly and inexorably he was being worn down. And then step by step the black man forced him towards the chair where his wife was sitting.

"Take Phyllis out, Paul," cried Irma suddenly. "Take her out."

Foot by foot, faster and faster the pair swayed towards the empty seat. Drummond was weakening obviously, and suddenly with a groan he gave in and crumpled. And then in a couple of seconds it was over. He was flung into the chair, and with a click the steel bars closed over his wrists. He was a prisoner, the family circle was complete.

With a heart-broken little cry his wife, who had torn off her gag, flung her arms around him and kissed him.

"Darling boy," she cried in an agony; then abruptly she straightened up and stood facing her enemy. And if her voice when she spoke was not quite steady, who could be surprised?

"You foul devil," she said. "Get it over quickly."

And Pedro's evil chuckle was the only answer. I glanced at Irma, and for the time she was beyond speech. Never have I seen such utter and complete triumph expressed on any human being's face: she was in an ecstasy. Standing in front of the bust of Peterson, she was crooning to it in a sort of frenzy. The madness was on her again.

"My love, my King: he has been beaten. Do you realise it, my adored one: Drummond has been beaten. You are here, my Carl: your spirit is here. Do you see him – the man who killed you – powerless in my hands?"

Gradually she grew calmer, and at length Paul spoke.

"There is no reason for more delay now, *carissima*," he said urgently. "Let us finish."

She stared at him broodingly.

"Finish – yes. All will be finished soon, Paul. But for a few minutes I will enjoy my triumph. Then we will stage our play."

She looked at each of us in turn – a look of mingled triumph and contempt.

"Ungag them, Paul; and Pedro – you attend to the white woman should she give trouble."

She waited till Paul had obeyed her – gloating over us, and the full realisation of our position came sweeping over me. Great though the odds against him had been, some vestige of hope had remained while Drummond was still free. Now our last chance had gone: we were finished – outwitted by this woman. And though nothing could have been more utterly futile and fatuous than Drummond's behaviour, I felt terribly sorry for him.

Still breathing heavily after his fight, he sat there with his chin sunk on his chest looking the picture of despondency. And I realised what he must be going through. Beaten, and knowing that the result of that beating meant death to us all and to his wife. And yet – angry irritation surged up in me again – how on earth could he have expected anything else? If ever a man had asked for trouble he had. Now he'd got it, and so had we.

All the fight seemed to have gone out of him: he was broken. And when I looked at the others they seemed broken, too – stunned with the incredible thing that had happened. That Drummond, the invincible, should have met his match at last – should be sitting there as a helpless prisoner – had shattered them. It was as if the Bank of England had suddenly become insolvent. And it was like Peter Darrell to try and comfort him.

"Cheer up, old son," he said lightly. "If that nigger hadn't caught you unawares from behind, you'd have done him."

And Drummond's only reply was a groan of despair, whilst his wife stroked his hair with her hand, and Pedro, like a great black shadow, hovered behind her.

"Possibly," answered Irma. "That 'if' should be a great comfort to you all during the next half-hour."

"All is ready," said Paul. "Let us start."

"Yes; we will start. But, as this is our last meeting, are there any little points you would like cleared up or explained? You, my dear Drummond, seem strangely silent. It's not surprising, I

235

admit; complete defeat is always unpleasant. But, honestly, I can't congratulate you on your handling of the show. You haven't been very clever, have you? In fact, you've been thoroughly disappointing. I had hoped, at any rate, for some semblance of the old form, certainly at the end, but instead of that you have given no sport at all. And now – it is over."

She fell silent, that strange brooding look on her face, until at length Paul went up to her.

"For Heaven's sake, *carissima*," he said urgently, "do not let us delay any longer. I tell you I fear a trap."

"Why do you fear a trap?" she demanded.

"They have come into our power too easily," he said doggedly. "They have walked in with their eyes open, it seems to me."

"All that matters is that they have walked in," she answered. "And now, whatever happens, they will never walk out again. Do you hear that, Drummond, I said – whatever happens."

He made no answer, until the Negro, with a snarl of rage, thrust his evil face close to him.

"I hear," he said sullenly.

"It matters not," she cried triumphantly, "if a cordon of police surround the house; it matters not if they batter at the doors – they will be too late. Too late."

She breathed the words deliriously; the madness was coming on her again.

"But," stammered Paul, "how shall we get away?"

She waved him from her imperiously.

"Be silent; you bore me." Once more she turned to the plaster cast. "Do you realise, my Carl, what has happened? They are all here – all of them. Drummond and his wife are here; the others are here waiting to expiate their crime. Their lives for yours, my King; I have arranged that. Is it your will that I delay no longer?"

She stared at the bust as if seeking an answer, and somebody – I think it was Algy – gave a short, high-pitched laugh. Nerves were beginning to crack; only Mrs Drummond still stood cool and disdainful, stroking her husband's hair.

Suddenly the wild futility of the whole thing came home to me, so that I writhed and tugged and cursed. Seven of us were going to be killed at the whim of a mad woman! Murdered in cold blood! God! it was impossible – inconceivable… Why didn't somebody do something? What fools they were – what utter fools!

I raved at them incoherently, and told them what I thought of their brains, their mentality, and the complete absence of justification for their existence at all.

"I told you she meant to kill us," I shouted, "and you five damned idiots come walking into the most obvious trap that has ever been laid."

"Shut that man's mouth," said Irma quietly, and for the second time Pedro's huge black hand crept round my throat – squeezing, throttling, so that half-choked I fell silent. After all, what was the use? Mad she might be, and undoubtedly was, but as she had said to Drummond, we were finished, whatever happened. And it was more dignified to face it in silence.

"We will begin," she said suddenly. "Paul, get Phyllis."

With a little cry, Mrs Drummond flung her arms round her husband's neck.

"Goodbye, my darling," she cried, kissing him again and again. But he was beyond speech, and at length the Negro seized her and dragged her away.

"Let me go, you foul brute," she said furiously, and Paul, who was standing by the stone of sacrifice, beckoned to her to come. Proudly, without faltering, she walked towards him.

"Lie down," he said curtly.

"Get it accurate, Paul," cried Irma anxiously. "Be certain that it is accurate."

"I will be certain," he answered.

And then for the first time I realised that there were ropes made fast to rings in the stone. She was going to be lashed down. She didn't struggle even when Pedro, chuckling in his excitement, helped to make her fast. And on her face was an expression of such unutterable contempt that it seemed to infuriate the other woman.

"You may sneer, my dear Phyllis," she stormed. "But look above you, you little fool; look above you."

With one accord we all looked up, and at the same moment a small light was turned on in the ceiling. And when he had seen what it illuminated, Ted Jerningham began to shout and bellow like a madman.

"Stop it, you devil," he roared. "Let one of us go there instead of her. My God! Hugh. Do you see?"

But Drummond was still silent, and after a while Jerningham relapsed into silence, too. And as for me, I was conscious only of a deadly feeling of nausea.

Hanging from a rafter was a huge, pointed knife. It was of an uncommon Oriental design, and it looked the most deadly weapon.

"Yes, Hugh – do you see?" cried Irma mockingly. "Do you see what it is that hangs directly above your wife's heart? It has been tested, not once, but many times, and when I release the spring it will fall, Hugh. And it will fall straight."

And still Drummond sat silent and cowed.

"But I shall not release it yet: that I promise you. There is a little ceremony to be gone through before our finale. The rest of them have seen it, Drummond, but to you as my principal guest it will come as a surprise. And after it is over, and the knife that you see up there is buried in Phyllis' heart, your turn will come."

She was rocking to and fro in her mad excitement.

"Paul has arranged it," she cried exultingly. "Clever Paul. Behind each one of you is enough explosive to shatter you to pieces. But Paul has so arranged it that even as Phyllis waits and waits for death to come – so will you all wait. You will see it creeping closer and closer, and be powerless to do anything to save yourselves. I shall light the fuse, and you will see the flame burning slowly towards this little box. And when it reaches that box – suddenly, with the speed of light, the flame will dart to the gun-cotton behind your backs. For the fuse that connects the gun-cotton to the box is of a different brand to the one I shall light. Paul knows all these things: Paul is clever."

And now the madness was on her in earnest. She walked to and fro in front of the altar stone, her arms outstretched, worshipping the plaster cast of Peterson.

"Is my revenge worthy, my King?" she cried again and again. "Does it meet with your approval? First she shall be killed before their eyes, and then they will wait for their own death. They will see it coming closer every second, until, at last..."

"Great Heavens! man," shouted Darrell to Paul, "you can't let her go on. The woman is mad."

But he took no notice: his eyes were fixed on the woman who had now become silent. She seemed to be listening to a voice we could not hear, and something told me that we were very near the end.

"Put out the lights, Paul," she said gravely.

I took one last look round the room: at Mrs Drummond, lying bound, with the black man gloating over her; at Irma, standing triumphant by the altar stone; and finally at Drummond. Even now I could hardly believe that it was the finish, and that he had nothing up his sleeve. But there he still sat with his head sunk on his breast, the personification of desolate defeat. And then the lights went out.

Once again we were plunged in darkness that could be felt, but this time it was not a rehearsal. In a few minutes that knife would fall from the ceiling, and the poor girl would be dead. And we should see it actually happen. The sweat poured off me in streams as the full horror of it came home; I scarcely thought of what was going to be the fate of the rest of us afterwards. To be lying there bound, knowing that at any moment the knife might fall, was enough to send her crazy. More merciful if it did.

"A model of Stonehenge, Drummond. You have realised that?"

At last he seemed to have recovered the use of his tongue.

"Yes, I have realised that."

His voice was perfectly steady, and I wondered if even now he realised what was coming.

"And the stone on which Phyllis lies is the stone of sacrifice. Do you think she is a worthy offering?"

"Do you really mean to do this monstrous thing, Irma Peterson?" he asked.

"Should I have gone to all this trouble," she mocked, "if I didn't?"

"And yet, when on one occasion you asked me, I spared Carl's life. Do you remember?"

"Only to kill him later," she cried fiercely. "Go on, Drummond: beg for her life. I'd like to hear you whining."

"You won't do that," he answered. "If I ask you to spare her, it is for a different reason altogether. It is to show that you have left in you some shred of humanity."

"As far as you are concerned, I have none," she said. "As I say, should I have done all this for nothing? Listen, Drummond.

"It was in Egypt, as I told you in my first letter, that the idea came to me. By the irony of fate, it was suggested to me by a man who knows you well, Drummond. You and dear Phyllis had been staying at the same house with him, and he was so interested to find out that I also knew you. He told me about this splendid game of hidden treasure, and it appeared that you had won. I asked him the rules, and he said they were exceedingly simple. Everything depended on having good clues: I trust that mine have been up to standard."

She paused, and no one spoke.

"From the game, as you played it then, to the game as you have played it now, was but a short step. Preparation was necessary, it is true; but the main idea was the same. I would give you a hidden-treasure hunt, where the prize was not a box of cigarettes, but something a little more valuable. And I would leave you to think" – her voice rose suddenly – "you poor fool, that if you succeeded you would get the prize."

She laughed, and it had an ugly sound.

"However, of that later. Having made my preparations, the next thing was to obtain the prize. That proved easier than I expected. Twice, but for one of those little accidents which no one could foresee, Phyllis would have got into a special taxi in London – a taxi prepared by me. But I could afford to wait. For weeks you were watched, Drummond – and then you went to Pangbourne – where you began to realise that I was after you. And then came the opportunity. A hastily scrawled note in your handwriting – Paul is an adept at that, and I had several specimens of your writing – and the thing was done.

"'Bring the Bentley at once to Tidmarsh, old girl. A most amazing thing has happened. – H.' Do you remember the note, Phyllis? I don't blame you for falling into the trap: it said neither too much nor too little, that note. And so I got the prize at a trifling cost. It was naughty of you to hit him so hard, my dear, as I've told you before. Paul said it was a positively wicked blow."

Once again that mocking laugh rang through the room, but I hardly heard it. With every sense alert, I was listening to another sound – the sound of heavy breathing near me. Something was happening close by – but what? Then came a groan, and silence.

"What was that? Who groaned?" Her words came sharp and insistent.

"Who, indeed?" answered Drummond's voice. "Why don't you continue, Irma Peterson? We are waiting for the theatrical display."

"Pedro! Pedro! Is Drummond still in his chair?"

Came that same throaty chuckle, followed by Drummond's voice again: "Take your hands off me, you foul swab."

"It is well," she said, and there was relief in her voice. "I should not like a mistake to occur now. And, with you, Drummond – one never knows."

"True," said he, "one never knows. Even now, Irma – there is time for you to change your mind. I warn you that it will be better for you if you do."

"Thank you a thousand times," she sneered. "Instead, however, of following your advice, we will begin. The sacrifice is ready; we have delayed enough."

Once more I became conscious of movement near me, and my pulses began to tingle.

"Just for the fraction of a second, Drummond, will you again see Phyllis alive: then the knife will fall."

The faint light was beginning behind the Friar's Heel, in a couple of minutes it would be all over. Unless…unless… My heart was pounding; my tongue was dry; was it the end, or were strange things taking place?

"The dawn," she cried. "You see the dawn, Drummond. Soon the sun will rise, the rays will creep nearer and nearer to Phyllis. And then… See…the rim is already there. It is coming, Drummond; coming. Have you any last message, you poor damned fool, for her? If so speak now for my hand is on the lever of the knife."

"Just one," said Drummond lightly, and to my amazement his voice did not come from the chair in which he was imprisoned. "Every beard is not false, but every nigger smells. That beard ain't false, dearie, and dis nigger don't smell. So I'm thinking there's something wrong somewhere."

There was a moment's dead silence, then she gave a little choking gasp. Came a streak of light as the knife shot down, a

242

crash, and on the stone of sacrifice lay the bust of Carl Peterson, shattered in a hundred pieces.

For a while I couldn't grasp it. I stared stupidly at the woman who was cowering back against the altar stone; at the crumpled figure of Paul lying on the ground close by me. And then I looked at the nigger, and he was grinning broadly.

"So it ain't poor dear Drummond in dat chair," he chuckled. "That is my very good friend John Perkins, and when you thought John was talking, it was really dis nigger what spoke, so you see you weren't quite as clever as you thought, my poppet."

Suddenly she began to scream hysterically, and Drummond raced round the chairs setting us free.

"Guard Phyllis," he shouted, as the door opened and Charles followed by the chauffeur came rushing in. It lasted about five seconds – the scrap; but that five seconds was enough. For when it was over and we looked round for Irma she had gone. Whether there was some secret door which we didn't discover, or whether she fled through the passage into the garage, we shall never know. But from that day to this there has been no trace seen of her. And I don't even know the ultimate fate of the various men of the house-party. Having caught the lot, including Charles, we put them in our chairs. And then Drummond lit the fuse and we left them bellowing for mercy.

"Let 'em sweat for ten minutes," he remarked. "I've disconnected at the junction box, but they don't know that I have. Now then, boys, once again – and all together – Froth Blowers forever."

We stood in the road and we yelled at the tops of our voices. And it was only when we'd finished that I suddenly remembered the sailor.

"That's all right, old boy," laughed Drummond. "Been retrieving any more bad plums out of wastepaper-baskets lately?"

And so the game ended, and I know that that night I was too tired to even think about the strangeness of it – much less ask. It wasn't till lunch next day, that Drummond cleared up the loose ends. I can see him now, lolling at the end of the table with a lazy grin on his face, and a tankard of beer beside him.

"You'll probably curse my neck off, chaps," he said, "for keeping you in the dark. But honestly, it seemed the only way. It was touch and go, mark you – especially for Phyllis, and that was where the difficulty came in!"

"For the Lord's sake start at the beginning," said Darrell.

"In the first place, I wasn't too sure that they really did think we'd been killed at the Mere. And so it became absolutely vital that I should not be caught. But how to arrange it, and at the same time lull her suspicions, and make her think she'd got me, was the problem. Obviously by providing myself with a double, which is where dear old John came in. He acts for the movies, and he'd grown that awful fungus for a part he has to play shortly. When it is removed, however, he really does look rather like me; moreover he's the same build. So off we set – me as a sailor, him as me – without the smell of an idea as to what we were going to slosh into down here.

"Then came an amazing piece of luck. We motored down – John and I – and we passed the house of last night. There was of course nothing suspicious about it – nothing to mark it as the spot we wanted. Except one thing, and therein lay the luck. As we went past the drive another car coming towards us slowed up, evidently with the intention of turning in. And sitting beside the driver in the front seat was the gent called Paul. That settled it."

"Why?" I asked.

"You couldn't be expected to know," he answered, "but I should have thought old Toby's grey matter would have heaved to it, especially as he spotted the astounding likeness to the late lamented Lakington. Don't you remember the message Phyllis scrawled with her finger, in the blood at the back of her seat?

LIKE LAK. It couldn't mean anything else, unless it was the most astounding coincidence. So we were a bit on the way, but not far. We'd found a house connected with them, but whether Phyllis was inside or not I hadn't an idea. However, being a bit of an adept at exploring houses at night, I intended to do so until you two bung-faced swabs went and made fools of yourselves at Stonehenge that afternoon.

"Never," he grinned cheerfully, "in the course of a long and earnest career have I heard two people give themselves away so utterly and so often as Toby and Dixon did that afternoon. It was staggering, it was monumental. And the man they deliberately selected to be the recipient of their maidenly confidence was Paul himself. Beer – more beer – much more beer."

"Damn it, Hugh," cried Sinclair...

"My dear lad," Drummond silenced him with a wave of his hand, "you were the finest example of congenital idiocy it has ever been my misfortune to witness. The stones of Stonehenge are little pebbles compared to the bricks you dropped, but I forgive you. I even forgive jolly old Dixon's scavenging propensities in wastepaper-baskets. Such is my nature – beautiful, earnest and pure. But you assuredly caused me a lot of trouble: I had to change my plans completely.

"Paul obviously suspected you: no man out of a lunatic asylum could possibly avoid doing so. And as I had no possible means of knowing that all he wanted to do was to get on with the job, I had to assume that he would pass on his suspicions to Irma, and proceed to rope the pair of you in. Time had become an urgent factor. So I wired Algy, and when he arrived, I told him by letter what to do. He was to announce loudly, that he proposed to go to the Friar's Heel by night, but as he valued his life, he wasn't to do anything of the sort."

He leaned back in his chair, and looked at me with twinkling eyes.

"You may be a damned idiot, Joe," he said, "but I looks towards you and I raise my glass. Had it remotely dawned on me that you were going there yourself, I'd have given you the same warning. But it didn't."

"You knew I was there?" I stammered.

"Laddie," he remarked, "hast ever listened to a vast herd of elephants crashing their way through primeval forest? Hast ever heard the scaly rhinoceros and young gambolling playfully on a shingly shore, whilst they assuage their thirst? Thus and more so, was your progress that night. Like a tank with open exhaust you came into action: like a battalion of panting men you lay about, in the most obvious places you could find, and breathed hard. You were, and I say it advisedly, the most conspicuous object in the whole of Wiltshire."

He frowned suddenly.

"You know what we found there, the others don't. Some poor devil who looked like a clerk – stone dead. What he was doing there, we shall never know, but it was perfectly obvious that he had been mistaken for Algy. The nigger had blundered, and it was a blunder which might prove awkward. You heard them talking, Joe – Paul and Irma: but it didn't require that confirmation to see how the land lay. All along I had realised that Phyllis and I were the principal quarry. If she got you so much the better, but we came first. And what I was so terribly frightened of, as soon as I saw that body, was that Irma would get nervous, and believing I was already dead, would go back, finish off Phyllis straight away, and then clear out. I still had no definite scheme; I didn't even have a definite scheme after I'd functioned with the nigger. In fact I didn't really intend to fight him at all.

"I suppose he must have smelt me or something; at any rate he came for me. And by the Lord Harry, it was touch and go. However" – he shrugged his shoulders – "I pasted him good and hearty in the mazzard, and that was that. In fact he is in an awkward predicament that nigger. I dragged him into one of those disused sheds, and handcuffed him to a steel girder. Then I put his victim beside him. And he will find explanations a little difficult.

"The trouble was that all this had delayed me. I hadn't got a car, only a bicycle – and that house had to be explored at once. My hat! laddie," he said to me, "I didn't expect to find you as part of the furniture. How on earth did you get there?"

"On the luggage grid of their car," I said.

"The devil you did," he grinned. "The devil you did! Joe – you are a worthy recruit, though when I saw you through the skylight I consigned you to the deepest pit of hell. But thank Heavens! you didn't give away the fact that you'd seen me."

"I thought you were one of them," I said.

"I know you did, old boy," he laughed. "What we'd have done without your thoughts, during this show, I don't know. They have all been so inconceivably wide of the mark, that they've been invaluable."

"Don't pay any attention to him, Mr Dixon," said his wife.

"My darling," he protested, "I mean it. Joe has been invaluable. The air of complete certainty with which he proclaimed the exact opposite to the truth, has saved the situation. I've been able to bank on it. And once I realised what that foul female intended to do, I wanted every bit of assistance I could get.

"The first alternative was to try and get you out of the house single-handed, but I dismissed that as impossible. I didn't know your room; the house was stiff with men, and – most important of all – that woman would have shot on sight.

"The second alternative was to get all the bunch into the house without arousing her suspicions. And when I heard her reading the letter she was sending Algy, I realised we were getting on. John and Toby could be brought in at a suitable time, and there only remained the problem of what I was going to do.

I confess I didn't think of it: John suggested the nigger. It was a risk, but it proved easier than I thought."

"Damn it, Hugh," cried Darrell, "why didn't you say who you were in the afternoon? You were alone with us, and if you'd set us free then we could have tackled the whole bunch."

"Because, Peter," said Drummond gravely, "it would have taken us some minutes to tackle them. It would have taken Irma half a second to kill Phyllis."

"At any rate," said Jerningham, "you might have let us know. Jove! old boy, I never want to go through twenty minutes like that again."

"I know, chaps – and I'm sorry. I'd have spared you that if I'd thought it safe. But then you would all of you have been acting, and I wanted the real thing. I knew that Dixon thought John was me, and would tell you so, too. And I wanted you all to carry on, as if you thought so. The rest you know. It was easy for me to talk every time instead of John, with the room in semi-darkness as it was. And I think you'll admit we staged a damned good fight."

"When did you spot it, Phyllis?" said Darrell.

"When I kissed John," she laughed.

"And very nice too," grinned that worthy. "Unrehearsed effects are always best."

Drummond rose and stretched himself.

"All over, chaps, all over. Back to the dreary round. Algernon," he hailed a passing waiter, "bring, my stout-hearted fellow, eight of those pale pink concoctions that the sweet thing in the bar fondly imagines are Martinis. I would fain propose a toast. But first – a small formality. Mr Joseph Dixon will place his hand in his pocket and extract therefrom coins to the value of five shillings. I will then present him here and now with the insignia of the Ancient Order, feeling that he has well merited that high honour. Our anthem he knows; he has already sung it twice in his cracked falsetto. The privileges attendant to our

248

Order you will find enumerated in this small book, Mr Dixon, and they should be studied in the solitude of your chamber, when alone with your thoughts. Especially our great insurance treble which guards your dog from rabies, your cook from babies, and yourself from scabies. Great words, my masters, great words. I perceive that Algernon, panting and exhausted after his ten-yard walk, is with us again, carrying the raspberry juice with all his well-known flair. Lady and Gentlemen – to our new Froth Blower. And may I enquire which of you bat-faced sons of Belial has pinched the five bob?"

# SAPPER

## THE BLACK GANG

Although the First World War is over, it seems that the hostilities are not, and when Captain Hugh 'Bulldog' Drummond discovers that a stint of bribery and blackmail is undermining England's democratic tradition, he forms the Black Gang, bent on tracking down the perpetrators of such plots. They set a trap to lure the criminal mastermind behind these subversive attacks to England, and all is going to plan until Bulldog Drummond accepts an invitation to tea at the Ritz with a charming American clergyman and his dowdy daughter.

## BULLDOG DRUMMOND

'Demobilised officer, finding peace incredibly tedious, would welcome diversion. Legitimate, if possible; but crime, if of a comparatively humorous description, no objection. Excitement essential… Reply at once Box X10.'

Hungry for adventure following the First World War, Captain Hugh 'Bulldog' Drummond begins a career as the invincible protectorate of his country. His first reply comes from a beautiful young woman, who sends him racing off to investigate what at first looks like blackmail but turns out to be far more complicated and dangerous. The rescue of a kidnapped millionaire, found with his thumbs horribly mangled, leads Drummond to the discovery of a political conspiracy of awesome scope and villainy, masterminded by the ruthless Carl Peterson.

# SAPPER

## BULLDOG DRUMMOND AT BAY

While Hugh 'Bulldog' Drummond is staying in an old cottage for a peaceful few days duck-shooting, he is disturbed one night by the sound of men shouting, followed by a large stone that comes crashing through the window. When he goes outside to investigate, he finds a patch of blood in the road, and is questioned by two men who tell him that they are chasing a lunatic who has escaped from the nearby asylum. Drummond plays dumb, but is determined to investigate in his inimitable style when he discovers a cryptic message.

## THE FINAL COUNT

When Robin Gaunt, inventor of a terrifyingly powerful weapon of chemical warfare, goes missing, the police suspect that he has 'sold out' to the other side. But Bulldog Drummond is convinced of his innocence, and can think of only one man brutal enough to use the weapon to hold the world to ransom. Drummond receives an invitation to a sumptuous dinner-dance aboard an airship that is to mark the beginning of his final battle for triumph.

# SAPPER

## THE RETURN OF BULLDOG DRUMMOND

While staying as a guest at Merridale Hall, Captain Hugh 'Bulldog' Drummond's peaceful repose is disturbed by a frantic young man who comes dashing into the house, trembling and begging for help. When two warders arrive, asking for a man named Morris – a notorious murderer who has escaped from Dartmoor – Drummond assures them that they are chasing the wrong man. In which case, who on earth is this terrified youngster?

## THE THIRD ROUND

The death of Professor Goodman is officially recorded as a tragic accident, but at the inquest, no mention is made of his latest discovery – a miraculous new formula for manufacturing flawless diamonds at negligible cost, which strikes Captain Hugh 'Bulldog' Drummond as rather strange. His suspicions are further aroused when he spots a member of the Metropolitan Diamond Syndicate at the inquest. Gradually, he untangles a sinister plot of greed and murder, which climaxes in a dramatic motorboat chase at Cowes and brings him face to face with his arch-enemy.